SUMMER
LIGHT,
AND THEN
COMES
THE NIGHT

SUMMER LIGHT, AND THEN COMES THE NIGHT

A NOVEL

JÓN KALMAN STEFÁNSSON

Translated from the Icelandic by Philip Roughton

HARPERVIA

An Imprint of HarperCollins*Publishers*

SUMMER LIGHT, AND THEN COMES THE NIGHT. Copyright © 2005 by Jón Kalman Stefánsson. All rights reserved. Printed in the United States of America. No part of this book may be used or reproduced in any manner whatsoever without written permission except in the case of brief quotations embodied in critical articles and reviews. For information, address HarperCollins Publishers, 195 Broadway, New York, NY 10007.

English translation copyright © 2020 by Philip Roughton.

HarperCollins books may be purchased for educational, business, or sales promotional use. For information, please email the Special Markets Department at SPsales@harpercollins.com.

Originally published as *Sumarljós, og svo kemur nóttin* in Iceland in 2006 by Bjartur.

FIRST HARPERVIA EDITION PUBLISHED 2021

Design adapted by SBI Book Arts, LLC, from the UK edition designed by Libanus Press, Ltd.

Library of Congress Cataloging-in-Publication Data

Names: Jón Kalman Stefánsson, 1963- author. | Roughton, Philip, translator.
Title: Summer light, and then comes the night : a novel / Jón Kalman Stefánsson; [translated by Philip Roughton].
Other titles: Sumarljós, og svo kemur nóttin. English
Description: First edition. | New York : HarperVia, 2021. | "Originally published as Sumarljós, og svo kemur nóttin in Iceland in 2006 by Bjartur"
Identifiers: LCCN 2021018628 | ISBN 9780063136472 (hardcover) | ISBN 9780063136489 (trade paperback) | ISBN 9780063136502 (ebk)
Classification: LCC PT7511.J53915 S8613 2021 | DDC 839/.6934dc23
LC record available at https://lccn.loc.gov/2021018628

21 22 23 24 25   LSC   10 9 8 7 6 5 4 3 2 1

Contents

[Now, we'd almost written that what made our village unique was that it wasn't unique at all; but apparently that isn't true. There are surely other places where most of the houses are younger than ninety years old, villages that can't boast of any noted individuals, no one who has distinguished himself in sports, politics, business, poetry, crime. We seem, however, to have one thing that other villages don't—there's no church here. And no churchyard, either. Still, repeated attempts have been made to remedy this particularity, and a church would undeniably make its mark on our community, the placid tolling of the church bells could liven up those who are feeling down; that sound heralds the good news of eternity. Trees grow in churchyards, birds perch and nest in the trees and they sing. Sólrún, the head teacher of the primary school, has twice tried to collect signatures for a petition requesting three things: a church, a churchyard, and a priest. But she's got thirteen signatures at most, which isn't enough for a priest, much less a church, and even less a churchyard—of course we die like everyone else, though many of us have reached an advanced age; percentage-wise, nowhere else in the country are more people over eighty to be found, which may perhaps be called our particularity number two. Ten or so villagers are approaching one hundred; death seems to have forgotten them, and in the evenings we hear them giggling as they play mini-golf on the green behind the nursing home. No one has managed to find an explanation for this high average age of ours, but whether it's our diet, our attitude toward life, or the position of the mountains, we've been instinctively grateful to longevity for how far it's kept us from the churchyard, which is why we hesitate to sign Sólrún's form, subconsciously convinced that whoever does so is signing his own death warrant, that he's summoning death directly. This is probably just nonsense, but even balderdash can seem convincing where death is involved.

Otherwise, there's nothing remarkable to say about us.

In this village, there are a few dozen detached houses, mostly medium-size and designed by uninspired architects or engineers; remarkable how few demands we make on those who have such a noticeable impact on our surroundings. Here there are also three six-unit rows of terraced houses and a few rather pretty wooden houses from the early twentieth century, the oldest dating back ninety-eight years, built in the year 1903, so dilapidated that big cars drive very slowly past it. The biggest buildings are the slaughterhouse, the Dairy, the Co-op, and the Knitting Company, none of which is pretty, but on the other hand, we have a nice little pier extending into the sea, built with concrete footings fifty years ago, no ships or boats ever dock here but it's fun to pee off the pier, to listen to the funny sound as the stream hits the water.

The village is more or less in the middle of the district, with countryside to the north, south, and east, and the sea to the west. It's nice to look out over the fjord, even if it's nearly devoid of fish, and has always been so. In the spring, the fjord attracts jovial, optimistic waders, sometimes you find a conch shell on the beach, while, in the distance, thousands of islands and skerries rise like a jagged row of teeth from the sea—in the evening, the sun bleeds over it and our thoughts turn to death. Perhaps you're of the opinion that it isn't healthy to think about death, that it drags a person down, fills him with hopelessness, is bad for the circulation, but we believe that one literally needs to be dead not to think about death. Have you, on the other hand, ever considered how many things depend on coincidence—maybe everything? It can be a damned uncomfortable thought; there's seldom any sense to coincidence, making a person's life little other than aimless wandering—sometimes seeming to go in all different directions before stopping, frequently, mid-sentence—perhaps that's precisely why we'd like to tell you stories from our village and the surrounding countryside.

We're not going to tell you about the whole village; we won't be going from house to house. You would find that intolerable. But we'll definitely be telling you about the lust that binds together days and nights, about a happy truck driver, about Elísabet's dark velvet dress and the man who arrived by bus; about Þuríður, who is tall and full of esoteric desires, about a man who couldn't count the fish and a woman who breathed shyly; about a lonely farmer and a 4,000-year-old mummy. We're going to tell of everyday events, but also of those that are beyond our understanding—possibly because there are no explanations for them. People disappear, dreams change lives, folk nearly two hundred years old apparently decide to make their presence known instead of lying quietly in their places. And of course we're going to tell you about the night that hangs over us and draws its power from deep in space, about days that come and go, about birdsong and the final breath; it will probably end up being quite a few stories, we'll start here in the village and end in a farmyard in the countryside to the north, and now we begin, here it comes, the cheerfulness and loneliness, modesty and irrationality, life and a dream—yes, dreams.]

The Universe and a Dark Velvet Dress

1

One night he began dreaming in Latin. *Tu igitur nihil vides?* It took a long time, however, to figure out what language it was; he himself thought that it was just made up, many things dwell in dreams, etc. In those years, things looked considerably different here in the village, we moved a bit slower and the Co-op held everything together. He, on the other hand, was the director of the Knitting Company, having recently turned thirty. He had everything going for him, was married to a woman so beautiful that the mere sight of her made some men feel peculiarly bashful, they had two children, and we expect that one of them, Davíð, will appear later on these pages. The young director seemed born for victory; his family lived in the biggest house in the village, he drove a Range Rover, had his suits custom-made, we were all gray in comparison with him, but then he began dreaming in Latin. It was the old doctor who finally determined what language it was; sadly, though, he died shortly afterward, when Guðjón's damned dog leaped at him, barking, and his old heart gave out. We shot that cursed dog the very next day; if only we had done it sooner. Guðjón threatened to sue us, but then got another dog that proved to be even worse, some of us have tried to run it over, but the creature is quick on its feet. The old doctor knew next to nothing in Latin, just a few words and the names of vital organs, but that was enough when the director managed to recall the aforementioned phrase.

Those who start dreaming in Latin are hardly woven of everyday material. English, Danish, German, yes, yes, French, and even Spanish, it's good to know some of these languages, they expand your world, but Latin, that's something else entirely, it's so much more that we hardly dare try to explain it further. But the director was a man of action, few things stood in his way, he wanted to have control over everything around him and thus found it frustrating when his dreams filled with a language that he did not understand at all. There was only one thing to do about this; go south to the capital, and sign up for an intensive, two-month private course in Latin.

He was so stylish in those years, almost to the point of impudence. He drove to the capital in his Range Rover, bought a new Toyota Corolla, an automatic, for his wife, to keep her from jarring those beautiful, slender legs of hers while he was down south, despite it being unnecessary to buy her a car, considering that there were more than a few who would gladly have carried her through all the streets of the village, along all the paths of life; but he drove south in a tailor-made suit, with a determined and impatient look on his face, his bearing confident but deep within him, which we naturally didn't know back then, tranquil dreams were spreading into what resembled a vast lake with a boat waiting for him on the shore.

2

We would have liked to have had an explanation, or explanations, for the profound transformation, metamorphosis even, that occurred in the director. He went to the capital and returned a completely different man, a man closer to heaven than to earth. Yes, he returned from the south fluent in Latin, which knocked us sideways, we didn't notice the metamorphosis right away, he still drove his Range Rover but his clothes were starting to look neglected, his voice was softer, his movements slower, and it seemed as if the man had got himself a new pair of eyes. The resolute glint was gone, replaced by something we found hard to name, perhaps absentmindedness, perhaps dreaminess, and, at the same time, it was as if he could see through everything, the confusion and the babel and the buzz that characterize our lives, worries about our weight, finances, wrinkles, politics, hairdos. Maybe we should all have gone to the capital to learn Latin and get new eyes; then our village would likely have lifted off the ground and floated into the sky. But we didn't go anywhere, of course, you know how it is; we were stuck fast in the magnetic field of habit. And it was habit, in fact, the soporific routine of everyday life, that accustomed us so surprisingly quickly to the new eyes, the wrinkled clothes, the changed behavior. People are always changing, anyway, finding new hobbies, dyeing their hair, cheating on their spouses, dying, it's hopeless trying to keep track of it all, and besides, we're busy enough trying to understand the buzz in our own heads. But just over a year after the director's Latin course, a delivery from abroad arrived at the post office, a box marked FRAGILE in nine languages. Ágústa, the post office's one and only employee, was so nonplussed by this that she didn't dare open the box, and we had to wait quite a few days before learning what was in it. You can just imagine the conjecture and speculation that this caused; there were various theories, which all, however, turned out to be very wide of the mark, because all that was in the box was a book, an old book, to be sure, and world-famous: *Sidereus Nuncius*, written by Galileo Galilei. The book was a first edition, which is no trivial thing, considering it was published more than four hundred years ago. It is written in Latin and contains this sentence: ". . . without paying attention to its use for terrestrial objects, I betook myself to observations of the heavenly bodies."

There's really no better description of the changes that befell our director, or the Astronomer, as someone called him after the contents of the package became known, after an old eccentric who died many years ago, probably with the intention of mocking the director, but the nickname stuck to him immediately and soon lost its biting edge. It was in fact his wife who told us about the book; she seemed to have a great need to tell as many people as possible about how much her husband had changed, and, believe you me, there were a great many eager to listen. She often wore black lipstick; if only you'd seen her in her green sweater, so beautiful, so attractive, she lived in our dreams, and some of us, for instance Simmi, who, at the time, was approaching fifty, a bachelor, a great horseman who owned twelve horses, was absolutely mad about her and thought at times that he should move away in order to restore some balance to his life. He started riding every day and was often seen passing by her house in the hope of catching a glimpse of her, if only for a split second. And one day Simmi saddled his bay horse, rode off, and saw her walking quickly away from her house.

He made a wide turn in order to ride directly toward her, and they met, she with those black lips, that delicate face, red hair, nose like a tear, eyes so blue, and wearing her green sweater under her fluttering coat, beautiful, a revelation, even, and no one knows how it happened, but Simmi, that highly experienced horseman, fell off his horse. Beauty unsaddled me, he would say later, but some maintained that he'd simply thrown himself off the horse, in a kind of desperation or momentary madness. He broke his thighbone, fractured his arm, and there he lay. There was no doctor in the village, the old one had died three days earlier, that fucking dog, that goddamn Guðjón, and no new one expected until a week later, we were advised to stay healthy in the meantime, those with heart troubles to keep calm, but then Simmi fell off his horse. She ran to him, tended to the poor bugger, her eyes bluer than blue. There was talk of sending him to a hospital in the capital, but we don't really like fuss or trouble so the vet jumped in and did a great job; Simmi has only a slight limp now. Those minutes that she knelt over him and breathed into his face, with her sweet, warm scent, are the best and most precious in his life, minutes that he loves to recall, over and over. On the other hand, it's unlikely that she would care to relive this incident, having recently discovered that her husband had sold his Range Rover, and the Toyota as well, in order to purchase the *Sidereus Nuncius* by Galileo. To him, it had been perfectly obvious, and he hadn't felt like talking about it, which was probably the worst part of it, she'd stormed out, furious and so desperate

9

that she could hardly breathe, the world had started to crumble around her, and then this horseman showed up.

It must tear something inside you, your heartstrings, for instance, when the person whom you believe you know inside out, whom you fell for, married, had children with, a home and memories, suddenly appears to you one day as a stranger. Of course, it's sheer nonsense to believe that you know someone inside out, there are always dark corners, sometimes even entire abodes covered in shadow—but in any case, she was married to a relatively young man who had some clout in our community, was a linchpin in the village, a man who had a real influence on our lives, an unpromising company flourished under his direction and earned some profit, he was a role model, he was our hope and anchor, but then he began dreaming in Latin, drove to the capital to learn the language, returned with new eyes, and sold his cars a year later to pay for old books. In comparison to all of this, one man's fall from his horse is trivial—though we're only speaking of the very beginning. The days rose in the east, they disappeared into the west, the Astronomer was hardly seen anymore at the Knitting Company, and Ágústa made numerous trips from the post office to the couple's house with new deliveries, some marked FRAGILE in nine languages.

Three or four weeks after the Italian Galileo rid the couple of their two cars, the Astronomer received an even older book, *On the Revolutions of the Heavenly Spheres* by Copernicus, printed in the year 1543. It cost a fortune, just slightly more than their house, but her patience, which some people truly miss, finally ran out when he received first editions of three books written in the seventeenth century by Johannes Kepler: the *Rudolphine*

Tables, Harmonices Mundi, and *The Dream, or Posthumous Work on Lunar Astronomy.* Before the arrival of these books in the post office, many had tried to talk sense into the Astronomer; the bank manager, the commissioner, the head teacher, a representative of the employees of the Knitting Company. These people asked, what are you doing to you and your wife, throwing your life into books, you're emptying your bank accounts, losing your house, you're losing your life, get hold of yourself, dear man! But it was all in vain, he just looked at these people with those new eyes of his, smiled as if he felt sorry for them, and said something in Latin that no one understood. There's no need to tell you the rest; about fifteen years have passed, now he has around three thousand books, and they're growing in number, they cover the walls of his little house, many written in Latin, like most of those that had deprived him of beauty, comfort, and a family life.

Shortly after Ágústa delivered the parcel containing Kepler's books, his wife moved to the capital with their daughter, while Davíð, on the other hand, remained with his father, who bought the two-story wooden house here just above the village center, the house had stood empty ever since old Bogga passed away in her bed there and no one knew about it until the wind changed and the stench wafted from the house over to the Dairy—loneliness exists in little villages as well. When the Astronomer bought the house, it looked like an old, crooked horse, half blind and dying, but he had the rotten wooden boards and broken windowpanes replaced with new ones—imagine if it was just as easy to replace a rotten worldview, a dying culture—and then he had the house painted pitch-black apart from a few white dots on three walls and the roof. The dots form the four constellations that he adores the most, the Big Dipper, the Pleiades, Cassiopeia, and the Herdsman. The fourth wall is completely black, it faces west, toward the sea, and symbolizes the end of the world. It isn't particularly uplifting, but at least the west wall is facing away from the road. The Astronomer's house is the first that can be seen of the village, when approaching it from the southern valleys; in the daytime it's as if a fraction of the night sky has fallen to the ground, onto the village. There's a big, openable window on the roof of the house, and late in the evening the telescope pokes from it, an eye that sucks in distance, darkness, and light. Now he lives there alone—Davíð moved down into the village when he was sixteen—and listens sometimes to the sound of the winter darkness pressing up against the windows of the houses.

3

When things were best, ten people worked at the Knitting Company, which is quite something in a village of four hundred souls. It was built in three months in the summer of 1983: 380 square meters, on two floors. The window on the upper floor overlooks the roof of the slaughterhouse and the fjord. The Knitting Company was built by the state; such buildings rise very slowly and so hesitantly that it's as if construction will be called off every day, and, little by little, people forget the purpose of the building. But so much is dependent on coincidence. The colors of the mountains, the cold you come down with in March, the speed at which buildings are built, two members of parliament winding up getting drunk together. One of them was a Progressive, the other from the old Social Democratic Party, and sometime late in the night they began betting on which of them would be quicker to set up a ten-person company in new facilities in his constituency. Thus did the Knitting Company come to be. Production commenced in the autumn of 1983 under the strong, enthusiastic management of its young director, who was on his way abroad, to conquer the world, when the Progressive MP offered him the job. The next ten years were lustrous and full of purpose. On the lower floor, the machines whirred; on the upper were the break room, toilet, and even a shower, besides a room allotted to the village's youth society for its headquarters. Good years. We felt as if this was the start of something big, were convinced that our village wouldn't start bleeding to death like so many other ones; whenever we looked at the director, we were filled with a sense of security. The machines whirred, socks, sweaters, caps, mittens streamed from them, and it could be a beautiful thing to go up to the Co-op, see perhaps five farmers conversing and all of them wearing garments from the Knitting Company; then there was beauty and harmony in the world, and we miss those times. But everything comes to an end, which, it seems, is the only thing you can count on in this life. *Tu igitur nihil vides*, the director dreams in Latin, changes into the Astronomer, sacrifices his SUV, house, wife, family life, and a bright future for the sky and a few old books. And one day in the mid-nineties, the machines on the lower floor were loaded onto a huge truck, which was followed by many heavy months, the sun and moon shone in through the windows of the empty room.

It would be unfair of us to blame the dreams of one man for these difficult, disheartening changes; you would likely lose faith in our fairness and even our credibility, and then what would be the point of our continuing with our account? The Knitting Company's machines went to another village out east, where the need was greater, where there was a higher number of unemployed, undecided voters, although it certainly would have made a difference if the director had put his foot down, it surely must count for something when such great talent, a new SUV, and tailor-made suits offer resistance. We can't remember precisely how long the lower floor of the building stood empty, but for a whole year the Astronomer continued to receive a hefty paycheck as the director of a phantom company. The rank and file, however, were immediately out in the cold: nine employees—seven women, two men. The men made other arrangements, spoke to their friends from football, school, the Rotary Club; this is a man's world. One of them, Gunnar, became an assistant to our electrician, Simmi, while the other man, Ásgrímur, usually called Ossi, became the assistant to the plumber, mason, and carpenter, dividing his working week between them and ending up, over time, quite multitalented and sought-after for all sorts of jobs. Ossi starts his day by thanking Providence for having sent the Knitting Company's machines to the east, considerably closer to the sunrise.

Of the seven women, five are still unemployed after all these years. Five unemployed women; that makes ten hands altogether. The other women were luckier. One of them is named Elísabet, and we'll tell you more about her later. The other woman, Helga, mans a telephone from 8 a.m. to 5 p.m., five days a week.

It was probably our head teacher, Sólrún, who found Helga her job. For quite some time, Sólrún had been worried about the stress that vexes modern man: the fast pace, the pressure, the way of life. She pulled some strings in the system, wrote letters, she spoke to influential people, and then Helga sat down at that phone and has been sitting there ever since. The job, which is a kind of experimental or innovative project, we're not quite certain what precisely to call it, involves listening to the person who calls, putting in a word or two, perhaps a sentence, but keeping calm no matter what comes up. It's as simple as that; yet not entirely simple. Some call just to chat, are lonely, want to hear someone breathing, while others call to rid themselves of all the intolerance, all the restlessness and anxiety that the short-winded present swirls up inside us. Sólrún believed that Helga's job would relieve some people's tension, alleviate the sting of loneliness in others. Concerning stress, she wrote in one of her letters: ". . . it's a phenomenon that builds up inside us and thus needs venting at times."

Helga is around forty, unmarried, she has one child and a soft and beautiful neck. The father of her child, a farmer from the countryside in the south, thinks about her quite a lot, about her neck, which he kisses often in his mind, and which we perhaps do, too. She likes her job, immerses herself in thick tomes about psychology, she reads books that try to define modern times, many of the books are in English, Helga often feels thankful for having lost her job at the Knitting Company. Some days are difficult, for sure; some people who call are so overwhelmed with stress that all they do is scream, sometimes they're furious, and then they flood Helga's ears with a torrent of abuse, which, for them, is cathartic; they feel better afterward but her ears still smart when she sets the table for herself and her daughter in the evening. One or two people have so deeply regretted losing their tempers over the telephone that they have sent her things that are supposed to betoken their remorse, their gratitude, their nice thoughts: Anton, the village's taxi driver, brings her flowers, red wine, a six-pack of beer, a bottle of vodka, a book, a puppy, and once a russet lamb with eyes that reflected the sky. The puppy has grown into a model dog, the lamb a sheep that spends blissful hours in Helga's garden. It is fun seeing her walking around the village; we recall her in our evening prayers and say, please protect Helga's beautiful head from exploding under that foul abuse.

By abuse, we don't mean solely the insults that people yell or say over the phone, tattered and troubled by modernity; now we're also, and no less, thinking about the five women, the ten hands, that didn't find work. They meet up twice a week and have done so ever since the Knitting Company's machines were loaded onto the truck; they keep each other company and help fill the void that comes with unemployment. Ten hands in a living room, ten unemployed hands that were once part of a chain of production, made their mark on daily life, but look at them now, what a waste of hands, and time passes. They don't always speak kindly of Helga, they would do her job better and skip all the clownishness, the psychology books, the russet sheep, wearing red shirts with black jeans, the ten hands launch themselves into the air like angry bees. And now men have begun calling her to discuss their marriages, complain about their wives, not enough sex; widowers, divorcés, and bachelors call and talk about their loneliness. We should complain about this to the Ministry of

Social Affairs, says one of them, or does this sort of work fall under the Ministry of Health? They aren't sure, and the months come and go. Together, the five women watch the home-design TV show *Interior/Exterior*, TV dramas, cooking shows, talk shows, it's actually a full-time job keeping up with both the TV schedule and the life of the village, though in recent years it's become more difficult to differentiate between them. But there are ten unemployed hands, a coffee table overloaded with cakes, oven-baked dishes, coffeepots, recipes, self-help books, popular novels, it's summer, it's winter, radiant summer light, pitch-black nights.

4

It would hardly be habitable here at the end of the world if the winter wasn't so long and the sky so dark. On winter evenings and nights, the Astronomer wanders around the village with his eyes on the sky, sometimes with a good pair of binoculars, and if he isn't outside, he sits at the big telescope that sucks distances down into the village, he pores over books, some in that ancient language, Latin, he stares at his computer screen and thinks a great deal. His hair grays, he is highly intelligent, he understands many things about the universe that we can't comprehend at all. Some of us have asked if God has appeared in his telescope, but the Astronomer doesn't talk about God, maybe it's enough to have the sky and Latin, stars never abandon us, though the same apparently can't be said about God. The stars are always nearby, even if we who are bound to everydayness find it a bit difficult to talk about nearness and stars at the same time; Reykjavík is a considerable distance away; Sydney is of course very distant, yet, even so, that's only a stone's throw compared to Mars, which even at its closest might be 56 million kilometers away, quite a long distance for the Astronomer to drive in his old Mazda, which can reach 110 kilometers per hour when descending long slopes. But of course everything is upside down and relative, most words have so many sides that they can make our heads spin, the person you live with, for instance, can be more distant than the planet Mars, neither a spaceship nor a telescope can bridge the gap. But no one lives on the sky alone, years have passed since the Knitting Company closed, around nine years since the Astronomer lost his director's salary, and what does he live on now? Living is expensive, even if you have no interest in high-pressure washers, a bigger television, the newest kitchen furnishings; we ponder this a bit but are afraid to ask the Astronomer about it directly, he who roams the surface of the earth, tall, slender, with thick gray hair, those in his presence instinctively lower their voices, try to avoid petty thoughts. We ask him about stars, the sky, Copernicus, but not much else and certainly not money. Even old Lára doesn't dare bother him with her stories, if only we were so lucky. Seen from a distance, she's like a fat little "r," she moves extremely slowly, but is suspiciously good at cornering us at the Co-op, the bank, the health clinic, and launching, without warning, into stories about her life, seemingly always starting mid-sentence. Her life has grown quite long, if it were possible to pull the years out as you would a measuring tape, it would easily reach Jupiter, though hardly back again. But why should we, ignorant and incapable, sunk to our ears in the monotony of everyday life, be bothered about a man who carries the heavens in his head and receives dozens of letters a year from all over the world, all written in Latin?

5

There are still people who go to the trouble of writing letters. And here we mean in the old-fashioned way: writing the words down on paper, or typing them into a computer and printing them out, putting the letter into an envelope and taking it to the post office, even if the addressee won't get it until the next day, at best, often considerably later. Isn't clinging to a lost world reactionism, blowing on cool coals? We've grown accustomed to speed; you type words into the computer, press a button, and they're at their destination. That's what we call brisk. And why then send letters by regular mail? We scarcely have the patience for such slowness—why use a horse-drawn cart when you have a car? Of course, words in computers tend to disappear, become nothing, become locked up in old programs, be erased when the computer crashes and our thoughts and actions turn to air; in a hundred years, let alone a thousand, no one will know that we existed. Naturally, though, we shouldn't care; we're living here and now, and won't be in a hundred years, but one day we come across old letters and something strange stirs inside us, we sense a thread that reaches from us back into the dimness of the past, and we think this is the thread that holds time together.

London, May 28, 1759

Now hurry home from this silly war, come right away and warm my breasts. I'm nothing, I'm lost without you.

The letters we send each other by email turn to nothing in a few years, and the thought, the feeling, that we've broken the thread, gnaws at us, the thread reaches us but goes no further, we create a void that will never be filled. We want, first and foremost, to display fidelity to our own time, not some possible future, yet are stuck with our gnawing guilt, as if we're committing a crime; we're really quite good at accumulating guilt. We feel guilty about not reading enough, about talking too little to our friends, spending too little time with our children, with the old folks. We're constantly on the move, instead of sitting down and listening to the rain, drinking a cup of coffee, warming breasts. And we never write letters.

Yet it does occasionally happen that we who live here, far from Highway Number One, sit down, write a letter, and take it to the post office. This makes Ágústa happy, gives her purpose and us a pleasant feeling that shivers through our bodies, similar to when we recall how nice it was to sip soda through a licorice straw, similar to when we go to the National Museum or visit an old aunt; we've shown the past our fidelity.

6

Back in the day, the post office was one of the hubs of the village, through which letters and parcels streamed, where there were two telephone booths for those who needed to make calls outside the county, and at which queues would often form on Tuesdays—the deadline for ordering alcohol from the south that was supposed to be drunk over the weekend. But now those phone booths have been taken away; gone are the days when Ágústa could listen in. Now the village even has its own liquor store, open from 1 p.m. to 2:30 p.m., Tuesdays and Thursdays; thus does everything change.

Thirty years ago, four women worked at the post office; Ágústa was very young then, and wore such thick, red lipstick that it resembled a stop sign, maybe that's why she's still unmarried, despite being middle-aged now. Four women thirty years ago, and now it's just Ágústa, besides the postmen, one who sees to the village and four who deliver the mail in the countryside. In December, however, Ágústa gets two of her nieces to lend her a hand, so young that everything quivers around them, the boys come with letters and postcards, they send anything to anyone just to be able to go and see them. Ágústa and the post office are one, like an arm and its sleeve. The postmen she manages with iron discipline; she's short, slim, light as a feather, it's perilous for her to be outside when the wind is stronger than twelve meters per second, she's hoarse and wrinkled, as only those who are big smokers can be, her hands sometimes resemble two curious little dogs.

We put a bit of thought into this comparison to dogs, because Ágústa is very curious and her nosiness has come very close, barely a finger's breadth, to costing her both her job and her reputation. Ágústa was called names, she was threatened, but she remained steadfast at all times, would not be misled and stayed true to her nature. But this all began in the mid-seventies, the world was different then, all of the Beatles were alive, you boarded planes without thinking about terrorists, roads were less easily traveled, more winding, distances were considerably greater, the world seemed bigger and the post office was still one of the focal points for human interaction in the village. Ágústa had worked at the post office for three or four years, she was well liked and extremely efficient, but there was a certain restlessness simmering inside her, dissatisfaction, she wasn't entirely content, there was something missing from her life. One day she opened one of the letters being sent from the village and read it. And it was so good, like inhaling cigarette smoke after a long abstinence, a feeling of well-being spread throughout her body, Ágústa sighed; one thing leads to another. She opened another letter, opened a parcel, opened a package, and became, over time, one of the top news outlets in the village, bringing us tidings big and small, informing us of expectations and disappointments; twice she revealed affairs, thrice warned parents when their teenagers, in letters to pen pals, gave indication that they were heading down the wrong path in life. You may find it strange that the people here put up with Ágústa's hands being like two curious dogs among all the letters and packages, knowing who got what, who were subscribers to pornographic magazines, or the *Crotch Times* as she called them, but you mustn't forget that the winter can be long, it can be slow and uneventful, there are so few of us, there's snow on the streets and the wind blows between our houses. Then it's not so bad to come up with some reason to go down to the post office, say something appropriate to Ágústa, return from there with news, some snippet, some gossip to munch on, to talk about over coffee, to make time pass. But as we said, Ágústa came close, a finger's breadth or so, to losing her job and reputation, she was accused of violating people's privacy, of betraying their trust, was

22

called a tattletale, a gossip, a snake, a witch. It was then that her smoking shot up from a little less than a pack a day to a little more than two; it has remained so ever since, making it safe to say that the verbal assaults, the criticism and slander, have shortened Ágústa's life by a few years—some of us have a thing or two on our consciences. But she wasn't sacked. The matter just faded away. Over time, she also learned to be more cunning, to modulate what she reported as if she'd got the news from others, which didn't really fool anyone, but you can get used to anything, it all becomes ordinary and a matter of course in the end. Without a doubt, her information was useful; Ágústa's curiosity has saved marriages, got people out of hopeless relationships, now we readily take advantage of the situation, have even sent letters solely to spread certain news, but times change, the number of post offices is constantly dwindling, they're closed or relegated to corners of grocery stores, and in that way lose their individuality, it's called streamlining, and email reduces the number of postmen. Ágústa's importance in our society has lessened, she's no longer the epicenter, yet it wasn't until letters and parcels began pouring to the Astronomer that we realized how dependent we were on Ágústa, her vigilance and curiosity. You can just imagine her discomfort when she opened the first letters and saw that they were all in Latin. Ágústa had become good at plowing her way through letters in English and the Scandinavian languages; she had excellent dictionaries. What do I do now, Ágústa thought, turning over the first letter between her tobacco-stained fingers. The next day, another letter arrived, then the third, and within a week there were six. This put a strain on Ágústa, dark circles developed under her eyes, she became crestfallen, we took notice of it, maybe she's got cancer, we thought, and cursed her smoking. Ágústa isn't one of those who give up, she's determined, a fighter, she spoke to Jakob, the truck driver, and a few days later, he brought her a Latin–Icelandic dictionary. But she had a hard time deciphering that language, and, what's more, the letters were all handwritten and the correspondents seemed to be competing to see who could write worse, dammit, those bloody bastards, said Ágústa. This disappointed us; we felt as if Ágústa had failed us, she sensed it, looked dejected sometimes, for no apparent reason. And more letters arrived, but gradually Ágústa stopped opening them, silence spread over them, mysterious silence.

7

What might he be thinking, we asked sometimes, meaning the Astronomer, how does he feel, what goes on inside those who have sacrificed everything, turned their backs on success, family, daily life? We were anxious to know, an inexhaustible topic of conversation on long winter evenings when the world seemed to have forgotten us and nothing happened except for the sky changing color. So it drew a great deal of attention when Elísabet hung up an announcement in the Co-op, in the same spot where old Geir and then Kiddi have advertised film screenings for thirty years:

WHAT MATTERS

Starting next Wednesday evening, the Astronomer will give a monthly talk at the Community Center about what matters. He will begin punctually at 9 p.m. Each talk, with an accompanying slide show, will last around 40 minutes. The talks are sponsored by the Nordic Council of Ministers. He will answer questions at the end of each lecture. Coffee will be provided.

It was a full house in the Community Center meeting room, the turnout nearly equaled Kiddi's best-attended film screenings, James Bond, *Die Hard*. Davíð and Elísabet had their hands full. Coffee, crullers, hors d'oeuvres, showing people to their seats, taking coats, it was an important night and we had butterflies in our stomachs, the big moment had arrived, soon we would learn what the Astronomer was thinking, what was written in those books. We drank coffee, munched crullers, hesitantly tasted the hors d'oeuvres, enjoyed ourselves, and said: What matters is that Arsenal wins the championship, that I get an erection tonight, that Goggi doesn't come too quickly, what matters is getting bloody well drunk enough this weekend. The whole time, the Astronomer stood there on the stage, behind the podium, staring into space, appearing not to care about anything, our chatter, the anticipation, that evening, his talk, as if he were gazing through the building's walls and roof at the evening sky, which grew darker between the stars as the autumn passed. He's above it all, we thought, not without admiration; he's a sage. Yet what was really going on was that the Astronomer had to hold tightly to the podium so as not to collapse, I won't survive this, he thought. Now and then, Davíð glanced sidelong at the stage, he won't survive this, he whispered to Elísabet, who was wearing a black velvet dress, it hugged her body, some people bit their nails, gnawed at their knuckles, what matters is a black velvet dress. You may recall that Elísabet worked at the Knitting Company, not for long, just the last two years, and, despite being barely more than a child, she soon became the unofficial assistant to the director, the fucking bitch, thought the five women who sat toward the front of the room and followed her with their eyes, just as well that looks can't kill. Elísabet lowered the room's lights but turned up the spotlights over the stage, she and Davíð took seats in the front row, closest to the stage, and the light from the spotlights fell over them like a fine mist. The Astronomer's heart pounded like that of a small animal caught in a trap, his body trembled, his hands quivered. We stared up at the stage, minutes passed, he said nothing, just stared into space, and some of us had begun to think that the Astronomer had gathered us there to tell us about silence, that that was what mattered, and that his books, then, must have been full of silence. Yes, of course, and our blather, chatter, and prattle disgust him, we blabber day in and day out about things that are worthless, the length of curtains, sizes of tires, and then we die.

In silence I store the gold; he who remains silent, keeps to himself, can discover various things, silence seeps in under the skin, soothes the heart, numbs the anxiety, fills the room you're in, fills the house, while outside the present blusters, it's a sprinter, a race car, a dog that chases its tail but never catches it. But silence is, unfortunately, afraid of people; it doesn't last long in a crowd, quickly flees. Someone coughed, someone swallowed, someone whispered and hid his grin behind his hand. Davíð closed his eyes and thought, I can't take any more, I'm not here, but Elísabet stood up slowly. She turned around and looked over the half-darkened room, probably meant to say something, looked at us, thought about it, the whispering dwindled, the grins faded, they vanished, we stared at her because there she stood. Only twenty-four years old, in her dusky velvet dress, with her long, dark hair over her shoulders, deep brown eyes, not exactly beautiful, but with something about her, dammit all, we thought, yet she isn't naked beneath that dress—and everything slowed down. The sky over the Community Center fell silent, the blood in our veins ran slower, nothing else mattered but this woman. The stage lights seemed to be drawn to her, to hold her like soft, almost see-through hands, she was wearing a dark velvet dress that appeared to be held up solely by her breasts, or by the gentle electrical current between the velvet and her nipples. Dammit all to hottest hell, thought someone in his powerlessness, soon the dress will slip down and not stop until her hips; dear God, let it happen, let the dress drop, allow my eyes to behold something beautiful, because there's a long winter ahead. Damned whore, damned cock gorge, muttered the five women to each other, and then the Astronomer opened his mouth, he said: There's room for everything in the breadth of the sky.

Such a statement comprises everything or nothing at all, and we didn't know which it was. With Elísabet standing there as well, it was impossible for us to think, digest words, but then she sat down and the Astronomer said, calmly, but at the same time so enthusiastically that we recalled the glory days of the Knitting Company: Immense is the expanse of the sky; it encompasses our beginning and our end. His voice was soft and dusky, like a velvet dress.

And that's how it began.

Once a month for ten years or so, the Astronomer was sure

to be found standing behind the podium on the stage of the Community Center. Nine years, that's how time flies, we wake sometimes to the melancholy call of the oystercatcher in the stillness of the morning, look outside and see that there's frost in the sky.

But despite that October evening nine years ago encompassing the expanse of the universe and a dusky velvet dress, the audience shrank rapidly in numbers as the winter went on, by spring it would have been newsworthy if ten people showed up to listen to the ticking of the universal clock in the Astronomer's talks, and it has stayed that way. I guess we should have listened better; we feel a bit guilty about that, one more cursed thing to feel guilty about, but you can't look past the fact that so many things need tending to, so dense is the daily snowfall, the quagmire. You have to put the kids to bed, tidy up the house, flip through magazines, paint a door, check under the car, call someone, *Interior/Exterior* might be on TV, maybe a Champions League football match, and there's undeniably more life in the Real Madrid players than in the Astronomer's talks. We do, however, drop in when there's nothing else going on, no match, one of the ping-pong table's legs broken, the coffee at the shop stale, have driven thirty times around the village, blathered enough about the newest gossip, we envy those who have an ADSL connection, have a hot tub, a good selection of DVDs. We poke our noses in, listen to the sky breathe through the words of the Astronomer, have coffee and canapés served by Elísabet, look at her and wonder whether she's bare breasted beneath her blouse or sweater or dress, then look again at the ghostly pale face of the man giving the talk, which, over the years, has become emaciated, the sharp nose seems even sharper, and, seen in profile, his head resembles an ax. The ten hands have stopped coming entirely, the stars are too far away, we want to think about things that are closer to us, they say, besides asserting that men attend the talks only to stare at Elísabet's breasts, the men hope that she notices them staring and sticks the tip of her tongue out between her moist lips, that bitch, nothing but deceit and knows only too well that the path to a man's will lies through his crotch.

The poor attendance has no effect on the Astronomer, he's just as inspired whether there are two people listening or fifty, but even if we're unnecessarily reluctant to attend, we're still happy, yes, proud of these lectures, they provide the village with an air of erudition, and are a welcome addition to its social life. It can be difficult to fill the evenings with life in a village of four hundred souls; seven or eight dances are held here per year, whist drives and bingo nights, as well as Kiddi's film screenings.

8

On good days, we call him Kiddi the Movie Star, he had a small role in Friðrik Þór's movie *White Whales*, very young at the time, and therefore knows the movie business inside and out. The screenings are held on the first and third Thursdays of the month, from September to the end of May, a poster of the film being shown is hung on Sunday and the program, put together by Kiddi himself, can be bought at the shop for 300 krónur. It contains descriptions of the director, the actors, sometimes the cameraman or editor, and the movie's subject. Around 1990, Kiddi took over from old Geir, who had by then been showing us films for more than twenty years, always with the same projector, which he set up in the back row of seats; toward the end, it was really worn out, coughed like a tractor on its last legs, was so loud that it would drown out the quieter scenes on the screen, had endless trouble with the focus, and the film's colors tended to merge into one. Geir died during a hilarious comedy at which we howled with laughter. It's good to laugh, heartfelt laughter is a mysterious blend of bliss and oblivion, we evaporate in it, hover above our personalities, become people more than characters. Sadly, we don't remember the name of the film, but it was before the interval and after a thunderous burst of laughter filled the room, those sitting closest to the projector began wondering why Geir was so quiet and serious, he who was so proud of his films and laughed with childlike joy whenever the audience laughed. Heiða, the agent, who held the licenses for all the lotteries, insurance companies, and newspapers in this part of the country, leaned toward Geir, tugged at him, and whispered somewhat loudly, what is this, man, are you dead, or what? Which really was the case—old Geir had stopped breathing, had died up against the projector and therefore couldn't laugh anymore. Since then, Heiða has been careful with her words.

It was pretty much a given that Kiddi would take over, the Movie Star himself, who had, in addition, assisted the old man for many years. Kiddi started by buying a new projector, saying that Geir had been too much in love with the old one, and soon began writing his own programs as well, in which he could share with us his thoughts, opinions, and knowledge about the films, quickly became quite clever at recapitulating the films' plots, his best summaries could stand on their own as fine short stories. His wife, Steinunn, embellished the programs with lissom illustrations connected, objectively or subjectively, to the films' subjects. Steinunn and Kiddi got together at one of the last of old Geir's film screenings. She had just moved to the village from Reykjavík, to work as a substitute teacher, short, petite, with long, dirty-blond hair and a particularly smooth gait, our attention had been drawn to the way she dressed, in expensive designer clothing, said those who were knowledgeable in such things. She showed up at one of the film screenings in pale-blue jeans, with the number 6 on her right knee and 8 on the left. Kiddi had a flask on him, it was something of a tradition to have a drop or two during screenings, well, some drink a bit too much and throw up in the toilet. Kiddi has never been shy, he's a man of the world, a movie actor and whatnot, and he walked up to the teacher-woman, of whom the rest of us were still a bit shy, asked, so how do you like it here in this place where nothing happens, and then offered her the flask: brandy. She took a sip, very carefully, Kiddi smiled, and then the film started. She took another sip during the interval, they chatted, Kiddi began staring at her knees, marked 6 and 8. What? she asked, a bit uncertain when she saw how he was staring down at her. Then he looked up, straight into her eyes, and asked, can I be number 7? Such a question is either life or death, a slap on the cheek or a kiss. They missed the second half of the film, you've got a mirror over your bed, she said, you don't like it? No, I'd like it if it were all around the bed.

9

That's how it was, but it would never cross anyone's mind to get drunk at the Astronomer's talks, despite it being desirable, perhaps, to numb the senses a bit against the menacing powers that come out of his mouth, the black holes that lurk in space like demonic spiders and suck up everything in their vicinity, meteorites, comets, moons, planets, suns, everything disappears into the insatiable black void.

Black holes are dead suns, said the Astronomer, which is also stated in the brochure that Elísabet publishes six times a year, containing excerpts from his lectures. One of these brochures tells a little about Johannes Kepler, who is something of a favorite of ours. His mother was accused of witchcraft, she was known to hit men with a wet cloth but took very good care of her son, who wrote the book *The Dream, or Posthumous Work on Lunar Astronomy*, the same one that cost the Astronomer his wife's patience, our fingers quiver slightly when we think of her. This book is about people who travel to the moon from Iceland. The Astronomer translated and read aloud the part that takes place in this country, Kepler lived in the seventeenth century, when Iceland was on the edge of the known world and often came close to falling off the maps. The head teacher, Sólrún, had the children do projects based on this account, and in the spring held an exhibition of their pictures. However, Sólrún didn't have the children do projects about black holes, which aren't considered particularly child friendly, black holes are worse than liberalism, worse than the United States, worse than the greenhouse effect, black holes are dead suns that were, in their time, many times larger than our sun—which has, however, been called the eye of God. They illuminate worlds for millions of years, then collapse into small yet dizzyingly dense points and become black holes. The history of black holes, it says in the brochure:

. . . undeniably recalls the story of Lucifer, the bright angel who was cast into hell, and what was bright became dark, the glorious became the devilish. Perhaps black holes are the instruments of the Devil, the most horrendous weapons in the eternal war against the Lord, who has grown so distant from us that it is difficult to stave off utter despair.

Cheers, one should say, away from me, Satan, or else: More light!

[The sea is deep, it changes colors and seems to breathe. It's good to have the sea so close by, because sometimes days pass without anything happening, and then we can look out over the fjord that becomes blue, becomes green, and then darkens, like the end of the world. But if it's true that standing still is speed's dream, then we should perhaps establish a sanatorium for city residents suffering from stress, and now we're thinking not only of Reykjavík but also of London, Copenhagen, New York, Berlin: *Come to the place where nothing happens, nothing moves but the sea, the clouds, and four pet cats.* The advertisement wouldn't be entirely truthful, but what advertisement is? Those who work in advertising have to be able to convince us that the useless is important, which is going quite well, because our lives are slowly filling with useless things and worthless moments; comforts pile up around us, with our heads barely sticking out above them.

In the old days, what people feared most was need, and misery: hunger, poverty, the cold; they dreamed of comforts: less toil, less hardship, to have time for themselves; they worked themselves to the bone, lived in dark, sometimes damp houses, it was a long distance to the doctor, even farther to schooling, they died before their time, had too few joyful moments, life was spent scraping through. But you know how it is today, we have everything of which our ancestors dreamed, live considerably longer, have better health, don't know hunger, feel hungry only when we're on a diet or get stuck in a bad traffic jam, we worry about our physiques, enlarge or reduce our breasts, fight against going bald, go to tanning salons, we dream of straighter teeth and are always looking for new recipes, many people work too much, and, with men, their penis sizes correspond to the length of time they spend working. We have it quite easy, yet don't feel well, because what are we supposed to do with all these days, with life itself, it's hard to work out why we are living. But at least our beach is beautiful, it's curved, a little less than a kilometer long, it's soothing to stand there gazing at something bigger than yourself. The ocean is eternal, it says somewhere, which, unfortunately, is utter nonsense, everything changes, the sun dies, seas dry up, great people are forgotten, but in comparison to a human life, the sea is certainly eternal. And just under thirty years ago, we also had the feeling that the Soviet Union and the Federation of Icelandic Cooperative Societies, the mother of all co-ops, were eternal. The Co-op was the center of the universe, it ran the grocery store, the Depot, the gas station, the convenience shop, the slaughterhouse, farmers deposited all their produce in it and made withdrawals in groceries, feed enhancer, gasoline, fencing material, Christmas presents, Easter eggs, they never saw any money except for when someone had to go to the capital to see the dentist. It was a time of stasis, a damned suffocating stillness, and behind it all was the Progressive Party, our beginning and end, we thought that things would never change, and there we were most definitely wrong. Remarkable how everything changes in the end, the Iron Curtain, black-and-white TV, typewriters, when will this progress stop, you don't have to answer that, we're just thinking out loud because now everything is changing so quickly that if you blink, you drop out of your connection with the world. Yet it wasn't until the Federation collapsed, rotten on the inside like the United States in our days, the rank, musty stench wafts over the ocean in the relentless western wind, that we truly understood the Co-op's supreme power. It is only when the chains break that you truly feel how heavy they were.

But here in the village lives a man who thinks little about the passage of time, about how everything changes, his name is Jónas and he painted the Astronomer's corrugated-iron-clad house. Jónas can change the world with his paintbrush; he changed a house clad with sheets of corrugated iron into the night sky.]

Tears Are Shaped Like Rowing Boats

1

Jónas is scrawny and wispy, of nearly medium height, he's fragile, don't step too hard on the ground near him or he'll shatter. Jónas grew up so slowly and quietly that we forgot about him for long periods of time, he never said anything unless spoken to, never really answered with anything but one-syllable words in a voice like a woolen thread, thin but early on with a touch of darkness, and easily severed. He did poorly in school, his teachers rarely bothered to ask him anything in class, let alone call him up to the blackboard, he slept little the weeks before exams, threw up twice over the exam desk and on one occasion fainted. Jónas never made any friends, nor, however, any enemies; the children hardly ever teased him, maybe because his father was Hannes, a giant of a man and the village's police officer, yet maybe more so because Jónas was so self-effacing that even the children were embarrassed in his presence—but the years passed. Jónas sat against the school wall and watched the other children play; this was in the seventies and eighties, he looked at his hands, which were so thin that the light shone through them.

He left school at the age of fourteen.

Then his classmates underwent growth spurts, while Jónas remained the same. The girls developed breasts, a gentle curve to their waists, the boys' hormones raged, they turned into a mad herd of bellowing bulls, they punched walls, howled at the sky, and got erections if a girl simply coughed. Jónas didn't seem to feel any such thing, he just pressed himself even tighter against the school's wall and then stopped attending, shut himself in his room. Hannes had to break his way through the door; he bribed, threatened, cursed, begged, but his son never went back to school. The boy is a moron, some said, Hannes talked to the foreman at the Dairy, they were friends, and on the dot of nine one Monday morning in February, Jónas showed up for work. Stick to the broom, said the foreman, and that was all the job description he was given. It was the late eighties, soon the Berlin Wall would be torn down and its fragments sold as souvenirs; man has an extraordinary talent for changing threats, death, and despair into cold hard cash.

Jónas had always had exceptionally pale skin, like a light bulb in darkness, stand next to me so I can read, said his dad when the electricity went out on winter nights in the years when there was still mad weather and the villages slept under blankets of snow. Yet despite his nearly unbearable shyness, Jónas was never seen blushing; he just became even paler when he was embarrassed, and we were terribly frightened that he would fade completely into the daylight and disappear. But two months after Jónas began working at the Dairy, he was seen blushing for the first time, and for no apparent reason; some of the girls, and even the women as well, looked down and kept their thoughts to themselves. The foreman was so excited at this turn of events that he called Hannes, who prepared a chicken for dinner that evening, cooked fries, gave his son half a beer and himself five and a half, now we celebrate! he said. Jónas didn't understand a thing, but sipped his beer and got drunk, you're as lightweight as a bird, said Hannes with a laugh, and then an unusually beautiful expression appeared on the boy's face, he opened his mouth and started talking about Icelandic moorland birds. He talked nonstop for an hour, with an enthusiasm that he'd never displayed before. Hannes listened, surprised at first, and then captivated, by the precise, sometimes sensitive descriptions, convinced that the lecture was a sign of awakening urges; now his son would finally become a man. The following day, the foreman even hazarded to assign Jónas a new task: a wall needed painting—although it was, of course, constantly hidden behind stacks of goods and was rarely seen, but the foreman is a discerning fellow and knows that what is hidden also needs care. He led the boy to the wall, which is three meters by three meters, pointed to a bucket of paint and a paintbrush, explained that we also need to take care of things that we can't see, this is your task for today, he added, treading lightly, as ever, due to the boy's shyness. What about the broom? Just lean it against the wall there. Should I paint the entire wall? Don't leave anything behind, said the foreman, there's more paint in the storage room if you need it, but this bucket should be enough. He patted the boy's shoulder amicably, walked away as slowly as he could manage, abrupt movements disconcert Jónas, went into his office, wiped the sweat off his forehead. Do you think he can handle it, somebody asked, yes, yes, the boy's becoming a man, soon he'll be looking at the girls, but we mustn't disturb him.

It was nearly noon by the time the director ventured to check on Jónas. The boy was standing there stock-still among several buckets of paint, staring straight ahead. The foreman stared for a long time at the wall, then walked up to Jónas, who had ruddy cheeks and a gleam in his eyes; afterward, no one would ever have considered stacking things against that wall. The foreman had two tables and a few chairs placed in front of it, and there people sit during their coffee breaks or when they want to think, calm down, get their bearings, they sip coffee and look at the painting, at the reddish sun stretching over half the wall and the sixty or so moorland birds that seem to be flying out of it, their figures a bit stiff, yet the birds still so vivid that in complete silence you can hear their wingbeats within the wall.

2

Once upon a time the world was so innocent that it was enough for the police officers here in the village to work part-time; perhaps, then, the road to heaven was shorter, and that to hell longer. The Progressive Party reigned in the countryside, it was in control of the co-ops that held the rural communities together and kept the bumpkins in their places, did the thinking for us and the best it could to keep everything as it always had been; it has always been easiest to manage those who never move. Perhaps, though, this has been turned upside down, because over the last few years there's been such great change that we can't even think anymore, all our energy goes into keeping ourselves from being slung out into the void. But have you noticed that the essence of man is often hidden from sight, that it's beneath the surface and maybe never emerges into the light of day? Nowhere in the public record are we told that although Hannes's main job was as a carpenter, the policeman's uniform was his life and delight.

This isn't me, thought Hannes when he put on his carpenter's tool belt every Monday morning, reached for his saw, cursed our obedience to the law, and let himself dream of a darker, more delinquent time, when he could toss away his carpenter's belt and wear his police uniform every day.

Hannes was a bigger man than most, 193 centimeters tall, broad shoulders, thick hands, not a speck of fat on him, the way he moved made you think of one of the big cats. He always had the better of it in fights, his arms seemed made of steel, he drank more than the rest of us, had done so since he was a teenager, which wasn't considered unusual; after all, the man belonged to the race of giants. The women were drawn to Hannes, he had a penetrating gaze that fell on things around him like the beam of a lighthouse. They thought, I would leave my husband and children for one night with him. Two sisters, gorgeous women, pursued him relentlessly for many years, you can have us both, they said, live with us both, having two women would be good for you, we're extremely imaginative, and we're not talking about cooking, but then, to all of our surprise, he married Bára, who was so delicate, with a bright head of hair, her body like a flower stem, said the old men about her. She'd left to attend university in Reykjavík; not, however, to learn all about delicate plants, as we'd expected, but about geology. She wanted to learn all she could about earthquakes, volcanoes, menacing forces. She was a good student and would have made an outstanding geologist, but at an Easter party here in the Community Center she saw Hannes fight; an active volcano, she thought, and two years later, Jónas was born. Bára had just completed her Bachelor of Science when Jónas was born; she thought she would teach at our school for three years and then continue her studies, specialize in volcanology, I'll specialize in you, she said sometimes to Hannes, but one day we noticed that the light over her head had begun to fade. The old doctor, the one who'd known a smattering of Latin, couldn't do anything about it, it was colon cancer, that flower of the devil, she went downhill rapidly, she withered, turned to nothing. Hannes held her with all his might, but against death we're powerless, the light of the world went out and Hannes lost his wife, the mother of their three-year-old son, and among the most delicate, finest things that our eyes had ever seen. There's always room for more justice in the world.

And then it was just the two of them.

The boy looked so much like his mother that Hannes hardly dared touch him, my boy, he said, sticking his hands in his pockets. Thus did the years pass. Father and son lived each in his own world, they spoke little to each other but liked watching television together, sitting together at the kitchen table, listening to the radio or the rain and looking out at the fjord, they lived in one of the old wooden houses that stand just above the curved beach. But now and then, usually late evening every sixth or seventh Thursday, Hannes settled into his armchair, called to his son, and said, bring me holy Hallgrímur. Then Jónas knew that what lay ahead were four or five days, and as many nights, of heavy drinking.

How often had he watched his hands reach for the poems of Hallgrímur Pétursson on the dark, heavy bookshelf: *Hymns and Poems*, in two volumes, from 1887 to 1889, *Poems and Verses* from 1945, in one volume, the two-volume biography of the poet written by Magnús Jónsson. First, the powerful voice of Hannes calls to him, then Jónas's hands reach up to the shelf; his memories are replete with this image of his own reaching hands. He grew slowly; for a long time, well past others of his age, he needed to use a chair to reach the books, his small hands grabbed the spines, and then he trudged with them across the living-room floor to Hannes, who sat in his armchair with a blanket spread over him, a plate of rye bread with mutton liverwurst, dried fish, and a bottle of vodka on the little table next to him. An endlessly repeated scene in Jónas's memory, like flipbook images or a filmstrip that starts playing in his head; his hands grow, he no longer needs to use a chair, but the books are as heavy as always, the trudge across the living room doesn't get any shorter, Hannes sits there in the corner and grows older. Many women would like to have hands like Jónas's; they resemble a butterfly's wings, the light shines through them. The boy is as delicate as Bára, but lacks her resolve and bright personality, she was delicate and strong, while Jónas is so fragile that we feared he could never bear the weight of life, which truly takes strange forms. Some people seem to have a deep pain woven into their being—in which case, strong arms make no difference, no matter how much one exercises, lifting weights or running fifteen kilometers, because you can't wrestle the darkness to its knees, can't run away from the shadows, can't escape the sadness that is black and gray and relentless. One evening, Hannes says to his son: Nothing would please me more, yes, it would make me so happy, if you would wear my uniform after I'm gone and become a man; then my life wouldn't have been lived in vain, it would soothe my sorrows, which it pleases the Lord over the angels and the heavens to let me suffer.

It was a November evening, four or five days and nights after

Jónas had brought his father the holy Hallgrímur, two empty bottles of vodka in the kitchen, three dozen cans of beer, Hannes having slept little, as usual; he'd read Hallgrímur, listened to Megas, Cat Stevens, Elvis Presley, lectured his son in vibrant language, Jónas still worked at the Dairy, which was perfectly fine, he stuck to the broom, occasionally spruced up the environment by painting birds, he had plenty of time to think, after work stayed home in his room, read about nature, about birds, drew, often locked his door, yet never when his father drank—then he left his door open and Hannes's faint muttering filled the room.

It would make me so happy, Hannes repeated, and it was nearly midnight. Jónas brushed his teeth with great care, as always, peed, washed his hands and face, went to the living room to say good night, Hannes looked up, raised his head, his rough-hewn head, good night, son, forever, good night, never let the shadows nab you, no, Dad, Jónas went to his room and fell asleep to the muttering coming from the living room, he was wearing his red pajamas. He woke early the next morning, his bedroom was still dim, he looked at his clock, which said seven, two hours until he had to be at work, plenty of time to read from the biography of an American zoologist who, for thirty years, had been in the habit of taking one month a year to hike in a particular area, the forests of America, the Rocky Mountains in Canada, the wilderness of Alaska, the Amazon, India, Madagascar, but once changed things up by sailing between Pacific islands aboard a small sailing boat; Jónas had read that far. "Sometimes, the sea is so blue," wrote the zoologist, "that I'm convinced that I'm dead and that the bow of the boat points to the sky." Jónas smiled expectantly, reached for the lamp, switched it on, and saw that the door to his room had been closed during the night and a large envelope had been taped beneath its handle. Jónas got out of bed, seized the envelope, the words *To my son* were written on it. He sat down on the bedside, his heart in turmoil, tore open the envelope, and read:

> *Dear son, please don't go into the living room. If you have any respect for me, or ever have had, please heed this final request of mine. I tried as hard as I could, but I've now given in to the shadows in my head. For me, the world's beauty is gone.*
>
> > *Fallen the forest that one time stood fair,*
> > *pale the plow's harvest, there's sorrow to spare.*
> > *Bounty abundant has now grown so rare.*
> > *Gone our delights, it seems like so long*
> > *since last that I heard even one bird's sweet song—*
> > *calumny now, and fear fill the air.*
> > *Living things shudder to see evening's gloam,*
> > *dark are the paths where my mind used to roam.*
>
> *The shadows have defeated me. I've fought; I applied all my strength and my manhood, but the war has been going on for too long and now I'm exhausted. I've never been good enough for you, forgive me, I only wanted the best for you. Don't go to the living room, because tonight I am going to hang myself. You must not find me like that, it's awful seeing a hanged man, and even worse if it's your father. The sight would burn itself into your conscience and blaze*

there all your life; that I don't want—so please don't go into the living room. Go straight out, but remember to get dressed first—a man mustn't be seen in red pajamas. Now it's twenty minutes past four, five hours since I drank the last drop, it's only weaklings that kill themselves drunk. I'm sober now. You're sleeping peacefully in your room, your mouth slightly open. I stood there for a long time just now, looking at you. I said goodbye to you. You're a beautiful boy, though I would have preferred it if you were a man. But you're my son. I'm going now, and you're all that I leave behind in the world of men. Be strong! Don't bend, ever! When you feel like crying, which will happen, it's nothing to be ashamed of; just go out for a run. There's nothing better for cleansing your mind or calming your nerves. Remember, though, that you can run to rid yourself of tears, but not the shadows. Now read this final farewell of mine to the end, and then get dressed, wear something respectable (not the orange shirt), and then go straight to Commissioner Guðmundur and Sólrún. I've left a letter for them in the vestibule, bring it to them but first tell them what has happened, be frank and avoid sentimentality, it deprives you of your self-control and dignity. Guðmundur and Sólrún will know what to do, you can trust them, but make sure that the rope that I used is destroyed. It's bad luck to keep it or use it for anything else; shadows cling to it, possibly death.

Now I'm going to meet your mother. I've never known a better person; she deserved so much more, but no one can withstand the power of destiny. But first, I must submit

*to punishment for my surrender. I will try to accept my
sentence in a dignified manner. I don't know what my
punishment will be or how long it will last; one day, or a
thousand years? It crossed my mind to drive south to ask
Jóhannes about this, because you don't discuss such things
over the telephone, but it's too late to go anywhere; my
decision has been made. In any case, I'll soon find out.
Be strong and be better than me.*

Your father, Hannes Jónasson

Jónas read the letter slowly, he groped at each word like someone fumbling for a landmark in darkness or a black fog, read
Hallgrímur's verse several times, stopped for a long time at the
words "bird's sweet song," felt the warmth stream from it, and
then he stood up, opened the door, his room is at the back of
the house, and he faced the hallway, a thousand-kilometer-long
tunnel, the dining room at a huge distance with the bookshelf up
against the wall. It took Jónas half his life to travel the entire way.

An hour later, Jónas left the house to go to Guðmundur and
Sólrún. He'd seen his father hanging from the rope, his head
tilted to the side, he'd stood there in his red pajamas as luke-
warm pee ran down his thin legs to the light-colored, speckled
living-room carpet. Hannes would hardly have been happy with
this, neither the pee nor the red pajamas; all you need now is
your teddy bear, Hannes said to Jónas when he saw his son in
those pajamas for the first time. Jónas tried to wipe up the pee,
erase the stain, he brewed coffee, ate a slice of bread spread with
liverwurst, gulped down two glasses of milk, drank one cup of

coffee, placed another full cup in the living room, went to the bathroom, moistened a washcloth, wrapped it around a piece of soap and cleaned off his genitals and legs, sat for some time on the edge of the tub and stared at the ceiling, stood up, shaved with Hannes's razor, put on clothes, but not the orange shirt, went back to the living room, looked for a long time at his father, who hung there heavy and lifeless over the living-room floor, like a sun that has collapsed on itself and turned into a dark rock.

3

We're buried here and there, rather randomly, around the countryside, you recall that there's no churchyard here, nor has there ever been one, and it's uncertain where we'll end up; it just depends on whatever priest we can get hold of. Worst is to die in midsummer, not because of the birdsong and the light, but because that's when haymaking is done; the priests are also farmers, and must tend to the farm work as well as their parishes; they really don't like having to miss out on good dry days because of dead villagers. But Hannes left this world of shadow and light in early winter, when frost covered everything, the earth was as white as an angel's wings, and it was little problem finding a priest; Jónas could turn to the east, south, or north, though not the west, which is the sea. He phoned the priest in the southern countryside, Jóhannes, of course he did, he and Hannes were old friends, numerous people attended the funeral. It was a beautiful day, the sky a polished pewter plate, the mountains so white that they faded into dreams. A beautiful day, and a lovely funeral. Jóhannes delivered a touching eulogy for his friend, now the shadows in your mind have dissipated, your pain is gone and you're awash in so much light that no earthly language can describe it. That light is also divinity itself. That light is eternal life. We who are here and feel your absence, yes, we who carry on in the faint gleam of earthly life, we pray that your sin not be judged too hard; your pain was immense, the shadows dark. Let us trust in eternal mercy. Yes, my friend, perhaps now, at this precise moment, you're lying on a grassy slope in eternity, picking berries with your Bára, having just said: I could never have imagined that something could be so green.

Jónas was sitting by himself in the front row, alone, with no hand to squeeze, darkness on one side, darkness on the other, he held firmly to the pew to prevent himself from plunging into the void. But the eulogy was beautiful, many had a hard time holding back tears, some were unable to do so, and then the ceremony was finished. Hannes Jónasson, carpenter, yet first and foremost policeman, was lowered into the cold earth, lowered beneath the frost, his body full of alcohol and the verses of Hallgrímur Pétursson, the soil rattled on the coffin lid and the man's aged aunts wept, two middle-aged men wept and six young women. Tears are shaped like rowing boats, pain and heartache pull the oars. Those who weep at funerals weep no less for their own deaths, and at the same time, the end of all the world, because everything dies and in the end there's nothing left.

4

It's been nearly ten years since Hannes was lowered into the darkness of the earth, ten years is not a long time, it's one thought, a reaction, yet the world can make a giant leap in less time, the climate can change, new species of birds can settle in a certain country, an empire can come to an end. Yes, the world can be shaken, while we sit at the kitchen table.

Shortly after Hannes's death, we lost our old Co-op director, Björgvin, who'd been with us for thirty years. Björgvin had long since become one with the surrounding mountains, he was nearly eighty, his skin ashen gray, his back bent, all his energy and focus went into blinking and breathing. For the last two years, Þorgrímur, the foreman at the Depot, had had to carry Björgvin up to the upper floor of the Co-op every morning and back down at the end of the day, the stairs were like the Himalaya mountains to his worn-out feet. He sat all day at his desk, his hands motionless on the desktop, blinking extremely carefully so as not to overload his heart, while the hairs in his ears grew unbelievably quickly, in the end filling them entirely, it was as if two hairy dwarves had been stuffed into them. For two years, Þorgrímur had had to carry Björgvin up and then down the stairs and breathe in his odor, which was like that of a piece of wet, rotting wood, and all that time, the huge Co-op wheel turned as if by itself. But everything vanishes in the end, it says somewhere, and these words suited old Björgvin well; it happened at the end of the working day.

Þorgrímur carefully carried the rotten old piece of wood downstairs, trying to hold his breath at the same time, but just as he stepped outside, a wind stormed in from the northeast, with violent gusts that tore old Björgvin from the foreman's arms and blew him along the Co-op building, across the parking lot, and out over the surrounding moor. There he swung, a few meters above the ground like a giant leaf, until his old bones could no longer hold together and old Björgvin, Co-op director for thirty years, a pillar of the district, was torn asunder and scattered over the moor. The only witnesses apart from Þorgrímur, who snorts contemptuously when anyone brings up the story in his presence, were two four-year-old girls who described this incident at home, each in her own way but essentially concurring: the wind blew the old man into the air, far, far away where the tussocks are, Hnoðri followed, barking loudly, and then the old man just broke apart, he burst and became food for the birds, but Hnoðri ran away because he was so frightened.

Bird food and hightailed Hnoðri; on these the story lives, and refuses to die.

Hnoðri was a dog here in the village; an adorable, good-natured creature, black with a white chest, beloved by everyone, of course he'd run barking after the old Co-op director, seen this as a game, and perhaps fate was in fact having a lark; it can be hurtful, but when Björgvin was torn into pieces, Hnoðri ran off eastward, whining; a farmer ran over him late that evening, around fifty kilometers from here, and the poor creature still running at full tilt.

A few weeks later, we got a new Co-op director—and it wasn't just anyone, but none other than Finnur Ásgrímsson who we finally hooked! As you will recall, Finnur had recently concluded an extremely long and distinguished career as a parliamentarian; he'd often occupied ministers' seats, we knew his face well from the newspapers and television, his voice from the radio, a man who'd played a significant part in shaping our society, had had an influence on big things as well as small, even down to our daily life, and now, as if nothing were more self-evident, he was here in our village. You can just imagine our excitement! Unfortunately, Finnur turned down whatever committee work he was offered, although he did agree to act as patron of the Youth Association, to give a speech on June 17, Icelandic National Day, and to write a short column for the *District Gazette*, which comes out ten times a year. He adapted quickly to the management of the Co-op, the bookkeeping and everything on the lower floor exemplary, of course, in the hands of Sigríður, and Finnur said that old Björgvin had made the right decisions all the way to the end—as might have been expected of him. Which gave us a little pause for thought.

After Finnur had finished familiarizing himself with and giving his blessing to the Co-op's operations, he spent a few days going around the village, shaking people's hands and chatting with them. He showed quite a bit of interest in the story of the Astronomer and was accompanied to the black house, but the Astronomer didn't answer the door, no matter how many times it was knocked upon or the bell rung. But Finnur was no less captivated by Helga and her work; she invited him to call whenever he wanted, day or night—at which Finnur wriggled as if someone had tickled him. Eventually, Finnur paid a visit to the garage of the commissioner and his wife, where Jónas was sitting in his police uniform.

5

Destiny takes strange paths—that is, if we accept that it exists; that our existence isn't dependent on the terrible power of coincidence. Hannes breaks beneath the weight of the darkness, the shadows catch him, he hangs himself, leaves a letter for his son and another for Guðmundur and Sólrún, in which he asks his friends to see to it that Jónas be given a full-time position as a police officer: "I believe this to be the only way to make him a man. It will be difficult schooling, but that's life; he has the bones to bear it; underneath his meekness is an unexpected and mysterious strength." Hannes was probably alone in this view, which, at best, seemed merely preposterous, wishful thinking. Sólrún, as well, said no, not a chance; the commissioner agreed with her, yet reluctantly; few things are more powerful than the last wishes of a deceased friend. What tipped the scales was Jónas's unexpected zeal; he wanted the position, maybe he was feeling dazed, in shock from his father's suicide, maybe he felt responsible, which was obviously out of the question, but the human mind takes paths no less strange than those taken by destiny. It was due to this surprising determination that just a few weeks later he was wearing the black uniform, pale and emaciated, as if lost in the dark of night. Sólrún had the garage turned into a temporary police station, providing Jónas with some security, at least; they added a desk, filing cabinet, computer, flowers; the walls of the garage were painted in soft colors and Sólrún hung up a poster showing the local avifauna. But Hannes's earnest, unreasonable, and cruel wish would turn out to have its consequences, or, as they say: a man hangs himself and the world changes.

Jónas held that position alone for one year. Most of us tried to help make the days bearable for him, but we took no responsibility for the nights, and never shall; nights are unaccountable, we grow a few centimeters taller or fourteen centimeters shorter and brown eyes turn yellow; a mouse attacks a cat, a dog becomes a snipe, and we kiss lips that we should never kiss. Sólrún advised Jónas to swim in the sea, it strengthens you, hardens you, gives you self-confidence, gains you the respect of louts, of whom there are plenty, believe you me, maybe not in the daytime, but the night drags forth many things of which we're not aware in the daylight. He just smiled, and that was also the only answer that he could muster, still paralyzed by shyness and insecurity in the face of his old head teacher. Sólrún is approaching forty, she and her commissioner husband have two children, Sólrún is tall, taller than Jónas, with somewhat long red hair, which she always ties in a bun that resembles a clenched fist, she studied philosophy at university, so clever that we don't always have the courage to talk to her, and swims in the sea twice a week, in any weather. Sólrún is thickset, like a seal or mermaid, she slips through the sea, which is sometimes as cold as death, the skin between her toes is like webbing. She swims far out into the sea, she's a flickering flame among the waves and the commissioner daren't watch her, but we do, following along with her through binoculars, from when she steps out of the car, slips off her coat, walks off in her sky-blue swimsuit, slowly raises her arms, undoes her bun, her hair falls and men sigh. Sometimes she dives down to the bottom of the sea, it's an entirely different world, it's like getting to the bottom of one's dreams, seeing the world through the eyes of fish and conches. But Jónas doesn't follow her advice, just as well, too, the first wave would have drowned him, the water's cold would have paralyzed him, the sea floor wouldn't have let him go. On the contrary, Jónas shows up punctually at eight o'clock five days a week, switches on his desk lamp, reads books on nature, reads his manuscript on moorland birds, which he constantly revises, rearranges, adding information, retyping chapters because nature is ever changing, it never stops. Sometimes the telephone rings, startling Jónas, a farmer complaining about his neighbor's sheep, some kids have written graffiti on a wall, there's a broken windowpane, a dented car, horse dung in the middle of the road, things happen, yet many of us still tried to protect him, we drove more carefully, put up better with the drunken commotions at night, were quicker to shoot dogs and bury them without undue fuss, but some things can't be prevented. The night is dark and long, it deprives us of our reason—and sometimes the world is not a whit good.

6

At some point, you should come to one of the dances here at the Community Center, we so look forward to them, they bring us a spark of life, the village smells of aftershave, hair spray, perfume, they're an especial godsend during the winters, which can be so long and inert, very little happens, we jump to our feet every time an airplane passes overhead. The dances are major events, the board of the Community Center posts the winter schedule in early September and we draw a red circle around the dates of the dances, we arrange for babysitters in time, go to the liquor store a few days beforehand, iron our clothes on Thursday, are fidgety on Friday, and Saturday is spent waiting. When evening arrives, we're so elated that we can't control ourselves any longer and shriek with joy. Jónas sits in his car outside the Community

Center, as tradition stipulates, in a cold sweat, his anxiety like a buzz inside him that has been growing louder all week, he listens to the shouts and shrieks that transform the village into a madhouse. Once we had to cut Jónas free from a seesaw outside the school; he'd been there for at least two hours, judging by how much snow had piled up on him, and his police car was gone as well, it was found the following day by an abandoned farmhouse just outside the village. They had shat in the driver's seat and pissed on the dashboard, people aren't always nice; sometimes they're bloody awful. One summer night, Jónas was pulled out of his car, the band The Soul of My Dear Jón was playing at a dance, it was a sweaty night, three guys tied him to the net of one of the handball goals outside the school, you're a fly, they explained to him calmly, then pointed at two women and added, they're the spiders. A bad night, but so bright, summer nights give free rein to certain things; the spiders cut Jónas's uniform off him with a sharp pocket knife. Don't wriggle like that, or we'll cut you by accident, they said, sighing heavily when they saw how white his skin was beneath his black uniform. How big is he, one of the guys asked, stretching his neck to see better, you mean how small is he, said another, laughing. One of the women slipped the knife carefully beneath his underwear, Jónas didn't make a sound, some animal species never react to aggression, that's their defense.

They didn't do this to you but to the uniform, Sólrún said as she cut him out of the net, but tell me who they were, anyway, and I'll have the earth scorched beneath them. Jónas shook his head, said nothing, and didn't need to, after all; a woman in her thirties from here in the village had confessed everything before a new day rose from the night's light. She gave all the names, including her own; her guilty conscience began rearing its head as she sobered up, and she even sent Jónas a letter admitting how ashamed she was, how bitterly she regretted her actions.

But what's done is done, and cannot be taken back, it changes your inner landscape in such a way that words are of little use. Jónas sat in the garage, read books on zoology, drew birds, started every time the phone rang, shut his eyes sometimes and never wanted to open them again. When it came to Jónas, almost all of us had something on our conscience; without realizing it, we'd begun to view teasing him at the dances as part of the fun, as we said, we take no responsibility for the night, but the incident at the handball goal appalled us, there was no way the night could be blamed for that. And maybe it was in a kind of attempt to absolve ourselves that we dragged Einsi, the originator of the stunt, excavator driver and pest controller, a real sleazeball, to be honest, out of his house and tore off his clothes, at first thinking we would lug him over to Selja, who raises calves in the summer, and let one of them suck Einsi, but we chickened out of that and settled for painting him all red, from his big toes to the tips of the hair on his head, yes, go ahead and shriek, we said. Þorgrímur paid the others a visit, two lads of twenty, so early in the morning that there was no way to distinguish between dream and reality, shoved them into his Willys Jeep, drove them up onto the high heath, pushed them out, and said, quick boxing lesson, up with your fists and defend yourselves; and then he got back in the jeep and made them hike home. A seven-hour hike, the rain will cool your bruises and sore spots, he said through the open window, and it really rained, sky and earth merged into one. And as it rained down on them, Gréta, the second spider, stood before her boss, Sigríður, and would have chosen Þorgrímur's hard fists and all the rain in the world over Sigríður's dressing down. On the other hand, it can be really nice to swim while it's pouring rain, because you're not entirely sure whether you're a bird or a fish. Sólrún swam out into the sea, dove down into the compressed silence, she thought about Jónas, and then she thought about Þorgrímur.

7

How damned proud we were to have been joined here in the village by someone as famous as Finnur Ásgrímsson; it was as if God had let a spark fall from the sky. You know how Finnur is: those slow movements, a bit as if he were trudging through deep snow; medium-size, stocky but not fat, his face coarse and chubby and forever expressionless, that blank look had been his trademark and to his advantage in politics; a reflection of determination and calm. He came to us with peace in his heart, contented with his victories, with being an important part of history, of having made a difference, the sun had shone on him while the rest of us lived in the half-light of everydayness, our decisions may perhaps move pebbles, but not rocks, let alone mountains. And because of all this, we dressed in our Sunday best the day that Finnur came to town. The Women's Association baked cakes with thick, soggy bottoms, whipped cream, and canned mixed fruit, there were sandwich cakes, striped-lady cakes, "love-ball" raisin doughnuts, the table at the Community Center sagged under the weight of all these treats, our mouths watered; now that's what we called a feast. We ironed our ties and dresses, the commissioner gave a speech, the chairman of the Rotary Club and district Progressive Party gave a speech, the chairwoman of the Women's Association gave a speech, we shouted hurray and Finnur smiled, he stood there among us and we felt like we were in a fairy tale, as if the center point of society had shifted to our community; we mattered. And the festive atmosphere only deepened when Finnur announced his intention, along with running the Co-op, of putting his memoirs down on paper; we shouted hurray once more, we adjusted our ties, smoothed our dresses, and sang the anthem "Iceland Carved with Bays," and Finnur went back up to the podium and said, I'm touched—your energetic, beautiful singing will certainly resound in my biography.

Did the sky not change color, did the mountains not shift from one foot to the other when Finnur began wrestling with his memoir? The first sentence came quickly and confidently: "I was thirty-one when I entered parliament," Finnur put a comma after "parliament," not a period, and then he reached for another sheet of paper and wrote the title on it in large capital letters: THE YEARS THAT MADE A DIFFERENCE. He leaned back, he ran his hand over the heavy, dark desk, he looked around the spacious office, he smiled because he had struck the right tone and we moved a little more quietly so as not to disturb his thoughts. "I was thirty-one," wrote Finnur with the fountain pen, because the ink is thick, it's like the night that spreads itself over the world. "I was thirty-one," his elbows on the heavy wooden table, to his left, a stack of five hundred white, empty sheets of paper, because that's how long the book was supposed to be, so short is a person's life. On the right side of the table were three thick folders full of newspaper clippings, letters, old speeches, photographs, "I was thirty-one," Finnur sighed and put down his pen. Thirty-one and now sixty-eight, time takes big steps. He looked at the sheet of paper in front of him, at the half sentence that was like a raincloud at the top of the page, heavy with memories, heavy with thirty-seven years, a man's life, thought Finnur, leaned back, and weeks passed. The moon expanded, it contracted. Moonlight is white but sometimes transparent, it kindles thoughts, feelings that we have a hard time handling, some draw the curtains of darkness shut so as not to lose their heads, while others sprout wings. No words fell from the cloud, which gradually dried up there at the top of the sheet, the sun shone in through the window, and the ink faded, a man's life.

The publisher phoned, a young man who wears leather trousers, has black hair, is thin but tends to put on kilograms easily, his face appears slightly greasy sometimes. Finnur, who wanted to connect with young people, their energy, had chosen him above others. Call me Jonni, the publisher had said at their first meeting; I want to publish people like you, Finnur. We both have duties to perform: you to tell what happens behind the scenes, the wheel of destiny, the decisions that changed the life of the nation; my duty is to publish your story, scrupulously prepare your biography, and deliver it to the readers. But just remember, Finnur, that in this business, there's only one rule: to be sufficiently straightforward, sufficiently candid. The book should matter, it should move people. You should tell of the disputes you faced, tell of the battles over complex social issues, of political opponents and comrades in arms, and you must never hesitate to dwell on personal difficulties; even if it's far removed from our goal, few things sell better than books with a certain amount of unhappiness, I would be a hypocrite to say otherwise. We've all experienced misfortune, why keep it quiet? And Finnur, you should also bring your readers into your marital bed, you should shed tears and you should feel hatred while writing. Be unsparing, warm, and honest. That's the golden triad of all good books.

And now Jonni, the publisher, called him.

What's going on, Finnur?

A man's life, said Finnur.

Yes, exactly, nothing more true, but send me what you've written, so we can decide together how best to proceed. Absolutely, agreed Finnur. And don't neglect anything, Finnur; remember, honesty is not only virtuous, but it sells as well. I agree completely! said Finnur, feeling a sudden burst of enthusiasm. Just straightaway, Finnur, we've got this! Straightaway! repeated Finnur, and he hung up, grabbed his pen, the voice that was carried by phone over heaths and mountains had swept away any torpor: "I was thirty-one when I entered parliament, and the years that followed made a difference." Much better, Finnur told himself aloud, and then he opened the folder of newspaper clippings: him standing at a podium, him sinking a shovel into the ground, him in parliament, him with foreign guests, him being interviewed, photographs of him and his family, his three children and his wife, Anna, who died three years ago, yes, life comes and goes. Finnur sat there at his desk, recalled the things that mattered, remembered a few speeches but rarely the occasion upon which he'd given them, he wrote, the days passed, piled up into weeks, into months, and the rest of us lived our dreary lives while Finnur put his illustrious years on paper.

Summer turned into a yellow and red autumn, the sky darkened, and then came winter. Jónas categorically refused to take off his black uniform, though his broom awaited him at the Dairy, walls to paint, he went to the garage punctually at nine o'clock, sat down at his desk, looked nervously at the telephone. This wasn't good, something had to be done, which is why Sólrún, as we were saying, drove down to the beach.

She stepped out of the car, let her coat slip from her shoulders, three or four binoculars trembled a little, she began swimming, became a flickering flame in the waves, turned into a seal and mermaid, dove down ten meters, where time passes slower and anyone who touches the seafloor sees everything with new eyes.

A few days later, Þorgrímur, the Depot foreman, is standing in Finnur's office.

It had been months since Finnur last heard from the publisher, and his enthusiasm had gradually faded, torpor had resettled in him, he looked at the phone, thought, I need to call Jonni. Still, Finnur didn't call and now Þorgrímur was standing in front of him, with his broad shoulders, brown eyes that looked at the world from a height of 190 centimeters, one hand constantly scratching his big nose, which he always did whenever he had to talk with others about himself. So you want to leave the Depot? said Finnur. Yes, thundered Þorgrímur, his bass voice so powerful that our eyelids quiver when he clears his throat, I'm being urged to become a police officer, he added, but this is certainly no easy decision for me . . . Finnur raised a finger, leaned back, narrowed his small, almond-shaped eyes. Decisions, he said, I had to make decisions—and no trivial ones, either!

He stood up slowly, went to the window, and said to the day outside: When I was a minister.

Þorgrímur waited for him to continue, slightly nervous, despite his powerful paws and his eyes at a height of 180 centimeters. Þorgrímur is a patient man, and he waited a long time. The clock on the wall above the door ticked, the afternoon advanced slowly over the village, the twilight streamed in through the window, making everything in the room blurrier, more obscure. Þorgrímur cleared his throat three times in as many hours, but Finnur never looked at him. Þorgrímur blinked, he had difficulty distinguishing Finnur's profile against the window where he stood. Þorgrímur backed away slowly, groping behind him for the door handle, opened the door softly, looked toward the window, squinted but could no longer distinguish what was twilight and what a man; he shut the door softly behind him.

8

The sun rose with difficulty over the mountains to the east and kindled a new day for us. The Astronomer switched off his computer, ate a bowl of porridge, and went to sleep, a wind blew from the north and it was snowing on the peaks. We pulled on our wool socks, thought about warm Danish pastries, anguish, and the coffeepot. Þorgrímur left his house and headed for that of the commissioner and his wife, a ten-minute walk for a man with such a large stride. He was wearing his policeman's uniform, he stepped into the garage, his figure filled the opening, Jónas was sitting behind his desk and didn't know whether to be happy or frightened. They looked directly at each other but were unable to say hello, because at that moment Sólrún arrived with a cake and her husband with a cake knife and four plates, he cut a piece for Þorgrímur and said, now it's the two of you, for which you have Sólrún to thank. Þorgrímur's thick fingers handled the fork with unexpected ease, those thick, powerful fingers possess a surprising sensitivity, four or five women here in the village can testify to that, they're always amazed at how agile and gentle they can be, and adept at feeling their way in the dark. They eat the cake, toast each other with coffee, Þorgrímur says something in his deepest voice and the others' eyelids quiver, not a word can be got out of Jónas but he drinks four cups of black coffee, he who never drinks more than one cup a day, and Sólrún leaves to go to work. Þorgrímur sighs to himself, relieved but also rueful, so shy, insecure, and clumsy in the presence of Sólrún, those brains of hers, that sky-blue swimsuit, that long red hair. Then the commissioner takes his leave, the office calls, my lads, he says, damned paperwork, and then it's just the two of them. Well, said Þorgrímur gingerly, now we're colleagues, from now on we stand together, as one man. They stood up and shook hands, a giant and an elf, the police car drove off, headed out of the village. Þorgrímur behind the wheel, Jónas trembling in the passenger seat, either from drinking too much coffee or from happiness.

[Time passes, it goes through us and because of this we grow old. In a hundred years we'll be lying in the ground, nothing but bones and maybe a titanium screw that the dentist affixed to a tooth in our upper gum, to hold the filling in place. Man doesn't last as long as titanium, and his story could be summarized as follows: what he has in his heart, what he has in his bones, in his blood, and then the movement of his hands one evening in October. Jónas probably doesn't think much along these lines, which is probably why he never seems to age, his skin is smooth and soft, and it's nice to see them together, he and Þorgrímur. A few months after Jónas sat there trembling in his seat, he sold his house, his father's house, and moved into Þorgrímur's, where he's safe, and early in the morning in spring and summer he goes out into the countryside around the village, hikes over hills and moors with his binoculars, a pen and notebook, and observes the birds, he likes snipes and godwits best of all, less so the seagulls, who glide over the abodes of the moorland birds and whine about death. Jónas has a serene air, as if he's untouched by all the things that torment us, the fast pace, the restlessness, we need bigger TVs, new mobiles, all he needs is to think about the curvature in the wings of moorland birds. What do we need to do to come so far?

Some people here want to see something suspicious in these

two living together, two men, but that's probably because we tend to connect everything with sex. You know how the times are. Hardly a magazine is published without an article or articles on sex: extramarital affairs, surveys about our sex lives, assessments of penis size, reviews of sexual aids. Somewhere we read that orgies and wild sex went hand in hand with the fall of the Roman Empire—but is man really anything besides flesh and bone, and perhaps a titanium screw or two?

At one time, faith was an anesthetic; it was both purpose and hope. At one time, there was science; at one time, a dream of a better world, less distance between people, and then everything changed. Days pass, centuries, and today faith is scarcely more than Sunday mass, science the property of scientists; and the dream of a better world is asleep on the newest sofa. Comforts besiege us, leaving us barely able to hold our heads above them, we doze off, we dream, and our dreams merge with the colorful pamphlets from travel agencies, they slip into television schedules, they're reproduced on the internet. It has been stated that the heroes of each age reflect their own society; in their own way, they're a description of the moment in which they live. Half a century ago, these were perhaps the astronauts; in them, we beheld the greatness of the human spirit, they represented the power of the sciences, new worlds, boldness. We're not saying that only these things characterized that era, absolutely not; symbols are always a giant simplification, and yet—the heroes of each age are in their own way a description of their society; our thoughts, dreams, and hopes; a hero is a goal, a beacon to follow, consolation in adversity, man needs heroes, it's in his nature; are the heroes of our times journalists, interior designers, and chefs?

Time passes, we live, and we die. But what is life? Life is Jónas, pondering the curvature in the wings of moorland birds, Jónas who falls asleep to the deep breathing of Þorgrímur; this is true, yet it's not all. And how wide is the gap between life and death— or is there a gap, and if so, what is it called? Is it measured in kilometers or thoughts, and do some people move from one to the other—there and back again?]

Should We Admit to Being Idiots?

1

The half-dark, cold morning air streamed in when the Depot's door opened; Sigríður walked in and shut the door on the January morning behind her. Kjartan and Davíð sat drowsily at the coffee table, Davíð trying to recapture the mood of his nocturnal dreams, Kjartan munching a sugar lump to keep sleep at bay. In those years, the Co-op was sometimes called the Women's Realm: on the upper floor reigned the motherly care of Ásthildur, the secretary, who prepared the coffee and saw to it that Björgvin, and later Finnur, were not disturbed, and had the tendency to cancel meetings on her own initiative, just as she pleased; those who wished to plead their causes had first to secure her goodwill. The lower floor—the grocery store itself and the gas station— was in the iron clutches of Sigríður, who had just turned fifty when she walked into the Depot that January morning in the late nineties, with the British group Massive Attack on the radio and Davíð tapping the beat.

Once, when Sigríður was young and the world was still in black and white, the boys buzzed around her; some of them she treated badly, those were unforgettable moments, and left their hearts in ruins, at the age of eighteen she was selected Miss Western Region, tall, thin, long blond hair; she tossed it and the

mountains changed shape. Then she began working as a recep-
tionist for the Co-op. We bought milk, biscuits, and potatoes and
admired her hair, admired her delicate face, but Sigríður married
a farmer from just outside the village, Guðmundur, frequently
called Guðmundur I'm Off.

Guðmundur held the district record in the 400-, 800-, and
1,500-meter runs, usually went by foot to retrieve the sheep from
the mountains, hardier than most horses. Whenever someone
pointed out a sheep high up on the mountain slope, Guðmundur
used to say, I'm off—hence his nickname. He's a hardworking
man, whereas Sigríður's nose is so petite, her arms so white, and
her shoulders so slender that for a time we thought she was too
delicate for that hard life. But as so often before, we knew little,
noticed nothing, understood even less; behind those beautiful
eyes, which caused some of us to lose sleep, dwelt an iron will,
an unshakable determination. Sigríður quickly worked her way
up to become, in just a few years, the sovereign of the lower floor;
even the Co-op director himself had to defer to her. It's been
years since she dumbfounded us with her eighteen years, when
she sprinkled her smile all around her like gold dust, although
her hair is still so damned blond, her body lithe, it resembles an
antelope's, and sometimes it's as if there's a vague tension in it,
waiting for release. Sigríður never lowers her guard, yet in spite
of this she often finds herself cornered at dances, by men who
have drunk half a bottle of vodka and just want to tell her that
she's holding up pretty damned nicely, better than all her peers,
the younger ones have nothing on her, one man confides to her
that he always feels restless in her presence, another asks whether
she ever thinks of him, a third wants to relive the old days, when

they shared a secret kiss. Sigríður, remember, we kissed all night, dammit all, we did nothing but kiss, and I'll never forget how soft and nimble your tongue was, I still dream of it; can I kiss you now? Oh, Sigríður, let's cast everything to the wind, the world and everyone else, and kiss each other as we did back then—and then we can truly say we lived. Sigríður, I'm married, I have children, I'm happy, but now I feel it so strongly, how I've never stopped loving you, come with me out into the night!

But it doesn't matter how much men try, what weapons they wield, old memories, the irresponsibility of the night, the fire of desire, it's all in vain. Sigríður just looks at them, they saunter out to their cars, pull out the vodka bottle from under the seat, pour more into themselves, think, oh life!—until they open the door quickly, vomit, and then doze off.

Sigríður closes the door of the Depot, goes to the counter, looks at the two colleagues, they're startled, the drowsiness abandons Kjartan, the dreaminess evaporates from Davíð's head, he's almost thirty years younger than Sigríður, in his eyes, she's a middle-aged woman, a ruthless dictator, he doesn't understand those men who can talk about her with the sweetness of a dream, with the excitement of desire, I see you've got your hands full, says Sigríður, as she raises the countertop's hinged panel and steps in behind it. We were just organizing our day, Sigríður, answers Kjartan, in a slightly dreary voice, he's holding a sugar lump between his fingers and desperately longs to stick it in his mouth. Sigríður looks from one of the colleagues to the other, then screws up her eyes, making them uneasy. Then she tells them that Þorgrímur has quit, which they'd probably already heard, and that that very morning he started his new job as a police officer, this all happened so quickly that it could take days, probably weeks, before the man she had in mind could take over Þorgrímur's job, this new man was quite far away and it was problematic getting in touch with him, so for the time being Kjartan and Davíð were to divide Þorgrímur's responsibilities between them, demonstrate their tenacity, show what strong stuff they were made of, that you could count on them. Kjartan puts down his sugar lump, puffs out his broad chest, and says in his deepest voice, you can trust us! Sigríður gives them a quick smile, hard to say whether it's friendly or derisive, nods, turns, leaves, the Depot warms up three degrees. The two colleagues stare at the door for several moments, and then Kjartan reaches for his sugar lump, sticks it in his mouth, goes to the counter, lowers the hinged panel, leans on the counter, and says, well. Davíð also leans against the counter and says, well, and there the two colleagues are, Kjartan a little above medium height but so portly that he appears shorter, a former farmer who moved to the village two years earlier, while Davíð is of course the son of the Astronomer, a sight shorter than Kjartan, thin as a reed but with the beginnings of a paunch, as if he'd accidentally swallowed a bowler hat, he sometimes stands in front of the mirror in the small wooden house, strokes his belly, and curses Kjartan's hearty lunches. There they stand until Kjartan says, now we need to think, and then they sit back down at the coffee table, Davíð nods off because naps are such a treat, you withdraw behind a heavy curtain into a world of your own. Kjartan opens his sandwich, pops the slice of ham in his mouth, puts a warm Danish pastry in its place, closes the two slices of bread over it, and takes a bite, eating is such a treat, your body is so grateful, the world isn't as thorny, Kjartan thinks pleasant thoughts. Then the sandwich is finished and he recalls the pain that he feels sometimes underneath his breastbone, in the vicinity of his heart, mild pains that come and go, doubtless just the pain inherent to existence, although it's safer, of course, to set up an appointment with Dr. Arnbjörn. He gives Davíð a nudge with his elbow, and the latter wakes with a start from his dreams, that's enough thinking, Kjartan announces, Davíð yawns, pours himself a cup of coffee, tries to give some thought to the responsibilities they face, but the only thing that comes to his mind is a particular piano melody, only its notes can express the kiss that a woman from the village pressed onto his lips almost half a month ago, can express the warmth of her tongue, a married woman of thirty, mother of two children, who smelled of tobacco and vodka and had heavy breasts. Davíð springs to his feet before the memory gives him an erection, to work, he says, clapping his hands. Kjartan sighs, remains sitting there with all 110 of his kilograms, you're a true child of heaven, he says, which is why you're so light, but I was born from the earth and have a few grams of hell inside me, which is why I'm so ungodly heavy, give me a hand. You have beautiful eyes, he added in his mind, because at that moment, a cloud drew back from the moon, a white light shone in through the large window above the door and fell on Davíð's face, making his dark eyes appear to burn with a dark fire, and Kjartan sighed. Yes, said Davíð, and he sighed too, it won't be a walk in the park keeping all this crap in shape, dammit. Kjartan said nothing, stood up slowly, heavy with flesh, though even heavier with unexpected sadness about his life, himself, his wife, about having experienced such a strong feeling, seeing Davíð's eyes burning, and side by side they set off toward the vast space of the warehouse.

2

I'm sure you're familiar with incidents like this, perhaps catch a glimpse of movement in an empty house, hear a creak in the attic where no one ever goes, a piano playing in an empty room. Such incidents can slink into our nervous system, we start sweating for no apparent reason, invent shadowy stories that disturb our sleep and fill the darkness with menace. Yet these stories are essentially positive; they bear the conviction of a world beyond ours. Whoever believes in such things is, despite it all, better equipped to deal with human solitude, is less acquainted with the precipice of uncertainty, is even blessed in some ways. Kjartan is a down-to-earth person and knows that in most cases, ordinary, if not scientific, explanations can be found for alleged ghosts: the whistling of the wind, the iridescence of the atmosphere, an optic nerve disorder. As a farmer, Kjartan frequently had to drag himself out to the farm buildings in the deepest winter darkness, the wind whined, the corrugated-iron sheets rattled against each other, ideal conditions for ghosts, yet nothing ever happened, probably because Kjartan is a rational man. Nor was Davíð lacking brains; he earned the highest marks in high school and in the Icelandic courses that he took at university, but he's the nervous type, chews his fingernails, bounces his right leg constantly while sitting, lives partly in dreams, switches on all the lights in his house on winter nights when the blackness of space seems to hang over the village with its sucking breaths, its bottomless darkness. And now they walk together from the coffee table to the warehouse, maybe twenty meters, pull open the big sliding door, turn on the lights, and the warehouse appears; endless stacks of pallets, a main corridor for the forklift and several narrow aisles branching from it, and over it all, twenty bare bulbs hang from long cords at a height of eight meters. Kjartan looks over the list of orders that he has brought with him, they go to work, nothing new except that Þorgrímur has quit, and so the days pass.

At first nothing happens, nothing at all, except that they both seem to feel something, without either of them mentioning it to the other. They sense an invisible presence, there's something that gets on their nerves, makes their breaths shallower. Kjartan feels as if someone is standing behind him; he turns around, but no one is there. Out of the corner of his eye, Davíð catches a movement, an indistinct movement, and hears a rustling sound; he looks to the side but sees nothing, and hears nothing but the wind outside and Kjartan humming out front.

One day, however, some sacks of feed enhancer fall from one of the pallets from a height of six meters, six 25-kilogram sacks. Two burst open on impact, the brown pellets shoot out over the warehouse floor, and a few hit black boots, size 45.

Kjartan is so startled that for a minute or two he stands there breathing hard through his wide-open mouth, his heart racing, the blood coursing through his veins. Two seconds earlier or later, and the sacks would have landed on his head and killed him. Davíð comes running over, shouting, what happened? Kjartan, ashen faced, points upward, at the gap in the pile on the pallet. The two colleagues sweep up the enhancer pellets, silently, glancing up now and then at the stack of pallets, inexplicable how this happened, says Kjartan finally. What do you mean, Davíð hesitantly asks, do you mean that . . . Do I mean what? Kjartan asks as his colleague's voice trails off.

Davíð: You know.

Kjartan: I know fuck all.

Davíð: Yes, you do, I mean, that there's . . . *something.*

Kjartan: There's always something.

Davíð: No, you know, those stories, about the woman and so on . . . haven't you felt something strange these last few days?

Kjartan: Felt something? No, what should I have felt?

Davíð: Come on, you know, as if we're not the only ones here, as if something's going on here, as if we're being watched and . . .

Kjartan: Come on, don't be ridiculous. There's no such thing; absolutely not.

Davíð: Do you mean that there's no such thing as ghosts? He pronounces the word "ghosts" as if he has dynamite in his mouth, which could explode at the slightest disturbance. Kjartan snorts, goes to the forklift, drives it up, and takes down the pallet of feed enhancer, they restack the sacks that fell off it, work carefully, put the pallet back in its place, then go and fetch a flashlight and spend the next hour wandering through the warehouse, going down the aisles and peering up at the pallet stacks, some so tall that they disappear above the light and into the darkness that fills the ceiling space. The following day, nothing of note happens.

Nor on the day after that. Kjartan starts having nightmares, dreams that he's alone in the warehouse, hears strange noises, things fall from out of the darkness, and then he loses his sight. He consoles himself with the thought that the night is one thing, the day another. And Jakob delivers merchandise in his big truck, it's loaded into the warehouse, he leaves with other merchandise, people come for sacks of feed enhancer, shovels, bicycles, skateboards. But early one morning, about a week after Kjartan barely missed being killed by falling sacks of feed enhancer, he hears something that sounds like a person is in the empty warehouse, even as if children are running barefoot down the narrow aisles. I don't eat enough, he thinks, that's the problem, and I sleep too little; it's just nerves.

After lunch, they're standing at the warehouse bay door, Kjartan goofing around imitating the truck driver, Jakob behind the wheel of his truck, Davíð laughing as he leans against a pallet, when suddenly a light bulb goes out in the northwest corner. The two men are startled, and Kjartan shrugs as if to shake off a chill, but then another bulb goes out, and then a third, fourth, fifth . . . at intervals of around five seconds; they hold their breath, look around, dead silence, more bulbs go out, the sixth, seventh, and the darkness draws quickly nearer, from every direction, presses in on them, they begin inching their way out, both their backs are sweaty when they come out of the warehouse. Kjartan pours two cups of coffee, Davíð's hand trembles slightly as he lifts his cup. Bloody wiring, says Kjartan when he finally feels up to saying something. Outside, late-afternoon dusk closes over the village.

3

It has been stated that life and death go hand in hand, that there's only a thin partition separating them, which is why we sometimes see the shadows of the realm of the dead. We mention death and ponder ghosts because at one time there was a farm where the Depot now stands, things happened there, the farmer went to Snæfellsnes peninsula for the fishing season, and returned one night to find his wife in the arms of a stranger, a black-haired, frighteningly handsome man, and the farmer, a fiery fellow, is reported to have grabbed a knife and slit the other man's throat, and then killed his wife as well, sinking the blade into her heart; then he set the farm on fire and everything in it burned: the farmer, the two corpses, the three children, two dogs, and dozens of mice. The grass grew slowly over the farm's ruins, but misfortune and a curse lay over it like a nightmare, people said they felt something, some saw apparitions and no one dared build a farm near there. Countless years later, however, one hundred fifty or so, we built the Depot over those ruins, which are located under the northwest corner. It was also a different era, the darkness having been defeated by electricity and compulsory schooling, and what are stories anyway, besides stories, they're a pastime, they can move us sometimes, of course, cause us to change our hairstyle, residence, gait, but none of them is capable of influencing the laws of life and death, they can't change the position of the stars in the sky, and no folktale cuts open the ground and releases 150-year-old darkness, ghosts, and misfortune.

Or, well . . . the night passed, followed by a dark morning.

Davíð arrived a little early, they'd forgotten to switch on the front-door light the day before. He pulled the keys from his pocket, put them back in his pocket, I'll wait for Kjartan, he thought, looked at his watch, half past eight. They were both supposed to have been there by then, and someone really should have been awake in this village at that time, but there was no one out and about apart from Elísabet, whom he'd seen pass the Depot earlier on her daily walk, otherwise there was nothing but the darkness and the front-door lights of the houses at its bottom. Davíð began whistling a tune to himself, at first a random melody that soon took a familiar form, he whistled "The First Kiss" by the pop group Hljómar. Of course he did. I'm twenty-four years old, thought Davíð, I've been kissed. The tune died out on his lips, he leaned up against the corner of the Depot, looked over the village.

They had played at the New Year's dance, Kjartan and Davíð's band, sixteen days earlier. The band from Reykjavík had canceled two days before it, which had created a panic, leading to them being called in at the last moment; the band was called The Good Sons, the name a reference to a record by the Australian Nick Cave, "The Good Son." The band has five members, who get together twice, three times a month in an old barn outside the village, where they play like madmen for three hours. One to get rid of stress, another to forget the disappointments of life, a third to escape memories, the other two most likely out of a simple love of making music, it had never crossed their minds to play at a dance; doing so took a repertoire, organization, and songs that get feet moving, but they simply had no other choice. The evening arrived and they shook like twigs. Davíð at the piano, Kjartan on guitar, and then the others, Ási on drums, Hörður on second guitar, or on trumpet for sadder numbers, and finally Ingvi or Ingvar on bass, for some reason we can never remember his name; let's just call him Ingvar. In any case, it was really Davíð's night, he rocked it, held the band together with his rhythm, he sang the slow songs, his voice youthful with a hint of darkness, his black hair hung down over his eyes, he was twice as good as the others put together, his shyness had vanished, and he drank almost nothing, unlike Kjartan, who'd already drained half a bottle of whiskey by midnight and had three hours to go. The whiskey turned him into a dim, rainy day, the others made him lean against the wall to keep him standing upright, and no matter what they played, lively, happy, yet simple songs by Geirmundur Valtýsson, cool-as-hell Stranglers tunes, leathery tight Presley hits, Kjartan always played blues riffs. The first kiss! Ingvi shouted into the microphone, but the rhythm guitar wept, I'm so lonesome I could die. Yet they dodged the bullet, just lowered the volume of Kjartan's guitar and raised that of Hörður's, who strummed his strings enthusiastically with his seven fingers, flashed his two shortsighted eyes over the dance floor, and the dance ended. The smoke-saturated room reeked of booze and sweat, Kjartan had long since finished the bottle, he can hold a lot of drink, having so much mass, and as he wolfed down fries from the Community Center kitchen and listened disconsolately to the reprimands of his wife and Ingvi, Davíð found himself penned in at a corner of the stage by Harpa, married, thirty-year-old mother of two, she pushed him ahead of her until the wall stopped them and the heavy, dark-red curtain separated them from the rest of the room.

She grabbed Davíð tightly by the back of the neck and kissed him openmouthed. The first kiss, and a fervid one at that, tasting of vodka and tobacco. She pressed her lips against his, her big breasts against his chest, her waist against his hard member, and he closed his eyes. What should I do now, he thought hesitantly, will she be angry if I stroke her tits, and should I then stroke them softly or forcefully, maybe pinch them, and what about her ass, should I touch it, I want to touch it so badly, I didn't know that women had such soft tongues. Davíð's left hand remained motionless on the woman's hip, the right one groped perplexedly up and down her back, like a giddy crane fly, he wondered whether they would kiss much longer, whether his tongue was as warm as hers, whether she enjoyed his kisses, his tongue, and what should he do with his hands? Only a heavy velvet curtain between them and the world, but a velvet curtain is sometimes heavier than the night, wider than the ocean, and Davíð's right hand groped at the air, now you'll touch her tits, or her ass, he ordered his right hand, but then Harpa began to undo his belt, slowly but surely. She unbuttoned his trousers, pulled down the zip, a female hand slipped into his trousers, his blue underpants, grabbed the cock that insecurity had softened, but that quickly hardened in her palm, Davíð's eyes widened, his mouth hung open, grab my tits, she whispered, no, under my shirt, unbutton it, God, those fingers of yours, get my tits out of my bra, you can have them, do you like them? Yes, he whispered in a broken voice. A few years ago they were more beautiful, firmer. They're wonderful, he whispered, because he'd probably never seen anything so beautiful. God, how wonderfully you lie, grab them, don't tickle, tighter, you're perfectly safe grabbing them, yes, like that, my love, you've never done this before? No, he whispers, red with eagerness, with shame. You've never been with a woman before? He shakes his head, has a tear in his eye. Oh, how beautiful, sighed Harpa, lift my skirt, take off my knickers. Davíð reluctantly let go of her breasts and his hands felt so empty, he bent down, hesitated, looked up at her, moved his trembling hands beneath her skirt, pulled her knickers down slowly, she lifted her right foot slightly, then her left, put them in your jacket pocket, she whispered. She pulled him farther into the wings, to a small table in the corner, he was breathing as if about to start crying or drown and she let her skirt drop to the stage, lay down on the table, spread her legs, pulled him to her, guided his cock into her, and he had never, never ever suspected that anything could be as wet, as soft, and as warm, and she stroked his face, she sucked his earlobe, she licked his eyelids, he began thrusting and she uttered low moans, like whines yet not whines, he whispered something hoarsely, happily, full of despair, my love my love, she sighed, come, it's all right, just come, and she stuck the tip of her tongue in his left ear and nothing else existed in the world but her breaths.

Memories aren't like clothes, which become worn with use; Davíð had thought almost uninterruptedly about this for sixteen days and the effects were always the same, a burst of emotion and an erection. Sometimes he was ashamed of the latter and tried then to focus on Harpa's eyes, which were dark, on the sweet scent that wafted from her scalp, on the smile that lit up her face when he met her at the Co-op, there was shyness in that smile, mischievousness, provocation, affection, there was passion. But if all this wasn't enough, he would go somewhere to be alone with himself and his warm memories, which is why he was behind the old Ford tractor when Kjartan appeared from around the corner. I'm having a pee here behind the Ford, shouted Davíð, he was almost finished but stopped as soon as he saw his colleague, because there are a few things in this world that you prefer to finish doing undisturbed.

They sat by the coffee maker until past noon. They spoke little, Kjartan finished what he'd brought for lunch before ten, he ate Davíð's lunch at half past eleven and was still hungry. Davíð tried to fall asleep on the chair because he who sleeps is unconscious of his surroundings, he's free from the chains of time, he can fly, he can die, he can do things that his conscience prevents him from doing while awake. Fortunately, they had no customers, it was very cloudy, a light snowfall, temperature around zero, January. Sometimes, it's as if January mornings seem to be pottering around braiding nooses, in which case, it's better to stay at home, go nowhere, hunker down and hope that the world forgets you. Kjartan munched a sugar lump, it crunched between his teeth, he cursed and Davíð started from his shallow, dreamless sleep, this isn't getting us anywhere, Kjartan said upon seeing his friend's eyes open a crack, no, Davíð agreed, and they stood up, went and got the long ladder that could be extended to double size, walked toward the warehouse, hesitated to open the sliding door, took deep breaths, and plunged into the darkness, it was around one o'clock. They went a few meters in, hardly able to see a thing at first, waited for their eyes to adjust to the darkness, and then set up the ladder, the light in the reception area appeared distant, like a faint gleam of another world. Are you sure we're right under the light bulb? Davíð asked, when can you really be sure? Kjartan said, and he took a new light bulb from his pocket. Which of us is going up? Heads or tails? Davíð asked, holding out a coin, heads, Kjartan said, Davíð shook the coin briskly between his hands and then slammed it on the back of one of them, looked down at it, sorry, friend, he then said, but I'll hold the ladder. I don't like heights, Kjartan muttered, yet he started climbing up into the darkness, which seemed to grow denser at every step, it was safer to shut his eyes, to keep the darkness from flooding in along his optic nerve, filling every thought, every memory. Hold the ladder steady, you bloody idiot, he shouted down to Davíð, I'm trying to! Trying, what do you mean, Kjartan shouted, opening his eyes, he saw nothing, not even the ladder, Kjartan, I hear something! shouted Davíð in a panicked voice. Kjartan cursed, inched his way down the ladder, followed Davíð out of the warehouse, they plonked themselves down at the coffee table, and Kjartan had already begun to reprimand Davíð for his weak nerves when the upper end of the silver ladder emerged slowly from the darkness, appeared to stand still for several seconds, and then fell at the speed stipulated by the laws of physics. The two colleagues started when it hit the ground. There's a natural explanation for this, Kjartan said.

The day passed; at five o'clock they went home.

4

The next morning, Davíð stopped in at Kjartan's, waited while he finished preparing his kids' lunches, cleared the breakfast table, kissed Ásdís goodbye, they didn't hurry to get to work, walked very slowly, what do you think it is? Davíð asked for the hundredth time and Kjartan shook his head for the hundredth time, do you think it has to do with the farm ruins? Kjartan shook his head again, thought about the woman and the mysterious itinerant in bed together and the woman had the face of Elísabet. People die, and then it's over, he finally said. So it's just in our heads? Kjartan grunted. Should we call Helga? I'm no coward, dammit, and she would just advise us to go down to the beach and gawk at the sea. She could lend us a book about, well, you know, such imaginings, derangement. But aren't they all in English? Probably. Can you read English? Maybe not scientific works like that, but I've got a dictionary. There's nothing wrong with my head, dammit, derangement, where do you find such words, open the damned door, Kjartan said, since they'd arrived, even though they'd walked so slowly that a snail would have exploded with impatience; we'll change the light bulbs, we'll fill the orders, derangement or ghosts or not, I don't give a damn about such things, Kjartan said, and he went in, well I do, muttered Davíð, following him reluctantly.

The day before, they'd been so disconcerted that they'd left the warehouse door open; Davíð peered into the darkness as Kjartan tried to call Simmi—without luck. We should let someone know about this, Davíð said, when Kjartan gave up for the time being. About what? You know, the sacks of feed enhancer, the electricity, maybe even the ladder, and that we both sensed . . . I don't know, something.

Kjartan: In other words, say that we scarcely dare to enter the warehouse for fear of burnt-out light bulbs? And admit to being idiots?

Davíð: I sensed something, you sensed something, it's screwing with our heads, to put it mildly, and why shouldn't we let someone know about it, you've got to be brave enough to face your fears.

Kjartan: They'll laugh at us.

Davíð: Look—

Kjartan: We're not saying a thing to anyone, not a single person, dammit, unless maybe about the wiring, I'm not going to make a fool of myself! He leaped up with all of his kilos, stared angrily at his colleague, who was balancing on the back legs of his chair, his head against the wall, the chair's front legs in the air, with a view of both the warehouse and the front door. I've always been afraid of the dark, announced Davíð. Kjartan snorted, stomped off toward the warehouse, tensed his shoulders but hesitated a few meters from the entrance, from the murky air that seemed to fill the opening. Why am I so bloody nervous, he thought, angry at himself, angry at Davíð, who sat there sipping his coffee, watching his colleague, and occasionally glancing at the front door. Something heavy landed on the roof of the Depot, probably a raven, which wasn't unusual, but Kjartan clutched his chest, Davíð splashed warm coffee on his right thigh. Bloody raven, Kjartan muttered after calming down, turned around, walked slowly and calmly over to Davíð, sat back down in his chair.

Davíð: I splashed coffee on my leg.

Kjartan: Did you burn yourself?

Davíð: A little, but nothing serious.

Kjartan: Still, you should put something cold on it, just to be safe.

You're probably right, said Davíð, and he stood up, removed his trousers, walked in his red pants over to the toilet, wet a cloth with cold water, sat back down at the table, placed the cloth on his thigh. I need to call Simmi again, it's going to take a bloody long time to get hold of him if I know him right, said Kjartan as if to himself, before looking at Davíð and adding, damn, your legs are thin. Half an hour later, the first customer of the day arrived.

A farmer from the countryside to the north, a tall, bony fellow, black haired, a slightly protrusive mouth, and a faint odor of sheephouse. Am I disturbing you, he said with a grin, as he leaned over the counter—his name is Benedikt. The two men just looked at him, Davíð having put his trousers back on. One of those quiet days, said Benedikt energetically, continuing to grin, well, you lads can have it the way you like it, but I need six sacks of feed enhancer and, um, I've backed up to the bay door . . . six sacks, if it's not too much trouble, or do I need to kick you into gear, maybe?

The two colleagues stared at Benedikt as if to weigh and measure him, then looked at each other, Kjartan nodded, rose slowly, almost as if against his will, approached the counter, raised his heavy left arm, and pointed toward the warehouse, Benedikt followed the finger with his eyes. I don't know what to say, Kjartan said slowly, hesitantly, and so quietly that Benedikt leaned forward instinctively, only that things aren't entirely as they should be here; look at how dark it is in there . . . Yes, you should turn on the light, Benedikt said. Kjartan looked at him with embarrassment and said, I wish it was so easy, I'm trying to reach Simmi and you know how he is, the bloody wiring is all worn out and useless, we can't even use the forklift, can't even get it to start, and . . . come in here with us, since you're here, and have a look at it. Benedikt looked from one to the other of the colleagues, Kjartan sheepish, Davíð on his tilted chair, his eyes half closed, and then he looked toward the warehouse door, you're hilarious, he said finally, and yawned.

He yawned, Benedikt yawned, a farmer of just over thirty, who lives alone, his wife had left him three years ago, a young woman from Akranes named Lóa, who couldn't stand the monotony of the countryside, good Lord, she said; a telephone call is like headline news, a car from outside the district such a grand event that we all rush to the window with binoculars, I can't bear it. She wasn't exaggerating, either; still, it wasn't so easy, when is life easy, sometimes she could look at Benedikt for long amounts of time, she loved how he took such big steps, found few things as beautiful as his slender chest, but his gait was gawky, he was simply too thin, it was hard to lay her head on his chest, beneath which was the heart that she could clearly hear beating, but to which she had no access. Benedikt never wanted to go anywhere, some nights he sat on the sofa and didn't let anyone near him except the dog, and looked at her so distantly, as if he were tremendously far away, on another planet, even. One day in early October, Benedikt drove her to Akranes, four suitcases in the trunk, a trailer hooked to the back of the car, loaded with all the things that tend to accumulate around us over time. Lóa gave her ex-husband a farewell hug, take care of yourself now, she said energetically, but had difficulty swallowing her tears when he got back in the car, so alone, so abandoned, his dark eyes looking very much as if something had broken within them, but then he raised his hand, smiled, or tried to smile, and drove off. Three years had passed, she still sends him wool socks in the autumn, Christmas cards, and one spring a white Boss T-shirt. Every now and then Benedikt calls her, you should try to find a good woman, Lóa might tell him, I don't think so, he then replies, yet not to elicit pity, just, nothing ever happens in that regard, fate had obviously determined that he would spend his life alone. Benedikt rarely participates in social events, but let himself be persuaded to attend the last New Year's dance, The Good Sons were on stage and it was late in the night when Þuríður, who works in the health clinic, dragged him out onto the dance floor, they danced for half an hour, he stepped on her toes a few times, and then she kissed him, grasping the back of his neck, perhaps to ensure that he didn't try to get away in his timidity. Then they left the dance floor, went to the door of the spacious foyer, stood there a few moments facing each other, the music boomed, the dance floor was a churning sea, and a man lay passed out against the big flowerpot, no way to hear each other without drawing closer and Þuríður did so, she drew closer, her lips touched his left ear and she breathed, she said: You have beautiful but sad eyes, Benedikt. And what could he say to that? But it was so nice to feel her close—and then Dr. Arnbjörn walked up, Þuríður disappeared with him out onto the wheeling dance floor, leaving Benedikt alone and vulnerable. He meandered out, down the steps of the Community Center, got into the village's taxi, take me home, he said to the driver, without even thinking about it, without making a conscious decision. The taxi driver is named Anton, he'd recently met a Polish woman in Flateyri and sent her a text message while waiting in his car outside the Community Center, she was sitting up awake in the Westfjords and answered it. Her name is Ester, said Anton to Benedikt, who sat in the front seat and stared out into the night, without knowing how he should feel. But the next day, he thought a lot about Þuríður, about her lips, her warm breaths, her voice. We were drunk, she did it out of pity, he said to his dog; and I also think there's something between her and the doctor.

Some people, however, like living alone, finding company in cups of coffee, the television, a book, silence, and not needing anything else, in fact, but the same doesn't hold true for Benedikt, except to a certain extent. We don't know how to explain it, don't really understand it, but sometimes he finds it great, best of all, to be alone with the dog, yet he's so lonely that we find it impossible to describe in words, there are only his hands on the kitchen table and time passes, or as a poem says: "There are wounds that lie so deep, so close to the heart / that even the rain against the windowpane can prove fatal."

And now he's at the Depot with Davíð and Kjartan he fakes a yawn in order to hide the discomfort that can grip him in the presence of other people, they're making fun of me, he thinks. It's like something strange is going on in there, Kjartan finally says. What do you mean? Benedikt asks brusquely. Kjartan takes a deep breath and says, very sheepishly, do you believe in ghosts? Benedikt snorts, ghosts are for children and tourists, he replies. Kjartan slams his hand on the table, startling Davíð nearly out of his chair, absolutely right, thunders Kjartan, seized with enthusiasm, even joy; this is simply some sort of damned emotional confusion, I knew it! I'm afraid not, Davíð says with a sigh, while Kjartan lifts the hinged panel, practically drags Benedikt behind it, such is his zeal, you're a sensible fellow, he says as if confiding in him, and then holds Benedikt in a bear hug, which the latter resists, trying to free himself from Kjartan's heavy arms, still convinced that the two colleagues are making fun of him, but Kjartan tightens his grip, you don't have marbles in your head like Davíð here, no black sins on your conscience like me, you live alone and know the darkness, and you know that it's nothing but air without light, you know that what's dead is dead and can't come back to life and will never move again. Naturally, I know this too, but my nerves have been playing tricks on me lately, maybe I don't eat enough, or at least don't have a varied enough diet and have been having stomach trouble, such a thing can of course get on your nerves, you know, Benedikt, science tells us so. But even if I know all this and even if I believe it, it's as if some demon has been hanging around here; the forklift won't start, we hear noises, catch glimpses of someone, and in the last few days, it's as if everything has got even worse . . . but anyway, I just needed a man like you here next to me, a man with his feet on the ground, to help me get a grip on things, Kjartan said—and then he stopped and let go of Benedikt. Well, Benedikt sighed, it won't do any harm to go in there with you. So in we go, Kjartan said, in a voice not quite as deep as usual. Benedikt muttered something, and they disappeared into the darkness.

Davíð stared in their direction for several moments, and then stood up and went into the office just off the break room, empty now that Þorgrímur had removed all his belongings, although the telephone was still there, Davíð lifted the receiver and called the speaking clock. When you're feeling upset, alone, maybe, or maybe afraid of the dark, it's an excellent idea to call the speaking clock, then at least you hear someone's voice, it even assures you that time is still in its place, despite all else, that it doesn't get thrown off track, and that there is thus no reason to despair. Davíð should tell Benedikt this; although Benedikt would rather call the emergency services number or shoot off a flare. Still, that would be useless, he would just receive a talking-to and be slapped with a big fine, the emergency services number, he would be told, was only for people in mortal peril, people in trouble at sea, in respiratory distress, pinned under a car, terribly lost in the barren wilderness while you're sitting there comfortably in your kitchen at home; what's the mortal peril in that? Davíð hung up, went back to the coffee table, sat there watching the clock on the wall, seven minutes had passed since the others had disappeared into the warehouse. Minutes so long, thought Davíð, that if I turned them into a rope they would reach the moon. He sat in his chair, leaned back, shut his eyes almost all the way, felt tranquility come over him as if his consciousness were being eclipsed in a fog, as if he himself had changed into a single note in existence, in infinity, just a single note and nothing more; and then they came out. Kjartan was supporting Benedikt, who'd stumbled over something and scraped his forehead, he felt slightly dizzy, blood dripped from beneath his black hair, the red spring of life. Davíð went and got the first aid kit, cleaned the wound, Benedikt stayed with them for another hour. Davíð wrote CLOSED UNTIL NOON on a sheet of paper and taped it to the door. Kjartan poured them coffee, Benedikt held his cup in his hands without drinking, feeling it gradually cool. They chatted, Benedikt didn't say a word about loneliness, despite it being a bird that pecks ceaselessly at the heart, but now and then he dropped out of the conversation, stared distractedly into space, his expression softened, the look in his eyes seemed sensitive, or regretful. They talked about the warehouse, exchanged stories about the ruins, there are various versions of them, Kjartan said that it could be difficult to think clearly in such palpable darkness, you start imagining things and once you started doing so, it was like losing control. Don't I know it, said Davíð, I've never sensed or noticed anything out of the ordinary at home, but hardly dare go into the living room at night; I always expect to see a dead man sitting there on the sofa—that's why I leave all the lights on at night.

Benedikt: Mama was clairvoyant; she often saw elves walking on the hayfield at home, and believed that my great-granddad was my dad's guardian spirit.

Kjartan: You've never seen anything?

Benedikt: No, and I've never sensed anything; Dad said that we had no imagination, but Mom always said that it just depended on your attitude, that you had to be open to other dimensions. I don't know, and have never given it any serious thought, except maybe when I was really bored, because some evenings are so dull that I would gladly accept the company of ghosts! Benedikt laughed, although there was little joy in his eyes. After he left, Davíð said: He doesn't feel very well.

Kjartan: We should invite him here more often, I like him and maybe it would help.

Davíð: Yes, you're right.

Silence.

Davíð: He just fell over in there?

Kjartan: Damned darkness.

5

The darkness can be friendly, it brings us the moon and the stars in the sky, the light of neighboring houses, the television schedule, sex, a bottle of whiskey; we mustn't decry the darkness.

Kjartan finally managed to get hold of Simmi, who showed up two days after Benedikt's visit, rumors about the situation at the Depot had begun circulating, the unusually slow-paced customer service, the forklift that wouldn't start, strange darkness, you can be sure that such news spreads quickly between us here. Probably few people here in the village, however, are quite as afraid of the dark as Simmi, which may be why he decided to become an electrician. Simmi said that the building's wiring was completely shot. In that case, would you kindly repair it as soon as possible, asked Kjartan, we can't see a thing in there and orders are piling up. It's going to take quite a few days to put back in order, said Simmi, and I can't start right away. But it's urgent, dammit, said Kjartan, who was beginning to lose patience. I'll need to order replacement parts from Reykjavík, replied Simmi with a ridiculous smile, glancing toward the warehouse and then asking, in a soft voice, is it true that you've sensed, umm, *something*? What are you on about? Something what? Simmi shook his head, it doesn't surprise me at all, it's absurd simply to build over ruins without taking the appropriate measures, now it's a case of revenge, it's actually what I expected to happen. Just concentrate on the wiring. Yes, that's what I'll do once the replacement parts arrive, but I think that this is about more than just the wiring, I think that something very serious is going on here, said Simmi, moving nearer the front door without taking his eyes off the warehouse, it's no joke alienating ghosts, and the way things stand, repairing the wiring won't be enough; we've got to make peace with these people. You're a hysterical chicken, growled Kjartan, taking one step toward Simmi, who bolted out the door of the Depot almost faster than the eye could see. Maybe there's something to what the fellow says, remarked Davíð from his chair, it would of course be mad, completely and perfectly illogical, yet it would explain everything, the feeling that you get in there, the insecurity, the sacks of feed enhancer, the ladder . . .

Kjartan: We need just one good night's sleep to clear our heads.

Maybe, said Davíð, closing his eyes, or maybe not. Kjartan looked at him for a few moments, watching as his face changed, became soft, dreamy, are you asleep, Kjartan asked incredulously, no, I'm just listening to the buzz in my head.

Kjartan: What bloody buzz? You're not going mad, I hope, and you're not going to drive me mad as well!

Davíð: I think we're both a little mad already.

Kjartan: There's nothing wrong with me.

Davíð: Then we'll just have to resign ourselves to this—he nodded in the direction of the warehouse—being a completely ordinary, normal situation.

Kjartan stared silently into space, and then shook his head: I hate clever people. Let's start again: what bloody buzz?

Davíð: I think it's nerves or dreams. But sometimes, especially if there are no interruptions, the buzz turns into images, like movies of my dreams. I can't explain it properly, movies isn't the right word, but whatever it is, it brings me happiness, or pleasure, yes, a great deal of pleasure.

I don't like it, said Kjartan, I bloody well don't like it, he reached for his lunch box and pulled out a sandwich, but just then the door opened and the parish administrator from the southern countryside walked in, a man in his early sixties, gray sideburns beneath his red baseball cap and unusually thick eyebrows that gave his face a fierce air, a little plodding and stiff in his movements and with a substantial paunch. He'd begun speaking even before closing the door behind him, said he'd heard about the situation, slung a worn, brown leather briefcase onto the counter, patted it, look here, lads, he continued, paying no heed to their silence or the bewildered expressions on their faces; in recent years I've busied myself collecting and transcribing stories from this district, the story about the ruins holding a high place among them; it's the jewel in the crown, I can safely say. And why do I say that, yes, the story is simply fantastic, I couldn't have penned it any better myself, but I've never had to search as widely for sources, I took one road and it branched into two and those two into four, might I bother you for a cup of coffee? he asked, and it took the colleagues a few seconds to realize that the coffee wasn't connected to the man's collection of sources and branching roads. Davíð stood up, poured a cup for the parish administrator, who sipped it carefully, four times, looking, as he did so, at the other two from beneath his bushy eyebrows. Kjartan looked down at the sandwich still in his hand, and then at the parish administrator, probably intending to say something, but the latter suddenly put down his cup and immediately took up the thread of conversation from where he'd left off: My extensive research has brought many peculiar things to light. The stranger, for instance, wasn't unknown to the farmer, but was in fact his half brother, half Spanish, according to some sources, as he was dark complexioned, or, as one source puts it, had a Slavic physiognomy. They were originally from the Eastfjords, the farmer moved here as a young man, whereas his brother spent many years abroad, at sea, on a whaler to be precise, and was never seen in these parts, and, umm, the woman, that is, the farmer's wife, had strong appetites that the farmer could never satisfy, yes, my boys, the appetites are dark and hard to govern, said the parish administrator in a low voice, groping with one hand in his jacket pocket for his glasses, holding the other hand up as if ordering Kjartan and Davíð to keep quiet, put on his glasses, began to rummage in his briefcase; yes, the story of the ruins is a story of jealousy, a story of passion, and a story of fire, my boys—fire. A fire that reaches out beyond the grave and death! He took some papers out of his suitcase, cleared his throat, and began to read. Kjartan and Davíð looked at each other, both smiling slightly, Davíð sat back down, the parish administrator read slowly and probably began reading around the same time that the commissioner went to the upper floor of the Co-op and spoke to Ásthildur, she hadn't seen Finnur, by chance?

No, she'd looked for him everywhere, here on the upper floor, at his house, but it was as if the man had vanished into thin air; Þorgrímur had been the last to see him and got the peculiar feeling that Finnur was merging with the darkness. The commissioner snorted, he stood over Finnur's heavy desk, muttered, is everyone here going mad, and then ran his hand over the thick stack of papers, read the title, THE YEARS THAT MADE A DIFFERENCE, Finnur Ásgrímsson's autobiography, he was dying to start reading it, but there stood Ásthildur, looking at him, her blue eyes, he breathed in her scent, she wore a kind of musk perfume and a lot of it, Finnur had often said nice things about her perfume. The commissioner was suddenly seized with a fervent desire for Ásthildur, he gasped, he thought, I'm going to take her here on the desk, unzip my trousers and, goddammit, fuck her here on the desk. Ásthildur was saying something about Finnur, the commissioner breathed heavily, trying to get hold of himself, he thought about Sólrún, fought against the carnal desires churning within him, he began to inch his way out, his eyes on the big painting in the heavy gold frame, portraying a cliff that rose proudly from a stormy sea, a penis in a billowy vagina, he thought, this is a picture of an orgasm, Asthildur followed him, jabbering Finnur this, Finnur that, the commissioner said yes, yes, half ran down the stairs, paying no heed to Ásthildur's bewilderment.

Am I having a midlife crisis, thought the commissioner as he stood there on the pavement and tried to settle down. How could I have ever considered this with Ásthildur, of all women, who's shaped like a barrel and wears that nauseating perfume; what's happening to me? He turned to enter the store and nearly ran into Sigríður, who gave him a quick glance—brown eyes! The commissioner watched her as she walked along the building, crossed the alley between the Co-op and the Depot, regarded her curvy figure, the hips that moved beneath her long sweater. Damn, he thought, flustered and frustrated, he looked at his watch, half an hour until Sólrún's next class began, he set off hurriedly in the direction of the school.

The parish administrator wasn't even halfway through his story when the door opened and Sigríður entered. Kjartan went to the counter, Davíð let his chair drop back to the floor and opened his eyes wide, the parish administrator nodded, impatient to continue. Sigríður raised the counter's hinged panel, said: Get me a flashlight. Kjartan promptly obeyed, coming as close to Sigríður as he dared yet not as close as he wanted. To her blond hair, gathered in a bun at the nape of her neck, her smooth face, with faint wrinkles extending from the corners of her eyes, the faint, delicate scent of perfume, her breasts like melon halves beneath her sweater. Kjartan handed her the flashlight, their hands touched, a feeling of joy blended with security welled up in him, she felt nothing, just lit the flashlight, looked at him coldly, and said: I trusted you, I gave you a chance. Kjartan muttered something about burnt-out light bulbs, shot wiring, a strange sensation, Sigríður snorted and then disappeared into the warehouse, holding the flashlight. The parish administrator took a deep breath, removed his cap, ran his hand over his thinning hair, cleared his throat, and said, damn.

A few minutes later, Sigríður emerged from the darkness. How extraordinarily beautiful it was to see her step into the light. Her delicate but determined face, blond hair, brown eyes, slender body, a string vibrated in Kjartan's heart, the parish administrator took off his cap again, laid it over his heart as if considering proposing to her, reciting her a love poem, singing the national anthem, whereas Sigríður looked neither right nor left, she handed Kjartan the flashlight, said, you'll be hearing from me, and walked out, so composed, the parish administrator opened his mouth but she was already gone, the door closed again.

Sigríður went into the store, into the office of the foreman, a small room built on a platform, two steps up, a desk, two chairs, a filing cabinet, a large aerial photograph of the village hanging on the wall behind the desk, the other three walls made of glass, and when Sigríður was seated at the desk, she had a view of almost the entire store, its shelves full of merchandise, the two counters, but this time Sigríður didn't sit down, she put on her green coat, went out, got into her car, drove extremely slowly out of the village, past the Astronomer's black house. Then she pressed a bit harder on the accelerator and when Guðmundur came out of the sheephouse and saw his wife's car approaching at high speed, he thought, something's wrong, and felt fear ignite inside him, deep in his belly, a tiny spot that grew quickly, filled his chest cavity, spread out into his arms, down into his legs. Less than three minutes passed from when Guðmundur saw the car until Sigríður slammed on the brakes in the farmyard, but there are few limits to what one can think and imagine during that amount of time. They had three children, all in their twenties, two girls, one a student at the University of Akureyri, the other married to a farmer in the northern countryside, and a boy now in his thirties, who ran a carpentry workshop in Akranes. There were four grandchildren; Sigríður had two siblings and Guðmundur four, making thirteen lives, to which were added his parents and her mother, for a total of sixteen lives and so much that could happen, innumerable possibilities, horrendous things that are best not discussed over the phone. Sigríður slammed on the brakes in the farmyard, got out of the car, walked toward her husband, the car's engine still running, the door wide open, Guðmundur's head was full of accidents, sudden tumors, stroke, brain viruses, even suicide, but now Sigríður walked up to him and had never looked at him this way before, Sigríður's eyes are so brown and there was no sorrow in them, there was probably nothing plaguing any of those sixteen lives and therefore he could breathe a sigh of relief, which, though, Guðmundur was unable to do, hypnotized as he was by the look in his wife's eyes, they'd been married for thirty years, he knew her laughter, her expressions, how she slept, how she drank her coffee, how she opened her mouth when she raised an ice-cream cone to her lips, thirty years yet she seemed like a stranger just now, he'd never seen those brown eyes before. Sigríður took her husband by the hand, she led him into the house, he nearly fell over in the vestibule as he bent to remove his boots but she dragged him inside and he just managed to keep his feet, they were in the hallway leading to the main bedroom, she was always a stickler for cleanliness, Guðmundur was the first farmer there in the area to start wearing a coverall in the sheephouse and for a few years he was the subject of others' smirks, now his boots leave a trail of dirty footprints in the hallway and she pushes him down on their bed, he in his coverall, in his boots, she unzips her coat, pulls off her long, red sweater, tears off her white shirt, there's no other way to describe it. Buttons rain over Guðmundur and he thinks nothing, just lies there on the bed and knows nothing, understands nothing, so bewildered that he doesn't get an erection until she has unzipped his coverall, unzipped his trousers as well, and bent over him with her mouth so soft and so warm.

They stayed in bed for the rest of the day, except to run out and shut off the car's engine, get some snacks from the kitchen, a bottle of vodka that they'd had for a year and a half, had drunk no more of it during that time than to just below its shoulders, yet finished it that night, it was incredible, this wasn't their life at all, he felt sometimes as if he was in a movie, as if he was with an unfamiliar woman, which was terribly exciting, even though adultery had never crossed Guðmundur's mind.

Sigríður went into the warehouse on a Wednesday and didn't return to work until Friday, and up until then had never missed a day of work in twenty years. That Friday, she was herself again, confident, slightly cold, she switched on the lights on the lower floor at the same time as Guðmundur tottered out to the sheephouse, exhausted, sleep-deprived, is this due to menopause, he thought, spreading udder balm on his sore penis.

Menopause?

We have our doubts about that. On the other hand, sometimes it's just an arm's length between sex and death, it has something to do with despair, with a mad thirst for life; and we speak of death because, despite our gleaming modernity, we're still afraid of the dark, we still fear ghosts, the incomprehensible that lies beyond life, and the night after Sigríður went into the warehouse, Lúlla dreamed—Lúlla lives here in the village, tells the future with coffee grounds and cards, she's married to Lucky Óskar, who, several years ago, won a million krónur in the lottery, twice, quit work, and slumped into fat and torpor in front of videos and computer games—yes, well, Lúlla dreamed that the farmwife from the story came to her and said that everything would return to normal as soon as they moved the Depot off the ruins, set up a cross over them, and consecrated the land. But even if we're tempted to believe in dreams and hardly dare ignore a woman's bidding, it would cost an arm and a leg to move such a big building, it would take millions, in fact, and where would we get them? The couple Laki and Begga, both raised here in the village, tried to burn down the Depot one night, after draining a bottle of vodka between them, although the only thing that ended up burning was almost all of Laki's hair and one of Begga's mittens.

The day after, Davíð said to Kjartan, it'll be fun to see Laki bald; I've never found it fun to see Laki, replied Kjartan, with or without hair. On the other hand, I'd be happy if Sigríður came to visit us a little more often. Sigríður! She can freeze a man just by looking at him! Kjartan looked at his friend, you're so young, he said, you don't understand it. I don't understand what? What she has. She's fifty, said Davíð, shaking his head. She's the kind of woman who can drive you mad without even blinking, I'm afraid I wouldn't be able to control myself if she gave me even the slightest sign. A sign? Yes, see, if she gave me a little encouragement. Dream on! said Davíð, laughing. You have a lot to learn, said Kjartan, and I should probably envy you that. And you're nothing but flesh. For several moments, Kjartan stared straight ahead, his expression dejected, with a touch of sadness, Davíð bit his lip. You're probably right, Kjartan muttered.

What Is Related to the
Noun "Apocalypse"

1

Kjartan grew up in the countryside north of the village, on a farm just over a kilometer above the fjord, he was a boy and the sea stretched out before him and changed colors. When he was barely twenty, Kjartan took over the farm's management, his dad had lost his right hand in the hay blower, it made a horrible noise, and since then, he's never been able to hug his wife tightly enough. The couple moved here to the village, they both took jobs at the Dairy, she works in the slaughterhouse in the autumn, works hard and quickly, one of those who deserves double pay, while we sometimes say to the old man: give us a hand, or you're all thumbs today! We find this funny, as does he, sometimes, but not always. Kjartan proved capable of handling the farm quite well for his young age, he's always been rather stout, downright pudgy starting around puberty, it's just his nature, his constitution, though he eats too much, cakes in the evening, has his pockets full of biscuits and chocolate during sheep roundups. There, though, he's best of all, of course runs very little, gets tired after three tussocks or ten steps, but has an immensely powerful bass voice, a proper "thunderer," can clear an entire mountainside of sheep with it alone, shouts "ho!" and the gravel starts sliding. He liked to sing during sorting, which was fine as long as he stuck to the low notes, women's knees trembled at the deepest of them, but his voice was so false when he went higher that it could conjure rain from a clear blue sky; dogs howled and the smoked lamb went rancid where it lay on slices of flatbread in the coffee lean-tos. Kjartan was well liked, he resembled his mother, had a jovial spirit and a mine of coarse jokes. No one built fences as beautiful as his, and he raised the best bulls in the area, farmers traveled long distances to borrow them, or loaded the cow in a wagon, drove to Kjartan, put her under a three-year-old bull, bolbolbol, said Kjartan in a low voice and the bull finished off in five seconds, its penis like an overgrown carrot. But let's not dwell on the sex life of cattle, it's so dull, the bull thrusts once twice thrice, foam wells at its mouth, its eyes bulge, and then it's all over, the bull goes back to grazing, the cow back to its own barn, it's so terribly simple, which, of course, it isn't for us, to our misfortune, or praise God, but Kjartan's wife is named Ásdís and they have three children.

For a long time, things seemed to be going as well as could be expected, as if Kjartan and Ásdís fulfilled the plans of God and the Ministry of Agriculture for that particular farm. The couple adapted their farming methods to the spirit of the times, we imagined Kjartan's beautiful fences gleaming in the sun far into the future, they had their children, made their mark on the social life in the area, Ásdís took correspondence courses, accounting, English, German, Icelandic, mathematics, she wanted to try to broaden her horizons a bit, and some evenings, after the children had fallen asleep and the darkness had switched on the farm's front-door lights, she studied at the kitchen table and Kjartan turned off the television, found something to read, and sat down with her there, the farmers' gazette *Freyr*, a whodunnit, togetherness is nice. But the human creature is what it is, yet it must be stated clearly, before going any further, that Kjartan loved his wife, called her his sunshine, Sunflower, Splendor, my Sky, and what the poet said is probably true, that love is the most powerful element, that it's the force that moves the wheel of life and prevents us from falling headlong into gray futility. But even if love can change everything, move countries, and interweave two different lives, it has no dominion over so base a thing as the flesh, carnal desires. The farm nearest Sámsstaðir is called Valþúfa, where Kristín lives with her husband, two children, and mother-in-law.

Around that time, that is, the mid-nineties, Kristín let herself be swept up in the fitness craze that spread through the Western world like a promise of redemption, new paradigms, new ways of thinking. Gyms multiplied so quickly that people lost count of them, there were soon considerably more of them than schools, far more of them than churches, which makes sense, fitness coaches have a stronger effect on our lives than priests, whose time, of course, is in decline, whose days will soon be up, with their black cassocks and their litanies on a God that no one has seen for more than two thousand years, though we'll still call on Him, no doubt, when the end draws near. Interesting coincidence, however, that we mention God and His priests, because above the entrance to Valli's Gym hangs the motto THE BODY IS YOUR TEMPLE, and those of us who have taken spinning courses there and pumped away on the exercise bikes for forty minutes, at the heaviest setting that our legs can bear, would agree that the sweat and exertion cleanse our minds and bodies so well that the wonderful feeling we're left with must be God. For forty minutes, you're outside time and life, there's nothing but the effort, your own breath, the hypnotizing voice of Valli at a great distance, and then this wonderful feeling that seems to fill all of existence. Yet Kristín hadn't come far in her personal fitness campaign when she first went to Valli's Gym, she was neither slim nor graceful, she was just a farmer's wife who tended to drink a whole glass of unpasteurized, unskimmed cow's milk in the evening, and eat a slice of cake along with it. She hadn't done sports, hadn't stretched her muscles since graduating from the high school in Akranes, intended to study to become an assistant nurse but then the years passed with her studying nothing. She hadn't done abdominal exercises for many years, her stomach was flabby, too soft, her upper arms too soft, the skin hung from them, until one day Kristín said to herself: I've got to get in shape. She watched the morning fitness program on TV's Channel Two, tried to imitate the cheerful smiles of the people on the screen, people who are in good shape smile, bought a tracksuit, shoes, start with short distances, she'd read in a magazine, and Kristín ran across the farmyard, headed toward the moor that spread out in all directions, an extensive stretch separating Valþúfa and Sámsstaðir, a large number of slopes, hills, hollows, horses roamed there all year round, sheep in the spring and also on nice winter days. How long are short distances, thought Kristín, already panting before reaching the fence, barely a hundred meters from the farmhouse. She leaned on a fence post to catch her breath, the dog sat down and wagged his tail happily, completely new to him to see a full-grown person running for no apparent reason. Kristín turned to look back, knowing full well that Pétur and his mother were watching her through the kitchen window, shaking their heads at her. Kristín cursed, walked tiredly back home, the disappointed dog at her heels, she pretended not to see the poorly concealed grin of her mother-in-law, went to take a shower, masturbated, a bit vigorously, even violently, imagining that she was with two unknown men at the gym, probably just to get back at those two in the kitchen, got dressed, went to the car, drove to the village, parked outside a white building, Valli's Gym, stood in front of the wall facing the parking lot, where, beneath the sign bearing the motto, a teenager had sprayed in red, gloating letters: LONG LIVE THE DICK!! Kristín entered the building, hesitated at the circular counter with health-food items lined up beneath its glass plate, energy drinks in the refrigerator, books on astrology on the shelf, and above her, a sheet of white eleven-by-seventeen-inch paper displaying the announcement:

> Valli reads Tarot cards, one-month reading 6,000 krónur, three-month reading 10,000, year reading 14,000, life reading, price by agreement (depending on the age and health of the subject). ATTN: Readings for longer periods are less precise!

The workout room is behind the reception counter, the gym's motto, THE BODY IS YOUR TEMPLE!, hangs above the door, and under the motto, Valli has recently hung another inscription, in letters half as large: REMEMBER THAT IF YOUR BODY FEELS WELL, YOU'LL FEEL WELL!

Kristín decided that she could wait no more, walked hesitantly into the room, two-meter-tall mirrors covered all the walls, considerably expanding the size of the room, always difficult to know just how many people were there, which bodies were reflections and which were real, loud, rhythmic music coming from the TV, a young female singer looked straight into the camera, her expression thoughtful, with just a touch of melancholy, her breasts almost completely visible, young and firm, two female dancers appeared behind her now and then, wearing skin-tight halter tops, pink G-strings, just as much of their breasts visible; we most definitely live in an age of exposure. Kristín turned away from the screen and looked around for Valli. At one time, Valli had been like everyone else; he worked for the power company, his wife worked at the bank, four children who grew up, a completely routine life, but then something happened and Valli said that he'd seen the light, to which someone answered, nothing peculiar there—you work for the power company. But Valli obviously didn't mean electric light; he meant the light that changes your life. He opened the first gym in the village, in a small, rented basement to begin with, open after work, as a kind of hobby. But Valli embraced the spirit of the times, changes were imminent, the fitness wave hit the Western world, articles and interviews in newspapers and magazines described how well people felt after getting in shape, with striking, persuasive titles such as "A Life with Fewer Worries," "I'm Happy," "Workouts Have Changed My Life," which naturally had an influence on us, and on top of that, Valli was granted a generous subsidy by the state to buy the white house that had stood empty ever since the old councillor had a heart attack over his prune porridge and his wife moved into a nursing home, where she began a relationship with her childhood sweetheart—a thread picked up fifty years later. The subsidy was granted under the auspices of the government's combined urban development and health program, under the slogan "Better Health, Better Community," and for the past few years, Valli's Gym has been open every day 7–9 a.m. and 12–9 p.m., we purchase annual passes and life would certainly be better, the sky brighter, and the village more beautiful if we used our passes more regularly, but we tend to get lazy in the summer and autumn, have no time in December, best if we can get in the swing of workouts in January and February and then again in the spring, so that we can remove our tops on sunny beaches in summer, apart from that, our annual passes gather dust and we smile embarrassedly when we meet Valli, who is always so radiant with fitness, health, and happiness, with highlights in his blond hair.

Have you come to work out? Valli asks, appearing beside her suddenly, as if springing up from the floor, and laying his muscular arm over Kristín's shoulders, well, I was thinking about it, Kristín answers, but Valli shushes her, leads her to a table in the corner, says, thinking and hesitating are tantamount to losing, and before realizing it, Kristín has taken off her jacket, her sweater, her socks, has stepped onto the scales, Valli has measured her blood pressure, her height, gently felt her body, almost like a doctor, he often says that he's both a priest and a doctor.

2

And new days have begun.

Valli prepared a detailed jogging routine, emphasizing that Kristín was to run short distances to start with, then walk a bit, then jog again, and so on. And Kristín jogged, sweatband, track-suit, running shoes, and the dog followed, she jogged, she walked, she disappeared between ridges, she sweated, she pedaled away on Valli's workout equipment, to the rhythmic music from the TV, the smell of sweat and warm bodies, she jogged away from the farm, ever more honed, more energetic, happier, now this is how you live, she thought, even if Pétur shook his head and his mother-in-law did the same, saying things such as fanaticism, idiocy, thank God she only did this while the children were at school, although the dog was happy, nothing beats running across moors with a human being, it's almost too good to be true. If the weather was nice, she ran every other day and skipped using the workout equipment, you've got to take advantage of the summer, which is so short that you could almost sleep through it. One day while Kristín was out jogging, she ran into Kjartan.

They were out of sight of their farms, and well out of earshot. Kjartan had walked out to the fence separating the two farms, both to feel the size of his farm with his own body and to check on the state of the fence, he brought along a sledgehammer, hammer, and pliers, and had fifty fencing staples in his jacket pocket. He met Kristín at a spot where the ground is somewhat soft and the fence tended to sink and lean forward, even lie down on its side as if in a bottomless depression. It was a mild day, the summer sky partly overcast, a light breeze, flies buzzed, spiders scampered in the grass, a snipe climbed into the sky, then let itself drop, making its characteristic warbling sound with its tail feathers. Kristín had tied her tracksuit top around her waist; she was wearing a white T-shirt and sweating. Kjartan was hot and sweaty from his struggle against the fence's depression, had removed his shirt, his thin jacket and sweater and T-shirt lay over a tussock. Kjartan is rather corpulent, rolls of fat hung like billowy clouds over the waistband of his trousers. Kristín had been jogging for twenty minutes without stopping, her clothes stuck to her skin, she'd just slipped off her sports bra, folded it, and stuffed it into her tracksuit pocket, to her great relief, her breasts seemed to take deep breaths, nor had she expected to run into anyone, it's rare that you meet anyone in the Icelandic countryside, you might see a car pass by, people doing various things at their farms, but nothing more, and now, there stood Kjartan, shirtless, and, letting his sledgehammer sink until its head rested on a tussock, he said the first and only thing that came to his mind: It's you! Yes, replied Kristín, trying to mask her breathlessness: It's you, too!

Thinking of nothing else to say, they both fell silent. Less than ten meters from each other, Kristín's sweaty T-shirt like a transparent glove on her breasts. It took a decided effort for Kjartan not to look, but it just wasn't enough, it's hard to control your eyes and of course easier to be a dog than a man, they immediately began sniffing each other, exchanging the latest news, Kristín's dog sniffed at the back end of Kjartan's bitch as if to say, here's something that I would like to investigate further. Kristín untied and removed her tracksuit top from her waist, put it on and zipped it up halfway, tried to do this slowly and nonchalantly to hide her nervousness, I'm jogging, she said with a laugh, almost apologetically, to get myself in shape. Well, I'll be! Yes, you have to listen to your body, said Kristín, and then she bit her lower lip and blushed, glancing down at Kjartan's overflowing belly, but he gave one of those deep, boyish laughs of his, said, it would do me some good to go jogging with you, and he slapped his stomach, which quivered beneath his palm, the tremors spread from there to his waist. She laughed, too, and wiggled her fingers, overcome with an unexpected, ridiculous need to sink them into that heavy flesh, to see them disappear into the fat. The dogs were running out of news to tell, Kristín's dog whined softly and tried to mount Kjartan's bitch. Smiling, the two humans watched, before Kristín shushed her dog and said, well, then, which Kjartan repeated, groping for his sledgehammer. Kristín unzipped her tracksuit top, hesitated, then took it off and tied it back around her waist, smiled at Kjartan and said, I get so hot when I jog. I can believe that, he said energetically, as he lifted the sledgehammer easily with his left hand and let it rest on one of the fence posts, and then, gripping the sledgehammer handle tightly, added, it must be great to jog in such nice weather. A fine sight met Kjartan's eyes, it was as if Kristín's breasts stretched toward him, they tautened her wet T-shirt, he could make out her brown nipples. Kristín scolded her horny dog, who was sniffing again at the bitch's rear end, and then jogged away, her breasts swaying, turned back after a few meters, raised her hand in farewell, and called out, I jog every other day when the weather's like this, nothing less would do, and then she was gone. The dog followed her, its loyalty and obedience stronger than its sexual instincts; yet another thing that differentiates dogs from human beings.

Kjartan let the sledgehammer slip from his grasp, his hands dangled at his sides, he looked downward and could feel every single gram of his overflowing flesh, I'm a rubbish heap, he thought, I'm fat as a pig, why the hell didn't I put on my sweater, she clearly couldn't bear the sight of this deformed waist of mine, and why the hell did I have to gape like that at her breasts, like some bloody pervert. Kjartan sighed, put his sweater back on, sat down on a tussock, stared straight ahead, and felt hungry, closed his eyes and envisioned Kristín, sweaty, glistening in her clammy T-shirt, which her oblong breasts had stretched out. He opened his eyes, assaulted by the fear that Kristín would tell everyone in the district about this, how he'd gaped at her breasts. He stood up heavily, gathered his tools, went home, and swore not to do any fence work the following week, and most definitely not after two days, I run every other day, she'd shouted, meaning: You stay at home, my good man.

Two days later, Kjartan is standing there in the same place, at the same time. Planting fence posts, working up a sweat, legs spread wide, sweater off; he keeps glancing around, restless, nervous, worried, doesn't understand what has got into him, go home, you fool, before she comes, before you turn yourself into a laughing-stock. But he doesn't go anywhere and is pulling the barbed wire taut when she appears, he pretends not to notice her, he's a busy man, thinks, hopefully she'll just jog on by. When she sees him, Kristín stops suddenly, the weather is even better today, hardly less than seventeen degrees, she has slipped off her sports bra, holds it in her right hand, the fabric of her T-shirt sticks to her wet skin, she'd just used the bra to pat dry her chest, stomach, lifted her T-shirt to cool off and her nipples had swollen slightly yet noticeably in the warm breeze. Hi, she says, because it would be stupid just to jog past him, he looks up and says in surprise, oh, it's you, loses control of his eyes for one, two, probably three seconds, letting them slip from her face down to her breasts, which seem to shout, no, scream, hey, here we are! Bloody fucking hell, thinks Kjartan, but then says without thinking: Oh, could you help me staple down the barbed wire here, I forgot the goddamn tensioner and really need at least one more hand to fasten the wire. I really don't want to mess up my exercise routine, she responds, almost dryly. He freezes; no, of course not, sorry, I'll sort this out, no worries, see you later, no problem. She shrugs, says, one staple can hardly hurt, but then I've got to get back to my run. Thanks so much, he says, I really admire your strength, I mean, to stick to your routine like this, really great, and he pulls harder on the barbed wire, which vibrates slightly as Kristín hammers in the staple, a few businesslike blows. Out of the corner of her eyes, she sees his thick arms, his overflowing belly, he's wet with sweat, she feels her breasts swing to the hammer blows. He's staring at my breasts, she thinks, these men have their brains in their dicks, stop gawking, you idiot, he orders himself. The wire is fastened, he lets go of it, she hands him the hammer, says softly, bye, and he says, bye and thanks for the help, unnecessarily loudly. She slips between the barbed wire and the top of the fence, takes a few steps, turns to look at him, he's resting his hand on a fence post, looking at her, sweaty, a gleam in his eye, he's nothing but flesh and she lets her eyes run down along his body, slowly, shamelessly, as if stroking his skin with her eyes, he swallows, she sets off jogging, stops after a few steps, turns and looks—and then something happens. Then it happens! An explosion inside both of them that paralyzes all thought, reason, erases the entire past and the entire future, because there's nothing else in the world but that very moment. Kjartan emits a half-stifled cry, tries feverishly to climb over the fence, presses his hand on the barbed wire, cuts himself, stumbles, loses his balance, falls, and hits his back on a fence post, it hurts, catches his trouser leg on the barbed wire, wriggles both furiously and giddily when she comes to him, when she throws herself over him and from her throat come sounds halfway between yelps and growls. I'm stuck, he pants, damned trousers, she says nothing, reaches out with her hands as if she were blind or in total darkness, feels her way down his body, searching for his belt beneath his heavy flesh, which she lifts, pushes aside, squeezes handfuls of twice and so hard that he flinches, finally finds the belt, undoes it, unbuttons his trousers, unzips them, he lifts his rear end, tries to help, damned back, he moans, and then, I'm free, as if she couldn't see that, as if she didn't see his thick thighs with their broken capillaries, as if she didn't see his black underpants that bulge, she tears off her shirt, he grabs both her breasts straightaway, like a drowning man, she grabs his bleeding hand and licks the blood, he pulls off her tracksuit bottoms, the two of them roll in the grass, simultaneously yell "Leave!" at the dogs, who prance around them, put your trousers under me, she pants, this damned grass is sticking into my ass, and that word, ass, deprives him of the last remnants of his self-control, he pulls and tears off his underpants, lies over her, she grabs a handful of his flesh, opens her legs wide, his broad penis fills her, she spurs him on with her heels, pounds him with her hands, viewed from a distance, they might have appeared to be fighting.

And then it was over.

Sitting on their own tussocks, they put their clothes back on, almost furtively, and regret kindled deep inside both of them, first as a vague suspicion, little ripples on a mirror-smooth lake that grow gradually and finally ruffle the entire surface. They said goodbye without looking each other in the eye, hurried away from each other, thought never, never again. When he returned home, Kjartan could not look directly at Ásdís, and Kristín had Pétur sit down in one of the kitchen chairs and cut his hair gently, paused to fondle his ear from time to time and he let his eyelids droop.

There is so much that we want, so little that we are able to do. The summer passed, with sunshine and rain and wind and calm. I'm going jogging, she said, I'm going for a walk, he said, to take a look at the fences, or else he said nothing at all, because he was the farmer and didn't have to explain to anyone when he went somewhere on his farm. He thought about her breasts, her buttocks, she thought about his broad shoulders, about sinking her hands into his soft, fat flesh. They always met in the same place and, viewed from a distance, they might have appeared to be fighting.

3

You mustn't feel as if this was easy for them; sometimes guilt can completely spoil the joys of the flesh. Kjartan, for example, loved his wife, which I'm pretty sure we've already said; you're my sun, he often said to her. My sky. My flower. Twice he sat on a tussock and simply wept after Kristín vanished from sight, yet they kept on meeting; we're so bad at controlling our flesh. Autumn came. On several occasions, Kjartan was on the verge of confessing everything; he had Ásdís accompany him on a long walk down to the sea, on a long drive and talked nonstop, but never about what he should have. He slept badly, remorse stirred in his dreams, emerged from his pores, he slept with a towel next to the bed, got up during the night, went down to the kitchen, turned on the light, drank a glass of milk, looked at himself in the dark windowpane, thought, I've got to stop this, thought, I've got to tell Ásdís about it. The situation affected his daily chores, in the barn he would stare distractedly out the window while the milking machines drained the cows dry, he could no longer watch a program or film on TV that had to do with infidelity, not even when Ásdís had settled onto the sofa next to him, with chocolates, soft drinks, and popcorn, he tensed up as if someone were pointing a pistol at him, couldn't keep calm, muttered some excuse, and fled out into the garage. A few years earlier, Kjartan had bought a 1955 Dodge, a jalopy, more or less, that had nearly been consigned to the junk heap, but since then he'd spent many fine hours out in the garage, fixing up the Dodge, which would soon see its dignity fully restored. But even those hours were no longer fine, he would sometimes just sit in the car's back seat while guilt tore at his heart like a noxious bird, he would be bent over the engine and suddenly think of Kristín's tongue, recall words that she had whispered to him.

But then Ásdís discovered everything.

Of course, she'd sensed that something was wrong, Kjartan was acting more nervous than usual, more distracted; he was paler, seemed tired and even as if he were avoiding her, sometimes. She was worried, suggested that he go to see the doctor, feared cancer, leukemia, an imminent heart attack. No, no, he assured her, I don't need to go and see the doctor, which was true, because there are no prescriptions against infidelity, it's not possible to buy drugs that deaden guilt, not yet, but science continues to make great strides. Kjartan hadn't told anyone about his extramarital affair, he had no friends in whom he could confide, while Kristín had a good friend in the village, Ólafía, called Fía, and one day in early winter, Kristín could no longer restrain herself, she simply had to reveal her forbidden secret, and she told Fía everything, because it was so hard, painful, even, to keep it bottled up inside, she opened her mouth and let it all spill out. To unburden her conscience, yes, most certainly, but perhaps also to make it known that her life possessed warmth and color, that it wasn't stagnant, the torpidity of the countryside, and she might even have embellished the story a little, made it more compelling, said that Kjartan always brought her flowers, that he had a thousand different nicknames for her, he was so sweet, he was so animalistic, wild. Kristín closed her eyes, as if to emphasize her words, then opened them, opened them wide, laid her hand over Fía's and whispered: Don't tell anyone, for God's sake; no one!

Of course not, are you nuts? Fía said, and she showered Kristín with questions every time they met, asked and asked, asked for details, even, it was as if she wanted to take part in that forbidden liaison, asked until she sensed Kjartan's unrestrained ardor and felt the great weight of his flesh. And the more she asked, the more eager Kristín became to tell the story, the telling itself became a pleasure. Or a continuation of the pleasure.

Many things can be said about human beings. Both beauty and filth can be found in most people. Man is a complex being, something of a labyrinth, easy to get lost in if you go looking for explanations. Once, Fía hinted at the affair in the hearing of a relative of hers. They meet regularly over coffee, her relative's name is Ragnar, called Raggi or Tabloid Raggi, because nothing gives him more pleasure than digging up and spreading stories about neighbors' problems, their money woes, alcoholism, unhappiness; he would have had a great career as a reporter for the tabloid press. Fía regretted it terribly, maybe it was envy that controlled her tongue, the devil always finds all the chinks, and she deeply regretted her words, felt desolate, wanted to cut out her own tongue. But even the most bitter regret can't take back what's been said, the words have set out into the world and live a life of their own; nothing can stop them. The news of Kristín and Kjartan's affair spread slowly but surely. On the other hand, accounts transform according to the mouths that tell them, that's their nature, no person tells a story exactly like the next, but the core of the story generally rolls along unchanged, and in this story, it's as follows, with variously discreet wordings: Kjartan from Sámsstaðir and Kristín from Valþúfa are having an affair— and a fiery one, at that.

Eventually, Ásdís got wind of this, though not directly—your husband is cheating on you with Kristín, they have sex once or twice a week on the moor between their farms, fuck like tailless dogs whatever the weather—no, it was more like an intimation, a subtle hint. An unsuspecting person might not have noticed anything, but Kjartan, of course, hadn't been himself and sometimes Ásdís fears it's cancer, dwindling passion, but then someone says to her, yes, it's only a short distance between their farms, or, does Kristín visit you often, or, did you know that Kristín is getting in shape, has Kjartan started jogging as well?—something along these lines. And then Ásdís thinks of how, over the last few months, he has taken so many walks—which is really unusual, in fact—and always to the west.

I would prefer it if you had a terminal disease, Ásdís thought when she looked at Kjartan that evening, he was sitting on the sofa, a drama series on TV, the children were sleeping, three, seven, and nine years old. Stomach cancer, she thought, that would have suited you, colon cancer, too, or bone cancer—that would have been best of all. Over time, no drug, not even morphine, would have been able to deaden her pain sufficiently, he'd shattered her will and personality into pieces. My love, you would have lain there in bed, moaned, screamed, cried, and then died. And I would have nursed you, and then been able to grieve for you. Ásdís smiles. Out of the corners of his eyes, Kjartan notices her smile and feels very uneasy, has difficulty focusing on the TV program, loses the thread of the plot. I'm feeling a bit under the weather, he finally says, maybe you have bone cancer, she gently replies. He looks at her in surprise, she looks at him with a tender expression, an expression that doesn't fit at all with the words "bone cancer." The house moves, sways slightly back and forth, Kjartan clamps his fingers on the sofa, tries to smile, produces little more than a grimace, come on, he manages to say, I'm just tired. He gets up, crosses the room, and now the house is a ship on a stormy sea, yet he makes it up to his bedroom, goes to bed without brushing his teeth, without peeing, without saying his prayers, which he hasn't of course done in twenty years, though now would truly be a good time to start doing so again. Kjartan lies down, looks at the ceiling, and thinks: My God, she knows, she knows, *she knows*! He's in a panic, he's so relieved, so sad and full of self-loathing, he hates Kristín with every cell in his body. Ásdís remains sitting downstairs, switches off the lights so that she can see out, and forgets to switch off the television, which half fills the room with the bluish light that has begun to illuminate people's inner walls and change their internal landscapes.

4

At first, Ásdís did nothing.

The days passed.

As calm and focused as a sociologist, she kept an eye on Kjartan, almost certain of his guilt yet not one hundred percent, maybe ninety-five, ninety-six, still hoping that she was wrong, that it was something else, depression, dwindling passion, cancer. Unfortunately, there was little to suggest any of these; she thought back over his actions, recollected his unexpected interest in walks, his frequent trips in a westerly direction, his strange restlessness before setting out, even shaving, combing his hair, and then his tendency to return in a peculiar mood, sometimes sad, sometimes almost shameful, sometimes angry, sometimes unnaturally cheerful. Details or moments that she'd noticed without realizing it now rose to the surface. Kristín's eyes when she glanced at Kjartan at the midwinter dance, Kjartan's hand on Kristín's waist at the same dance, Kjartan's abnormally constrained voice when he said Kristín's name, the trembling of his hands when they met Kristín and Pétur at the Co-op. I was blind, thinks Ásdís, it was right before my eyes all winter, but I was so entirely focused on my studies that Kjartan took advantage of it. Ásdís thinks, she recalls, she trembles, from fear, pain, perhaps from hatred, she looks out the window and stares for a long time at the frolicking puppies that their bitch gave birth to in January, one of them has a white star on its forehead, just like the dog at Valþúfa.

It all pointed to only one thing.

Her certainty slowly rose from ninety-six to ninety-nine percent, the percentage point that was missing was the thread that kept her dangling over the abyss. Yet a single thread can't hold a person up for long; the fall opens beneath your feet, the chasm pulls at you. No lethal disease, just base, shitty infidelity.

Infidelity—betraying one's partner, having sexual intercourse or establishing a loving relationship with someone other than one's partner—is related to the noun "Apocalypse."

And now it was Ásdís who couldn't sleep.

She lay there staring at the ceiling, uncertainty, conflicting feelings, churned violently within her. She lay there listening to Kjartan's deep breathing, which was interrupted from time to time by his irregular snores. I'll ask for a divorce, he makes me sick, no, it's my fault, I was so selfish, so distant, I always say, not now, later, tonight, tomorrow, I've had enough of doing myself up for him, dressing like a slut here at home. She lay there, unable to sleep, and the night covered everything. She thought, I haven't taken good enough care of our home, I've neglected the children, all my energy, all my concentration went into my studies, I think only of them, I think only of myself, and now I'm being punished. We've got to cultivate our relationships, she thinks. She lay on her back, breathed deeply, the sky so dark over the countryside. No! It's not my fault, maybe a little bit, but not more, I don't want to grant him the pleasure of reproaching me because it's he who betrayed me, betrayed his children, betrayed himself. It's he! Or no, it's I, I'm to blame. Ásdís rose silently, went downstairs, took off her blue nightgown, stood naked in the vestibule and looked at herself in the big mirror. Her breasts are close to medium size, once firm, but falling now, as if they were having trouble keeping awake these days. Her waistline is straight as a boy's, no attractive, sexy curve that ignites desire, her belly ugly, wrinkled and far too flaccid following three pregnancies. She looked at her body, flabby from lack of exercise, I'm ugly, she said to her reflection, I'm unexciting.

Thus passed the days and thus passed the weeks. Ásdís swung from one mood to another, she was irritable, pettish, kept a close eye on her husband, waited for something that could eliminate that last one percent, waited for the thread to snap and plunge her into the abyss. One day he set off west.

For a long time, he'd been hanging around outside, noticeably restless, continually looking toward the house but unable to see her in the living-room window behind the flowers on the windowsill, before finally setting off. Slowly at first, but then gradually increasing his speed to a brisk clip before the ridges and hills and slopes shielded him from view. He's on his way to her, thought Ásdís at the living-room window, inhaling the scent of the flowers as her body slowly grew numb. She sat down, couldn't remain on her feet, the living-room clock counted the seconds, counted the minutes, devotedly kept track of the time, looked after it. Ásdís gathered her strength to stand up, went to the stairs, listened for her children, the eldest, Kolbrún, was at home recovering from the flu and Diljá, the youngest, was playing with Lego bricks in her sister's room. She returned to the living room, got a videotape ready in case Diljá came downstairs, didn't have it in her to look after her now, afraid that she would lose control of herself and start scolding her for no reason. The living-room clock did its duty, had counted twenty minutes, tick tock, it said continually, tick tock. Ásdís sat motionless in her armchair, calm on the surface, incredible how little the surface can tell us. She sat there as if she were recalling the conjugation of German verbs, cake recipes, the plot of a book, which cow was going to give birth next, while inside her everything was topsy-turvy, she followed Kjartan in her mind, beheld everything in her mind's eye, she quivered with hatred, even had a murderous impulse, pure and simple, she was desperate, overwhelmed with sadness, anger, and that was actually the best feeling, worst when she was assailed, seized entirely by her impulse, making her arms twitch, but then it passed, burst like a soap bubble and left behind a bitter sense of shame and a deep disdain for herself. She sat there, that cool, blue April day, the sun high in the sky but the living-room clock holding time in its hands. Then someone walked through the farmyard.

He was back!

He'd finished his fuck.

Once again, he had betrayed everything that was beautiful and good. How could he look at his children without batting an eyelid, without burning to ashes, she should tear out his eyes, he would be grateful, over time. She jumped up, went into the kitchen, started making bread dough, and was busy with that when he came in, didn't make herself available, was listening to the radio as well. Kjartan wanted to talk to her, was eager, wanted to organize their summer holidays, we should go abroad, to Copenhagen, imagine it, the Tivoli and Bakken for the kids! Yes, and Istedgade for you, she thought, sinking her hands into the dough, conceivably to keep them from encircling his neck. Ásdís's aloofness silenced him, he drew back to the living room, I should take a shower, he muttered, and did so, went to take a shower, washed off the smell of Kristín, the warm water flowed over his broad shoulders. When he came back to the kitchen she was gone, she had to pop out, Kolbrún said. Where? I don't know. Kjartan went into the living room, stood at the window with binoculars but didn't see the car anywhere, Valþúfa can't be seen from Sámsstaðir, knolls and hills block the view.

Ásdís is seated at the kitchen table at Valþúfa, Kristín has just returned home, her mother-in-law, Lára, prepares coffee, Pétur is busy outside, a tall, round-shouldered man, thin, almost emaciated, with a coarse face, somewhat serious, almost always taciturn, some are convinced that he never changes moods. The April light is still blue, but soon evening will arrive, with its darker colors. There has never been much contact between the two farms, one wouldn't call it discord, but rather a kind of deep-rooted resentment that Kjartan and Pétur inherited from their parents and their parents' parents; the heat from the friction that is sometimes generated between neighbors in the countryside. Perhaps we're so used to living in relative isolation that we don't know how to relate to our neighbors properly, we're not accustomed to having to show consideration for others, something that could be called a lack of social maturity, lying deep inside us.

Lára is surprised by the visit, while Kristín is terrified, sitting stiffly in her chair as the sweat dries on her skin, as Lára sees to the coffee, takes out this and that to go with it, wonders about the reason for the visit, says well then several times, says yes indeed, too, asks the news, asks about the livestock, the haymaking, the condition of the hayfields, Ásdís answers, but does nothing more than that, and sometimes there are silences, during which Lára rocks nervously. Ásdís doesn't touch her coffee, a full cup in front of her, black liquid that slowly cools, Lára's temper flares when she notices, Sámsstaðir scum, she thinks, nothing but presumption and arrogance! She abruptly abandons polite small talk, crosses her slender arms, purses her thin lips, and says nothing. For a long moment, not even a fly is heard, but then Lára sips her coffee noisily, the other two look at her, she sticks a biscuit in her mouth in something of a dither, but regrets it immediately. She bites it slowly and carefully, Ásdís and Kristín stare straight ahead and listen, Lára chews slowly in the hope that it's less noticeable, but in doing so, has to chew for what seems forever, though she eventually swallows, quite substantial, these biscuits, her skinny face has reddened slightly, she reaches for her coffee cup, drinks a bit too eagerly, gulps, coughs, again Ásdís and Kristín look at her, then silence returns. It's remarkable how silence can distort time, the minutes act differently, they seem not to want to pass, they're a motionless sky. Kristín listens to the heavy beating of her own heart, a bass drum that someone strikes with a decisive, urgent rhythm: boom! boom! boom! Her skin still tingles from the salt that her sweat left behind, she senses the smell of Kjartan rising from her neck and filling the kitchen, the smell of kisses, breaths, sweat, and semen, she'd asked him to come on her stomach, the heavy, sweet aroma of male semen. You were running, says Ásdís suddenly, so unexpectedly that they're all startled and Lára is so bewildered that she grabs another biscuit. It's as if the silence intensified at these words, despite its having been deep enough already, and at its bottom sits Lára, not knowing whether to chew slowly or quickly, trying unsuccessfully to make the biscuit dissolve in her mouth, Ásdís and Kristín appear to be waiting for her to finish it, so she decides to chew it quickly, finish it, she munches it, smacks her lips, swallows, her forehead sweaty. Then Kristín says: Yes. Just one yes, one or two long minutes after the question.

Ásdís: And you haven't had a shower yet?

Kristín: I just got home.

Ásdís: So it's best that we let you go and take a shower, you probably need to wash, clean yourself up, you must have sweated a lot with the effort. Ásdís's lips part, revealing her teeth, white but not quite straight. Damned bitch, thinks Kristín, looking at her mother-in-law, who is staring furiously at Ásdís. Yes, I put a lot into it, Kristín then says.

Then go and wash.

She paused between each word. Each like a stone that Ásdís pulled from her mouth and lined up in the middle of the kitchen table: THEN GO AND WASH. Lára snorts, she's about to say something; she stares angrily at Ásdís and the unbearably full cup of coffee, but then the visitor gets up, slowly pushes the chair back, and says calmly, coldly: I hope you enjoyed it. She walks out of the kitchen. Walks out of the house. She's crazy, declares Lára, in a shrill voice, before adding, with gusto, Sámsstaðir scum, those . . . then falls silent, stunned, almost frightened when Kristín hurtles toward the front door, tears it open, and squawks into the dwindling April light: Oh, yes, I enjoyed it! I bloody well did enjoy it, every damn moment! Standing in the farmyard next to her car, Ásdís turns to look at Kristín. Hi, Pétur, she then says, though Pétur is nowhere to be seen. Kristín slams the front door shut.

5

Shortly after lunchtime two days later, Ásdís says to Kjartan, go with Diljá to the village, here's a shopping list, and then go and pick up Björgvin and Kolbrún from school and take them to see their grandparents. Can you do that? I have to stay at home and study.

Two days have passed. Two days of hell for Kjartan, who is having a harder time sleeping at night, he slinks down to the kitchen, makes a sandwich, chugs milk, eats some crullers, and the black night is at the window. Ásdís says little, and he's been waiting, expecting at any minute for her to say, I know everything, or, you're a goddamn piece of shit, or, I've applied for a divorce, or, here's the knife, take it and cut off your balls. But instead of the knife, she hands him a shopping list and sends him to the village. He is completely convinced that she knows, or at least has strong suspicions, and has started longing for a reaction, anger, for her to scream at him, but then just finds himself sitting behind the wheel with a shopping list in his pocket and Diljá bouncing in the car seat. The car drives slowly down the side road, I'll talk to her tonight, he thinks, after the children have gone to bed, I'll admit it all, I'm a bastard, a dirty, fat bastard, he turns onto the main road, shifts into third. Ásdís is sitting in the living room, listening to the car as it drives away, listening as the sound of the engine fades, then gets up and goes into the pantry. Uses a stool to reach the top shelf, takes the single-action pistol used to dispatch sheep and lambs and a box of bullets, goes back to the living room, puts on her coat, slips on her shoes. The thermometer reads seven degrees Celsius, there's a gentle breeze, the sky is partially overcast, and it's dry, though raining in the mountains to the southeast. The bitch and the puppies are outside, so blissful that they can't think of doing anything but chasing their own wonderful tails, which can never be caught, or else running back and forth and leaping into the air. Ásdís picks up the puppy with the star on its forehead, it wags its tail, tries to lick her face, can't, and settles for licking her hand. She carries it into the laundry room, through the separate entrance at the back of the house. Crouches holding the puppy, which shoves its nose enthusiastically up the arm of her coat, poor dear, she says, pushes it slowly and carefully down on the floor and shoots it in the back of the head. Puppies don't think about death, they're just carefree and believe that life is eternal, and then it's all over. Ásdís goes and gets the next puppy, the third hops around her and whines when it doesn't get to go, too, waits at the door, scratches at it, and bounds in when Ásdís opens it, barks twice, perhaps to ask, hey, where are you? And what could one answer, what happens to dead puppies, do they get to go somewhere with their irrepressible happiness? Ásdís couldn't immediately catch the third, it ran away, thought that this was a game, agile and quick to avoid her grasp, but then got its head stuck in one of Kjartan's trekking boots. Moved its head slightly when it felt the shot, its heart beat hard but then beat no more. It took Ásdís some time to get the bitch, which had hidden in the cowshed, she lured her out with blandishments, the bitch crawled to her on its belly, trembling and whining, dogs have sensitive noses and death can be smelled. Afterward, Ásdís dug a deep hole, it wasn't easy, the ground was still hard after the winter, but it's good to toil, it clears your mind, then she looked for some time at the bitch and her puppies down in the hole, tried to arrange their corpses better, thought something, filled the hole with earth, patted it down well, over and over, then went back to the cowshed and from there to the henhouse just off it, grabbed the half-asleep rooster off its perch and clamped it under her arm to immobilize its wings, went to the garage and came out with a small machete, changed her grip on the bird, grabbed it by its neck, slung it quickly onto a barrel standing up against the shed, and cut off its head. Took a few steps backward and watched the headless rooster flutter around the farmyard, flapping its useless wings as life gushed out of the stump of its neck. Then it dropped dead, and would never again flutter out into the black night to fetch the morning sun from down in the deep, its final day had dawned over the farm. Ásdís went back into the house, washed her hands using a lot of soap, drank a glass of water, and then phoned her parents. Yes, Kjartan and the children had just arrived, she could hear the children in the background and moved the receiver to her right ear, with which she couldn't hear as well. Can the kids stay with you and Mom tonight? No, I need to talk to Kjartan, just tell him to hurry home. Ásdís hung up, went out, opened the garage door, sat down behind the wheel of the Dodge, started the car, the *Elvis Presley's Greatest Hits* tape started playing on the car stereo, she backed out, parked the car between the farm buildings and the house, shut off the engine but let Elvis keep singing, even raised the volume, One thing I know, I loved you like a baby, bent down to pick up the headless rooster, placed it on the driver's seat, went and got some of Kjartan's clothes that she'd set out earlier, along with a few record albums, letters, and wedding photographs, arranged these things carefully on the front seat, poured gasoline over the seats, over the rest of the car, sat down on the ground with her back against one of the front wheels, shut her eyes for a moment, opened them again, looked down toward the road.

It takes about half an hour to drive back from the village, under normal conditions. One moment Kjartan pressed hard on the accelerator and the car dashed forward, but in the next, his anxiety flared and he slowed down, shifted to a lower gear, coasted along at 40 kph, at one point pulled over to the side of the road, hurried out of the car to vomit, leaned with his right hand on the hood but nothing came out. Sámsstaðir is the first farm that one sees upon rounding the slope of Mount Kollafjall, which stands in a deep semicircle behind the group of nine farmhouses that form the settlement called Kollabyggð throughout Iceland's recorded history. Sámsstaðir, however, quickly disappears behind the landscape's contours, and doesn't reappear until the turnoff to Valþúfa is far behind. At that point, Kjartan sees smoke rising. At first, he thinks some absurd nonsense, my life is in flames, or something like that, which was perhaps not nonsense in a metaphorical sense, but then he realizes that it's the Dodge that's on fire, no doubt about it—and nothing metaphorical either. Instinctively, Kjartan pressed down on the accelerator, the car skidded sideways as he took the turnoff to home too fast, but he gunned it and tore up to the house, slammed on the brakes, got out. Ásdís had her back turned to him, staring at the Dodge awash in flames, the headless rooster, *Elvis Presley's Greatest Hits*, clothing, and photographs. Kjartan took a few steps forward, stopped, and would have given anything, the salvation of his soul, ten years of his life, to feel anger, even fury, because this was his Dodge, burning there, countless winter evenings of work had gone into it, for two years, tranquil, pleasant hours, he and Elvis Presley, sometimes Björgvin and Kolbrún, sometimes Ásdís with hot chocolate or coffee. But he didn't feel any anger, didn't feel anything, in fact, except perhaps numbness and then those two words that hung like motionless birds in his head: Of course. Then he began walking slowly, very slowly, toward the burning car and Ásdís, feeling every single kilogram in his body, no small number. Ásdís turned, maybe fifteen meters between them, turned her left side toward him, the fire seemed to enlarge her, expand her, she raised her arm, held it straight out, and then he saw the gun. And it fired.

6

A bullet travels fast, even one fired by a single-action pistol normally used on sheep. A fraction of a second from when it is fired until it hits or misses its target. A fraction of a second is just a snap of the fingers, but it can also become a very long time, it can expand to reach over all your days. And so it was for Kjartan. He saw the gun, heard the report, and then the moment expanded into eternity, in the middle of which he stood waiting for a bullet. He would come to ask himself a thousand times, day and night, in sleep and waking, happy and sad, drunk or sober: had she meant to hit him?

7

About ten minutes after the shot was fired, they were seated at the kitchen table. He wasn't allowed to confess anything, which hurt, it would have lightened his conscience, the admission of sins is cleansing, it is purifying, but Ásdís said only: I know everything and I will never forgive you for betraying me and our children and our life together. Kjartan started talking, he didn't want to explain anything, he just wanted to open up, to say that he didn't understand what had happened to him, that he had tried so many times to break it off, that he was a bastard, a damned idiot, he wanted to talk about his sleepless nights, his malaise, he wanted to say to her, Kristín is nothing compared to you, my God, nothing at all, you're so much better, what a damned idiot I've been. These are the things he wanted to say, and maybe even wanted to cry, he longed to cry, he needed it. He wanted her to scream in his face, he needed it, he wanted her to rebuke him and would accept every rebuke, he wouldn't try to defend himself, not a word about her having been so pre-occupied with her studies that she neglected all else, and that perhaps they hadn't put enough effort into their relationship, but instead had simply let time pass, love is a fire and the fire dies out if it isn't fed. But he wasn't allowed to say much; she raised her hand and he fell silent. There's a nice house for sale in the village, said Ásdís, and there's a job opening at the Depot, I've already spoken to my uncle Þorgrímur about it, the place is yours if you want it. Kjartan listened, dumbfounded, almost frightened, at first could say nothing, a big, hard lump in his throat, but finally he sighed, and in something of a soft voice, he said: Sell the farm? Yes, said Ásdís. Kjartan looked around as if in need of help, as if hoping the refrigerator would say something, the coffeepot, the radio, the walls, the house itself. But no one came to his aid, so he said the only thing that came to his mind: But we've been living here almost an entire lifetime.

We've often talked about selling, said Ásdís calmly, a little coldly, before listing all the reasons they'd come up with the past few years, that there wasn't a great future for such a modest farm, living in perpetual anxiety of failing to make ends meet, of being unable to provide their children with the best, of spending their entire lives struggling. Times are changing, in a few years, ten or twenty, only big farms will be left, at least three, four times the size of our own, those who stubbornly stick to smaller farms waste away in constant toil and disappointment. You've said this yourself, many times, and your brother has said it often, too. But Mom and Dad, said Kjartan, groping for arguments, grasping at straws, we can't do this to them! Ásdís stared at her husband across the kitchen table, things became a touch colder there in the kitchen, she said, there are many things that we can't do to others, yet do all the same. Kjartan looked down at the table, and wished that he never had to look up again.

Ásdís: But we aren't living for them. And there's no need to attribute sensitivity to people who don't have it; you can of course always hold on to a piece of land for a summer cottage for them and your brother. But it's like this: I'm moving to the village, and I'm inviting you, in spite of it all, to come with me. I'll ask you this only once. Kjartan sighed. Then he went out to extinguish the Dodge, it went slowly, the car burned, his life burned. It was only after he'd extinguished the flames and stood there staring at the blackened remains of his beloved vehicle that he noticed the silence around him, how quiet everything was, and then he remembered the puppies, their clownish joy of life, remembered the devoted bitch. They're inside, of course, he thought, and headed to the door to let them out. He was nearly there when Ásdís stepped out, looked at him from the top of the steps, where are you going? she asked slowly, just to let the dogs out, I . . . He stopped when he saw her expression. I, she then said, but said no more, didn't need to, just looked down at him and he understood—the silence, the puppies' absence, he knew what had happened. How can I explain this to the kids, he thought, as things slowly grew darker within him.

And Kjartan sold the land, every single blade of grass, every tussock and hill above the house and the hiding places of his childhood and the view over the broad fjord with all its islands, all its rocky islets, he sold the animals, the machinery, the buildings, and then they left, moved away, but how does one bid farewell to a mountain, how does one bid farewell to a tussock and blades of grass and the rocks in the farmyard?

[Why have I lived, asked our aunt on her deathbed, we opened our mouths to reply, without knowing the answer, but then she died, because death is still a good step ahead of us.

We've seen the night fall over the mountains and have stood outside as a mild tremor passed through the air, the birds looked up and then a ball of fire rose in the east. Why do we live; is it safe to answer such a question? Perhaps not, do we have any tasks besides kissing lips and so on? But sometimes, and especially right before sleep overcomes us at night and the day has passed with all its restlessness, when we're lying in bed, listening to our blood, and the darkness comes in through the windows, sometimes there awakens the deep and uncomfortable suspicion that this newly passed day was not used as it should have been, that there's something we should have done but we simply don't know what it was. Have you ever considered that, throughout our history, we have never had it so good as now, that individuals have never had more opportunities to have an impact on their environment, that it has never been as easy to participate, to change things, but rarely has there been such lack of will—how is this possible? Perhaps the answer can be found in another question: who profits most from this situation?

Why have I lived? Our aunt's name was Björg, she was married twice and had three children. Her first husband fell from a cliff while gathering seabird eggs, a thirty-meter fall, he was just over twenty years old, and six months later their son was born. Björg's second husband overturned their Russian off-road van, it rolled over four times on its way down the slope and ended up in a river, he was stuck behind the steering wheel, his head half submerged in the water, which slowly washed away his life. Björg was in the front passenger seat, her legs broken, and she could do nothing but watch and say his name so many times that her lips numbed; she was around fifty at the time. She died in her nineties, and sometimes we said that she was evergreen, because, despite the deaths of the two men she'd loved, her joy and faith in life seemed unshakable; everything was better when she was there. We were thus a bit dumbfounded by that dying question of hers, but perhaps it didn't betray any despair, perhaps Björg just sort of said it, intending to answer it herself, but then death came. Which means that we'll always live in the uncertainty that there was a shadow deep inside Björg, but when do we really know another person, we often see little more than the surface, beneath which may be worlds that we can scarcely imagine. We had no suspicion of Hannes's despair, back in his day; we could never have imagined that the director of the Knitting Company would transform into the Astronomer, nor did we know that Kjartan would have so much trouble reining in his sexual appetites, that such a tranquil person as Ásdís was capable of decapitating the rooster, shooting the puppies, we'll never forget their exuberance. Nor will we ever forget Björg's question: why did I live? Might these accounts of life and death in our village and the surrounding countryside be a sort of answer to that question, and the uncertainty that derives from it?

We speak, we write, we tell about big things and small to try to understand, try to grasp something, even the essence itself, which is, however, constantly moving away, like a rainbow. Old stories say that man cannot behold the face of God, that doing so would destroy him; and without doubt, it's the same for what we seek—the search itself is our purpose; the result will deprive us of it. And of course it's the search that teaches us the words to use to describe the splendor of the stars, the silence of the fish, a smile and sadness, the end of the world and summer's light. We do have a task, apart from kissing lips; do you know, by chance, how you say "I desire you" in Latin? And how you say it in Icelandic?]

A Man Thinks About Many Things in a Forest, Especially When a Big River Runs Through It

1

One day in February, the green bus stopped with a heavy sigh in front of the Co-op, the door opened, and out stepped a man wearing trousers so red that his legs appeared to be engulfed in flames. It had been a little more than a week since the light bulbs burned out and darkness fell over Davíð and Kjartan; since the sacks of feed enhancer nearly killed Kjartan, since they saw the ladder fall to the ground; they had difficulty finding certain merchandise in the dark and felt rather ill at ease.

Apart from Sigríður and the two sworn brothers, no one had entered the warehouse, we learned of Benedikt much later, and Sigríður said that there was nothing to worry about, even if you couldn't see your hand in front of your face, the wiring was shot but Simmi was waiting for replacement parts from down south and a new foreman was expected to show up at any moment. There's nothing unusual going on, she said, and what the hell should it be, anyway, but the two colleagues work slowly in the dark, it's nerve-racking, and it's hard to blame them for thinking constantly about the ruins under the floor, we've just got to be patient with them. Sigríður has always been very convincing; there was nothing unusual going on, except that at home Guðmundur had a sore penis, his sex life had suddenly become so unpredictable and wild that sometimes he couldn't wait for his wife to come home, but at other times he most definitely could; she was like bad weather.

Nothing unusual going on, of course she was right, rational to think in such a way, but what do we really know, when all is said and done? Sometimes our existence has so little to do with rationality—perhaps it was ghosts, pure and simple; people nearly two hundred years old, now out and about. And you know what that means: proof of life after death. It's no small thing to gain such proof; in fact, it may be the biggest thing of all. Then it wouldn't be so difficult to live, so distressing to lie down to sleep on the darkest winter nights. And Elísabet used all this to her advantage, skillfully and shamelessly, when she announced the Astronomer's February talk and hinted that he would discuss matters that touched on life and death and—take note—the gap between the two.

This talk had an extraordinarily high turnout as well. The evening arrived and there was hardly an empty seat. In fact, almost all the villagers seemed to have come, apart from those who couldn't leave the house for health reasons, or because they had young children to look after or a television program to watch; there was also a sprinkling of folks from the countryside, for example the parish administrator, who sat there in his baseball cap, legs spread wide. Elísabet served coffee, tea, crullers, and canapés, absolutely delicious, an eighteen-year-old girl from the village gave her a hand, remarkable how easily and quickly they served these refreshments to the audience, coffee never seemed to be missing in anyone's cups or a canapé on their plates. Elísabet slipped between people with the coffeepot, which never emptied, one more round in her tight-fitting shirt and we instinctively began thinking about the distance between her nipples; why does she dress like that? The Astronomer waited patiently at the podium, not a sign of nervousness, nowadays feeling as confident in his talks as he was during the heyday of the Knitting Factory. Finally, Elísabet dimmed the lights, the chatter faded, and the Astronomer said: Tonight I would like to talk about the possible confines of the universe, the possible confines of existence.

You can just imagine how our ears pricked up.

Normally, very few of us would have bothered to spend the evening on such speculations, we have plenty of other things to do with our time, and studies show that these kinds of ruminations are conducive to alcoholism and the overuse of sleeping pills and antidepressants. The Astronomer said that man would never understand life, would never comprehend its dimensions, its nature was beyond the power of our imaginations but at the same time so obvious, so simple that there was no way to grasp it. With these words, our heads began to spin. The Astronomer has a high forehead, his eyes change color according to how he feels, a whole new language came to him in a dream, how can you keep up with a man like that? In fact, we barely understood half of what he was saying, and on top of that, Elísabet let us down by not publishing an excerpt from this talk in the *Brochure*. Yet we do remember this statement of his: Some insist that death is the direct continuation of life and that therefore it is wrong to say that people die, they simply pass from one dimension to another. Accordingly, the dead are not dead in the meaning of gone, they're all around us, surrounding what we call life as the sky surrounds the earth. Or, in other words, those who die move beyond the confines of the universe, where the ultimate life, eternal life, at the margin of the cosmos, is beyond our sight. These are of course ancient theories, he added, waving his hand, before going on to talk about the murmur of the cosmic microwaves, a steady signal that radiates in all directions from the margins of the universe. Probably a reverberation of the Big Bang, but perhaps the echo of conversations in other worlds, the murmuring of the dead.

Thus did the Astronomer conclude his speech: the murmuring of the dead! Fortunately, Elísabet switched on the light. We sat there silently, various thoughts flying through our heads, as he gathered up his notes, drank a glass of water, looked around the room, and asked, any questions, but with a smile so mischievous that it baffled most of us, though not all, there are always some who lead us through the darkness. The parish administrator ran his hand over his face and cleared his throat, and Helga, you remember, the woman who answers the telephone and reads psychology texts in English, took a deep breath and started to get to her feet, but Björgvin was quicker than both of them, he stood up, the self-same director of the Agricultural Bank, called Björgvin Jr. while the old Co-op director was still among us, he's also on the board of the Dairy Association, of the Community Center, and the Co-op; we're so few in number.

At one time, Björgvin dreamed of a life with Ágústa, of the post office, though it remained but a dream, as things often do, the world is full of dreams that never come true, they evaporate and settle like dew in the sky, where they transform into the stars in the night. Björgvin never dared to take the first step, Ágústa waited for him to do so, they danced together at the village dances, their hands touched once, twice, three times, but then Björgvin married Sibba Jónsdóttir, who, at the time, was as slender and short as a piece of string, but so sprightly and quick in everything that we were sometimes dumbfounded in her presence. One evening she pulled Björgvin onto the dance floor, it was at a village dance, bloody good fun, with loads of drinking, and they danced, Ágústa was wandering around the dance floor with that red lipstick of hers, bright as a stop sign, she saw Sibba stand on tiptoe, lay her right palm on the back of Björgvin's neck, pull his face down to hers, their lips opened, their tongues met, it was a long and passionate kiss and Ágústa went home with a broken heart. Björgvin and Sibba got married, had four children, Sibba is no longer as slender as a piece of string, she's so wide that Björgvin can barely reach his arms around her, which he has perhaps in a certain sense never done. And now he stood up, as impeccable as ever, in his blue pinstripe suit and red tie, the years have given him respectability. He has also gained a lot of weight, looks as if he's carrying a sack of cement on his stomach, his hair turned gray early on, those who have gray hair think a great deal, and in a responsible manner, but now he was on his feet, glanced around, greeted a few faces, and those who received a nod from his head felt chuffed indeed. Björgvin stuck his thumbs under his wide, green suspenders, gave them a little tug, slid his thumbs up and down but didn't clear his throat, because a man like Björgvin never needs to clear his throat, he just speaks, the murmur of the cosmic microwaves, indeed, he said, does the murmur by chance resemble the jingling of coins when our machines at the bank count them? We smiled, laughed softly, Björgvin certainly had a knack, and in a flash we envisioned the enormous coin-counting machine of the heavens, counting for the dead when they make deposits to the bank of eternity. The Astronomer kept smiling, he and Björgvin know each other well, an acquaintance that goes way back, and they were on excellent terms when the Knitting Company was running, no shortage of important meetings then, evenings during which cigars were lit and cognac poured into widemouthed glasses. It's nice to drink cognac while the evening leans against the windows, you toast the darkness, the only problem being, though, that Björgvin had the tendency to get a little too drunk, he lost his grip on his tongue and ended up talking too much about his friend's wife, especially about her eyes, which, however, it was possible to forgive; after all, a famous novel states: "The light of the world is in your eyes, and the darkness as well." Still, it had been quite a few years now since they sat together in the thick fog of cigar smoke, and now Björgvin said, smiling and looking alternately around him and up at the stage: No, there's probably another explanation for this murmur of the cosmic microwaves of yours, though I strongly suspect that what your scientists detected was the echo of the Sewing Circle of Eternity, but all joking aside, I wanted to thank you for your informative lecture, I should of course come more often to listen to you, to air my dusty brain cells a bit. That said, I would like to hear, for my personal curiosity, your opinion on certain, what should I call them, incidents here in the village, though incidents is perhaps not the right word, but rather rumors. These, of course, being a kind of foolishness in which we let ourselves become tangled, but still, I would be curious to have a scientific assessment of them, I refer, naturally, to the stories about the Depot, Lúlla's dream, and the case of Björgvin and Finnur, yes, it would be interesting to hear your opinion on these—your scientific opinion.

Björgvin fell silent, stuck his thumbs back under his suspenders, looked at the stage. They faced each other, these former colleagues, for perhaps the first time in many years, or ever since Björgvin had tried to get him to give up "that bullshit," meaning: Latin, costly ancient books, sacrificing his family. Björgvin had probably never forgiven his old friend for turning his back on prosperity, because that decision, that act, or whatever one can call such madness, was directly antisocial, subversive to the community, completely ignored our *values*. Ever since then, their relationship had been arid, the minimum possible in a village of four hundred souls. Perhaps what Björgvin considered the worst crime, though, was his former colleague's treatment of his wife; how the hell was it possible to sacrifice your future with a woman like that for the sky, a dead language, old books? You should think about getting help, Björgvin had even told him, talk to a psychologist, a psychiatrist, there are drugs for such aberrations, to which his old colleague had asked in return, do you mean that there are drugs for life? Since then the years had passed, and now they stood there looking at each other in the Community Center, with the silence buzzing around us, and finally the Astronomer opened his mouth, he said, you're ageing gracefully, Björgvin.

Björgvin was so surprised that he sat down, glanced at Sibba, who nodded, and then Björgvin sighed quietly, looked at the stage, the Astronomer placed his hands on the podium, his full gray hair combed back, his thick black sweater making his face look even paler. No matter how rapidly the sciences advance, he said, we'll never free ourselves from fear of the dark, and that fear may grow even deeper, because contemporary man—by which I mean city dwellers, we here can hardly be classified as contemporary men—no longer knows darkness, it's been wiped out by excessive lighting, over-plentiful electricity. People no longer know how to deal with the darkness of nature, no longer know how to find their way in the dark. My foreign friends have told me many stories about this, how children even start crying when they suddenly find themselves confronted by the darkness of nature. I expect that some would call this degeneration. And perhaps this applies to us, too, almost no one here is out and about after darkness falls, as I well know, most are chained to their televisions, computers, sex lives, or sit there half submerged in their hot tubs. Be that as it may, I can say very little about these things, the Depot, and those two, Finnur and Björgvin, but I remind you that Finnur used to be a politician and it's in their nature to disappear—evaporate—as soon as they step aside and lose their power and influence. Man is what he does, and politics comprises power and authority; take these two away from a politician and you've got nothing left, why be surprised when they evaporate and vanish, as Finnur did? As far as the Depot goes, I have hardly anything to say, I haven't discussed it with my son and therefore know very little about it, but some say that all existence is subjective, that is, that everything in your mind automatically exists. If we take one step forward from this idea, things become real as soon as we come up with them here, he said, tapping his finger on his head, gray with wisdom. Ghosts are perhaps little other than a state of mind, but every state of mind is in a sense reality itself, and vice versa, of course. Otherwise, there are theories that not only posit life after this one, but also suggest that there is such a small gap between the world of the dead and the living that it can take very little, an unexpected change in the weather in someone's psyche, perhaps, for the curtain that separates the two worlds to be torn apart. Such things have already happened, sometimes without consequences, sometimes with terrible ones. There are recent stories of entire mountain villages in Nepal and Peru being mysteriously deserted, in big cities people disappear as if the earth has swallowed them or the sky has sucked them up, in a village in Wales sixteen perfectly healthy men and one dog lost their minds in one afternoon, all they were doing was watching a football match at the village pub. And why shouldn't something like that happen here; but I see that Elísabet would like to say something, so I wish you good night, he said, completely unexpectedly, came down off the stage, and walked out, we heard the door close.

Which really rubbed a few people up the wrong way.

The nerve of that snob, behaving like that; we come here, sit here listening to his grandiose philosophical and scientific bosh, but when we feel like asking a question, he just walks out. Those remaining stood up to leave, chairs scraped the floor, there were sighs, well then, said someone, and someone else said, bloody hell, but wasn't referring to the Astronomer's abrupt exit or his disquieting description of the torn curtain, the murmuring of the dead, the end of the world, because now Elísabet had stepped onto the stage, she went and stood next to the podium, didn't want to stand behind it, nothing was allowed to cast a shadow on her, she always had to reveal all, seduce the world and even the sky as well, no wonder that it hid behind the clouds sometimes. But bloody hell, the way she's dressed all the time, the way she carries herself, bloody hell, the way that she is. In tight-fitting T-shirts, in denim skirts, black fishnet stockings, and, for the umpteenth time, clearly wearing no bra. She moves, and some swallow. She's wearing light-colored lipstick, light eyeliner, which may be why we thought of a lioness or a tiger, no, a panther, and there she stood, in red Adidas shoes, which completely clashed with the rest, her face not exactly shapely, her dark eyes a bit too far apart, even as if space had been left for a third, her nose a little wide and upturned, her nostrils big, her hair long and dark. We say dark, but to tell the truth, it seemed to darken as the day passed, and even turned pitch-black at night, though we didn't really know that for sure, Elísabet always sleeps alone, goes home from dances early, she who baffles men or drives them mad with her breasts, I would give my right hand to see them, my left to touch them, but how then would I embrace her? She stands there on the stage, so damned striking, despite those worn red Adidas, and says: Someone is on the way.

Someone is on his way here. Sigríður contacted him after Þorgrímur quit, and he was going to take over the Depot. You all know him, he left here six years ago to venture into the world, as he worded it. He's coming tomorrow, I'll welcome him, no one else will do.

2

The day after Elísabet's announcement from the stage, the green bus stopped with a heavy sigh in front of the Co-op, the door opened, and out stepped a man wearing trousers so red that his legs seemed awash in bright flames. Elísabet had awaited the bus in the cold January wind, bundled up in a green coverall, orange woolen gloves, black hiking boots, and a fur hat that resembled the head of a teddy bear—and then the bus arrives, he steps out, legs ablaze, and she says: You've arrived. The man smiles, smooths his dapper mustache with his thumb and forefinger, doesn't take his eyes off Elísabet's face, the driver, wearing a sweater, steps out, opens one of the luggage bays, grabs a suitcase, sets it on the ground next to the man, bids him farewell by tipping his finger to his forehead, and then the bus crawls away with gasps and coughs, no reason to linger in the village, very few passengers and all of them sleeping. The man who the bus leaves behind is thin, of medium height, about ten centimeters taller than Elísabet, with black hair, Slavic features, a thin nose, high cheekbones, dark eyes, there's something nonchalant about him, how he stands, he's wearing a heavy brown coat that's halfway between an overcoat and a jacket. Yes, we know him, but haven't seen him these six years since he left to venture into the world, after stating that he was leaving forever, leaving this bloody backwoods behind, took a job on an ocean liner, sailed to Europe, left the ship, roamed from one town to another and took various jobs to support himself, then sailed to South America, where he stayed for a little over three years, sailed down the Amazon, wound up in adventures, spent time with an anthropologist studying natives deep within the rain forest. Six years, during which he'd sent three lousy postcards, all from South America, addressed to no one in particular, just the name of the village, to everyone from him. Hard to say what news they carried of his life, the handwriting looked most like squashed ants. Even Ágústa, despite her being accustomed to various things, was at a loss, but as the postcards were for everyone, she taped them up on a window of the Co-op, and there they still hung when he got off the bus, three postcards side by side, the pictures facing outward, looking over the village and the mountains on the other side of the fjord, the text facing into the store. We'd often lingered there inside the Co-op, trying to pick out a meaning from the squashed ants, we even made special trips to the Co-op when boredom besieged us with its weapons, the village's dreamers preferred to stand outside and stare at the pictures, lose themselves in an exotic city, a mountainside covered in forest, in the uncanny light of the Amazon, it's fun and a bit dreamlike to stand there with both feet firmly planted in an uneventful existence, often in more or less crappy weather, and stare at photographs of exotic places, bright colors that had by then begun to fade, of course, warm light and the postcards like an advertisement from heaven. The rest of us, who aren't quite so inclined toward dreams, tried with little success to decipher that handwriting, just as we try to do all our lives, and with little success, to decipher the complex signs of heaven and earth. But forgive us this digression; he has arrived, his name is Matthías and he stands there in his red trousers, the panting bus drives away and he hugs Elísabet, no one has got to do that in six years, and he was also the only one here who got to hug her before, but then he left and we never knew what happened between them. They're still hugging when Sigríður comes out of the Co-op, where she's been sitting in her office, immersed in accounting or who knows what else, her computer buzzing, she greets Matthías with a handshake, nods at Elísabet, it's no small thing to see them standing so close to each other, it's actually more than we can bear. Sigríður speaks, Matthías listens, looks at her, appears to agree, he says something and Sigríður laughs, Elísabet seems to smile, she looks down, and then Sigríður shakes Matthías's hand again, throws a fleeting glance at Elísabet, goes back into the Co-op, into her office, closes the door. Matthías picks up his tired old suitcase, he and Elísabet go into the shop, sit down, have coffee and flatcakes with smoked lamb. You're looking exceptionally well, says Matthías.

Elísabet swallowed the morsel in her mouth, smiled—or grinned—and said, lovely of you to say, and I'm very glad that you're back, I'm in desperate need of a lover, and if you're the same person I knew, I have something to look forward to. Matthías leaned back, rested his hands on the nape of his neck, his dark, almond-shaped eyes glinted, his Slavic features gave his face an air of mystery. Elísabet spoke calmly, as if commenting on the weather, asking for another cup of coffee, Fjóla, the cashier, and Brandur, the gas pump attendant, heard this clearly, heard every word, they stood behind the counter, I'm in desperate need of a lover, Elísabet had said, Fjóla and Brandur looked at each other, he licked his lips.

Elísabet did not take her dark eyes off Matthías, who had started to laugh, but then stopped suddenly, gave her a peculiar look, perhaps happy and sad at once, then shook his head and said, you never change. Yes, every day, I just don't show it. Why have you never left, like me? She shrugged; my destiny is here.

Matthías: We know nothing about destiny.

Elísabet: I was waiting, then.

Matthías: For what?

Elísabet: I don't know, but if I find out, I'll let you know. But sometimes I like living here, it's beautiful, quiet, I can get in touch with myself.

Matthías: But it's a bloody backwoods.

Elísabet: That just depends on you, on what you want, how you are.

Matthías: A backwoods is a backwoods; no attitude can change that. Hardly anything happens here, an entire winter can fit on a single postcard, people are always lethargic, those looking for a bit of movement go away, kaput!

Elísabet: Not if you're self-sufficient. And of course things happen here, the weather is always changing, the sky appears to move, sometimes it even seems to lean a little, in which case nothing in life is safe, the light is never precisely the same here, but sometime I need to tell you about the last days of Björgvin, the old Co-op director, it was none other than Finnur Ásgrímsson who replaced him.

Matthías: The minister?

Elísabet: Yes.

Matthías: He came here?

Elísabet: Yes, and started writing his memoirs here but didn't manage to finish them, he just disappeared, or, to be exact, he merged into the late afternoon.

Matthías: People don't disappear, they leave. I suspect that that can apply particularly to a former minister.

Elísabet: You're entitled to your opinions, but what happens pays little consideration to our opinions.

Matthías sighs: I never had any chance of beating you in an argument—and clearly, that hasn't changed! But last I knew, the Knitting Factory had been closed, there were dreams full of Latin, and . . .

Elísabet: Yes, I was coming to that, you should see him now!

Matthías: I saw his house from the bus.

Elísabet: The night sky.

Matthías: What?

Elísabet: We call his house "the night sky."

Matthías: Oh, of course. And he gave away all that he had for books.

Elísabet: Well, you might say, rather, that he gained a new life. Woke up one morning with such a different view of life that he'd actually become a different person. He looked around and couldn't relate to anything, it was all foreign to him. That house wasn't his, nor the furniture, not even his wife, and why hang on to something that has never belonged to you?

Matthías: A bit drastic, wouldn't you say? Do you mean he experienced a kind of revelation?

Elísabet runs her index finger slowly along the brim of her coffee cup, she has small hands, Matthías, captivated, watches the finger move: When Tolstoy, the Russian writer, turned fifty, his life changed completely; we can call it a revolution, without any fear of exaggeration. He was one of the greatest writers in the world, had written *War and Peace* and *Anna Karenina*, an energetic man, even impetuous, enjoyed drinking, gambling, was a passionate hunter with a huge sex drive, too huge, felt his wife, but one day everything changed. All his accomplishments, the work of a lifetime, suddenly seemed ephemera, even his family seemed alien to him, his body brutish, sex crude—he had to start all over again, his life, his writing, and nothing was as it had been.

Matthías tears his eyes from her index finger, looks aside and says: I read *War and Peace* once.

Elísabet: But maybe we shouldn't be so surprised by such radical change, because if you think about all the contradictions in the world, it's almost unbelievable that it doesn't happen more often. For example, most of us believe in God and Jesus, and attach a great deal of importance to their words, we memorize the Commandments and know certain sayings of Jesus—if we can speak of a core common to all Western cultures, it's surely the teachings of Jesus, yet we live from day to day as if we've never heard of Him. With guns in their hands, people declare life to be sacred. If there was a grain of intelligence in the world, we would all have left for Reykjavík, to study Latin and start new lives—maybe making life around us more beautiful.

Matthías: I could tell you so many stories about stupidity in the world, and will hopefully get a chance to do so, but what does he do, or, should I say, how is he supporting himself?

Elísabet: Well, he holds a monthly talk here at the Community Center, for which he's paid a stipend out of Nordic funds, you wouldn't believe how many funds and grants exist to support small, isolated communities.

Matthías: Once a month; he can hardly be living on that.

Elísabet: No, there's also another thing that occupies most of his time and around which his life revolves, even if he never mentions it; I believe that people here know little or nothing of it. He belongs to some sort of international association, the name of which I can never remember, he became acquainted with it soon after he started studying Latin—its simple aim is to save the most important aspects of our culture from extinction. It's a hugely wealthy, secret association that supports people like him; he corresponds with many others like him, and last year two of them came here to the village, extremely secretively, I must say; only Davíð and I saw them. Interesting people, a woman of forty from Hungary, I think she had a doctorate in philosophy and a good position at the university in Budapest, married and with one child, but she turned her back on everything just like our Astronomer, extremely intelligent, as dark skinned as a Gypsy, very beautiful, I suspect that there was something between them, at least I hope there was.

Matthías: And who was the other one?

Elísabet: A German, a former football star, lean and agile in his day, of course, but now so fat that he struggles to move—apart from his tongue, which he loves to wag, it hardly ever stopped, but unfortunately, he had such bad breath it made me want to kill myself, incredible that the Hungarian survived such a long car trip with him.

Matthías: And what did he talk about, this German footballer, did you speak to him in German?

Elísabet: Well, a little, and then in English when my German failed me . . . He went on about anything and everything, as is common with talkative people, they dash from one topic to the next, east and west in the same sentence, but he always came back to that activity or task of theirs, which revolved around saving what was salvageable from dying cultures. In short, they claim that our culture, the Western one, is on its last legs, and—

Matthías raised his left hand: Those who have traveled through Europe would have difficulty contradicting them, and anyone who has watched at least a little American television would surely agree wholeheartedly—and celebrate the fact as well! But I don't really understand what exactly this salvage work comprises . . .

Elísabet looked at him intently, as if wanting to touch the lines in his face with her eyes: They see Latin as a kind of hard disk, storing everything that matters, I'll explain it better later, but I liked that Hungarian woman, she was so full of life that it was impossible not to find her captivating. She didn't give much weight to clothing, went around half naked, the German didn't seem to care, seemed insensitive to it, which we can't say of our Astronomer, fortunately. She was so beautiful.

Matthías leaned forward a little: But tell me something, was this Hungarian woman more beautiful than Davíð's mother?

Elísabet gave Matthías an inquisitive look. I don't know, no, probably not, but she had that Slavic look, for which we Icelanders seem to have a weakness.

Matthías grinned, and then said: I thought of her sometimes, when I was in the forest.

Elísabet: *You* thought about her?

Matthías: A man thinks about many things in a forest, especially if a big river runs through it.

Elísabet: Did you think about me?

Matthías: Yes. But listen, you shouldn't stare so intently at people when you talk to them. Most people move their eyes, look aside, down, and so forth.

Elísabet, with her arms crossed, and without taking her eyes off his face: Often? And how, then?

Matthías: I'll answer you if you move your eyes a little, look out the window, for example, look, there you can see the night sky. That's better, you were suffocating me with those eyes!

Elísabet: Can I look at you now?

Matthías: Just remember to look elsewhere once in a while; Jesus, you haven't changed!

Elísabet: Often? And how, then?

Matthías: Often and how, what?

Elísabet: Whether you . . .

Matthías: Yes, whether I thought about you, quite certain, the whole package, flesh and spirit, though it varied from day to day. There were days, sometimes many, when I barely remembered that Iceland existed, which is a damned good feeling, but then there were other days, maybe the most difficult ones, when what I thought about, when I was thinking, was you—meaning I could never get away from you. Maybe that's my destiny. But I'm sure you prefer me not to go into detail, not now, because they weren't all beautiful and noble thoughts; some were pretty damned lewd!

Elísabet: Have you been with many other women?

Brandur and Fjóla exchanged glances.

Matthías: Six years is a long time. I'm not asexual.

Elísabet: Did you keep track of the numbers?

Brandur holds his breath, Fjóla raises her arm, but then seems not to know what to do with it, there is no new customer. Elísabet does not take her eyes off Matthías's face, it's difficult to read her face, she's good at hiding everything behind an impassive expression, her eyes are dark and unfathomable. She stares him straight in the face, looks aside once or twice so as not to overdo it. Matthías looks up at the sky. Are you counting? she asks. He shakes his head, looks at her, grins, and says, I can count them all up if you want. Instinctively, Fjóla leans forward to hear better, pushing her hips and bottom back a bit, Brandur sits down, he listens and stares at Fjóla's bottom. Nine, says Matthías finally, causing Brandur to blink. Were you with them often? Sometimes yes, sometimes no. Did you love any of them? No, unfortunately not. What women were they? What were they like? Matthías smiles, seems embarrassed, well, some were just faces, you know, you meet a person and then it's done. Suddenly he grins, glances at Fjóla and Brandur, and says: Once I was with an Indian woman, she belonged to a tribe that lives in the rain forest and has little interaction with so-called civilization. Louis, a friend of mine, is studying the ways of life of the Amazon Indians and took me with him to one of the villages. We stayed there for two nights, and the first night I woke with a woman on top of me, sometimes I think that I actually dreamed it, but she was everywhere with her tongue and fingers, I couldn't resist. Did your friend know? I think so; of course he never said a word about it, but we slept in the same hut, barely two meters between us. Didn't you find it awkward, doing that in front of him, or was it just better that way? You don't think like that in the rain forest, it's so replete with life and death that it changes you, changes the rules, yes, maybe at first I was a little uncomfortable, but then I simply didn't care anymore. Was she beautiful? I don't know, it was so damned dark! But she was eager, she was like a wild beast, she called the shots, she came and then she was gone. I didn't sleep anymore that night, and the next day the village women started giggling every time they saw me, it was a bit uncomfortable . . . She wanted to be on top, Matthías says suddenly, looking Elísabet straight in those Gypsy eyes of hers, Louis said that it was customary among the indigenous women of the Amazon—because that way, they're in control. Brandur had stood up, maybe wanting to see Matthías as he spoke, but stooped in order to hide his persistent erection, Fjóla had sweated a little under her arms.

Elísabet: Of course they want to be on top, it's much better. These were interesting years for you.

Matthías: I don't know, I've certainly experienced a lot, changed my ways of seeing and thinking, which is important, perhaps the most important thing. But now I'm back, I'm taking over the Depot, I'll have a good salary, plenty of free time for my own interests, enough summer holiday time to go abroad—plus I get my princess. I'm not a princess. I know that, I didn't really mean it, are you a queen, maybe? Stop being stupid, I'm a witch, and it's I who get you, not vice versa. But in any case, while you were off on your travels, a few things happened here, I mentioned a few of them already, apart from the extramarital affairs, suicides, record sales of sleeping pills and antidepressants, yes, and my sister goes swimming in the sea three times a week, in any weather, and the men watch her through binoculars, and Kiddi the Movie Star married a teacher, and our Brandur is coming ever closer to winning the title of Icelandic Champion of Correspondence Chess; am I exaggerating at all, Brandur? But Brandur didn't answer, he just took two steps backward, which put him behind the candy counter, while Fjóla grabbed a box of Malta chocolate bars and began counting them. Brandur, Elísabet explained to Matthías, is participating along with about sixty other people in the Icelandic Correspondence Chess Championship; there was an article about it in *Morgunblaðið* last year. Applicants are sifted through before being invited to participate; it's no competition for beginners. Brandur is assigned eight opponents in the first round, and if he draws white, he sends out eight postcards showing his first move, and then waits for replies. This reminds me of the trolls, said Matthías. What trolls? Hello! shouted a troll, and a hundred years later, another troll's reply came: yes, hello! Don't listen to him, Brandur, Elísabet said, it's actually really exciting, the Agricultural Bank reproduces the games on eight chessboards, and Brandur comes to move the pieces every time he sends or receives a postcard, while the rest of us ponder the moves. People come from the countryside expressly to write down the new moves, but no one is allowed to make suggestions to Brandur, under penalty of him being disqualified—and anyway, he needs no advice.

Matthías sniffs a cigarette, you can't smoke in the shop? That's new, he says, lays the cigarette on the table and it rolls over twice, and then he takes a deep breath: I thought about it often, how it would be to see you again, if and how you'd be different, whether you'd be happy to see me, whether you'd given it any thought, in general, and, no less, how I would feel about it. Brandur's round face, slightly flushed, appears beside the licorice wheels, and the redness spreads to his forehead and up to the crown of his half-bald head. Elísabet runs her hand slowly up her cheek, it too disappears in her black hair. I've also thought, continued Matthías, after enduring Elísabet's gaze and silence for a few moments, about how it would be to return here, to my home village, which is such a tiny and ridiculously insignificant place when you're out traveling the world, well, it may be enough to go to Reykjavík to realize that, and Reykjavík isn't that remarkable, either. And now you're here, says Elísabet. Yes, it seems so. Matthías looks over at the counter, looks at Brandur but without seeing him, Brandur sits down next to Fjóla, and then Matthías turns his eyes back to Elísabet and says: It's difficult to control your feelings, sometimes just impossible; I came back because nothing else was possible. He says this softly, looking down, as if speaking to the floor, how are things at the Depot, otherwise, he asks, in a slightly louder voice, yesterday on the phone you mentioned inexplicable incidents, ghosts, even—which is no trivial thing . . . There were two fellows working there, Davíð and, what was the other one's name . . .

Elísabet: Kjartan.

Matthías: That's right. Kjartan and Davíð. I remember Davíð quite well, a damn smart boy, like everyone in his family, in fact, what's he doing here, why didn't he go to university? He did go, but came back after two years. And hasn't returned? Not yet; he said he missed the bus. There are other buses. Not always. And what then? You'll have to ask him yourself, but you remember how Davíð was as a child. He's pretty much the same, his head always a bit in the clouds, and sometimes people like him get lost between what we call reality and imagination. But this Kjartan, what about him, what's his story, wasn't he a farmer out in the sticks somewhere? Yes, in the valleys to the north. And why didn't he stay with his sheep, why should they have had to pay? There's a whole story behind that, says Elísabet, and her eyes appear to expand. With a grin, Fjóla turns to look at Brandur, who tries to smile back, suddenly seized with irrepressible desire for her, despite never having thought about her when he's at home, alone with his hand, pornographic magazines, his imagination, Brandur is unmarried, no one knows if he's ever been with a woman, and Fjóla's hips are too wide for his taste, her bosom too big, yes, it's just too imposing, too firm, too authoritarian, too self-assertive, and now everything has suddenly changed; he stares at her. A long story? asks Matthías, Elísabet shrugs, maybe fifteen minutes, well, I'll eat while you tell it, he says, Fjóla Fair-eyes, he suddenly says, in a slightly louder voice, without taking his eyes off Elísabet, fry two eggs for me, beat the yolks together with a generous helping of skyr, put the whites on a slice of rye bread and pepper them well. Just like in the old days, says Fjóla cheerfully, straightening her back. Hopefully they're not too old, replies Matthías, looking down at his hands as if they could reveal to him how much time has passed.

Fjóla goes to work, Brandur watches her fry the eggs, beat the yolks together with the white skyr, cut a slice of bread, her arms stout and strong, her big breasts that sway as she stands there beating the eggs, legs spread wide, is love like this, thinks Brandur, laying his hand on his chest as if to trap the buzz in his heart. Fjóla steps out from behind the counter, taking the coffeepot with her, smiles at both of them, yet slightly more widely at Matthías, then goes back to her place, Brandur wants nothing more than to look at her, not just now, but always, because she is more beautiful than the summer.

Matthías looks down at his plate, lifts his spoon, and mutters something about the weather.

Elísabet: Yes, you think for a moment and ten years pass.

3

Both Fjóla and Brandur sat behind the counter as Elísabet told Matthías the story of Ásdís and Kjartan, and then she was finished, although stories never end, continuing, as they do, long after we add the final period, and besides, we never fully grasp whole stories, only ever really take in fragments and must resign ourselves to that fact. Elísabet wet her lips with the tip of her tongue, which glistened slightly, the tongue is a muscular organ in the mouth of most vertebrates, it plays an important part in the digestive process and is, in addition, one of man's main vocal organs. Matthías stroked his delicate mustache with his thumb and forefinger without taking his dark eyes off Elísabet's face, his eyes small but brimming with life, his hair thick, disheveled, probably never combed. And how are they now, he asked, has she forgiven him, do they sleep in separate beds, and what about the children, you haven't completely finished your story. Yes, it's finished, said Elísabet, but some things cannot be forgiven, may not be forgiven, you make a mistake and your days are never the same again. You're cruel. No, realistic. So do they sleep separately? I gather from Ásdís that she has to settle for the sofa every now and then, not often, maybe; she earned her diploma via distance learning, has taken courses offered by the university at Bifröst, started working for my brother-in-law, the commissioner, and is his right hand. And the children? They've settled into village life, wouldn't want to live anywhere but here, everything's close, their playmates are right around the corner, for children, that's important, but they'll never forget the puppies, nor will I, said Matthías, and he stood up, put on his coat, brown and heavy, of coarse wool. If you put up your hood, you'll look like a monk, she said. Nothing is further from me right now than the idea of chastity, he said, half smiling, half apologetic. Just as well for you, she said, getting to her feet, and Fjóla and Brandur exchanged a glance. But what about Kristín, said Matthías, as if suddenly remembering her, yes, and that poor husband of hers? Elísabet shrugged, I expect everything has changed for them, Pétur felt guilty for neglecting her, Kristín blamed his indolence, she told him, you start snoring as soon as your head hits your pillow, while I lie beside you and have nothing but my hands; but are you afraid of ghosts?

Matthías: Of course I am. I mean, I'm afraid of them if they exist. I mean, they bring death with them, and I'm afraid of death. Why do you ask?

Elísabet: Well, you'll have to lug this fear of yours out to the Depot and deal with the ghosts there.

Matthías: Ghosts! Yesterday you said this was about getting Simmi to come and repair the wiring.

Elísabet: Don't pay attention to what I say.

Matthías: What do you mean?

Elísabet smiled, which she doesn't do often, we realized, she smiled, her red, rather fleshy lips parted to reveal to Matthías a row of white teeth, a tiny gap between her incisors, two in her lower gum are crooked, leaning toward each other, as if seeking support. Sometimes I say things just to make the days pass, or to change them, to shake things up, shock people with scandalous statements, give a jolt to the tranquility hanging over us and surrounding us, but now I'm going home, go talk to the lads, they'll be happy to see you, relieved to be rid of the burden of responsibility, and let me know if you encounter a ghost, that would be a great relief, then we would finally know that there's life after this life and would have nothing left but to find out how it is, though it's perhaps better to know as little as possible about that. Matthías, appearing puzzled, looked at Elísabet, glanced at the counter where two heads were visible, on them a total of four ears, he ran his hand over his mustache, swallowed, even as if gasping for breath, and then said quickly and softly: You know of course that I left mainly because of you? Elísabet didn't answer, just looked at him with those eyes of hers. He glanced again at the counter, maybe I wanted to find something greater than you, I imagined that it would then be easier to return, to you, I mean. And? And what? Did you find it? No. Yet you're back. Matthías held up his hands, as if in complete surrender. She looked at him for several long moments, and then said, raising her voice a little: I have a long dressing gown of red silk, thin and nicely transparent, quite revealing, yet leaving something to the imagination, I'll be wearing that, and nothing else. Elísabet went to the door, opened it, went out into the cool February day, the light had begun to change, as if the air were growing denser, he followed her, she crossed the parking lot and headed home, he stood there watching her. Brandur and Fjóla had stood up, did you hear that, she asked, did I ever, Brandur had difficulty standing still, she's going to strip for him! And she can't be bothered to hide it, Fjóla muttered, looking away when she felt Brandur's eyes on her. Then she shook her head, those sisters have always been a little strange, she said, and it's not surprising, you can hardly say they were taught their manners. Brandur swallowed, his face was slightly flushed, he rubbed the nape of his neck, he scratched his throat and said pensively, hesitantly: It's nice when women undress. Fjóla looked at him in surprise and Brandur added, in a panic: Maybe nothing more beautiful in the whole world! Fjóla said nothing, she went to Elísabet and Matthías's table and began clearing it, a car drove up to the gas pump, Brandur walked quickly to the door, grabbed the handle, eager to get outside to cool off, his ears were uncomfortably warm, but just as he opened the door, Fjóla said: For today, you'll have to settle for sticking your nozzle into gas tanks, Brandur.

4

On the way to the Depot, Matthías stopped for a moment at the Co-op window to take a look at the three postcards, smiled to himself, perhaps recalling where he'd bought them, where he'd written them, and then he went on, looked to the left, Elísabet had reached the Agricultural Bank, would soon slip behind the post office for a shortcut home, and some men would have given their right arm, three months of health, their car, and even the dog to be the one she was waiting for.

Matthías walked past the Co-op. Nonchalantly, a bit of a swinging gait, in monkish outerwear, he stopped at the corner, looked at the alley that separates the Co-op from the Depot, sometimes called Berlingssund. He stuck his hands in his pockets, stood there, and thought. It's good to think with your hands in your pockets, a kind of serenity, softness, comes over you, sometimes melancholy or wistfulness, and he who stands like that with his hands in his pockets, leans his shoulder against the wall of a house and thinks, is dependent on no one, for a few moments he is free. Then Matthías took his hands out of his pockets and continued on his way, and at the same time a woman stepped out of the Co-op with a man at her heels, they saw Matthías bend down, pick up a pebble, and put it in his pocket, then stand there motionless, he seemed lost in thought, the man and the woman looked at him, the woman's name is Rósa, a farmwife from the valleys to the south, she's on the parish council, knows how to organize things and get them going, few things happen in her parish without her finger being on them, Rósa often sits on a chair against the wall and plays wistful tunes on her violin for the hens in the farmyard, for the dog and the children, and sometimes a curious calf comes to listen. The man lives in the village and is none other than Daníel, the vet who treated Simmi's broken leg after he fell from his horse. Sometimes Daníel smells of whiskey, he dreams about Rósa, he writes her love letters that he reads to the night and his twelve-year-old cat, then punches holes in them and puts them in a folder, the back of his hand brushed her coat as they came out of the store, a current passed through him and life was beautiful. He stands next to Rósa, relishes the happiness of the moment, and watches Matthías open the door to the Depot and disappear into it. Inside the Depot, Kjartan was on the telephone, trying to contact Simmi yet again, the replacement parts had arrived and he could start his repairs, now the darkness would be defeated, Davíð was sitting in his place, his chair tilted, the nape of his neck against the wall, his eyes half closed, his breathing as if he was sleeping. It's risky to get too close to your dreams, they can weaken you in the face of life, replace your will, and what is a man without his will?

5

It was toward evening when Matthías knocked on Elísabet's door, but no one came to answer and he looked around unsuccessfully for a doorbell. Doorbells can be blaringly loud, and if you don't have one you can pretend not to have heard it when someone knocks at your door, continue to enjoy your peace and quiet if you're not in the mood for conversation. Matthías hesitated, then grabbed the handle and opened the door; it was dim inside. He said nothing, didn't call out, hello, it's me, he just went in, took off his shoes, the monk's cowl, walked down the hall, and then saw her, he saw Elísabet.

Three days passed, with not a sign or peep of them.

Kjartan lay in bed at home and slept for sixteen hours straight, a deep, dreamless sleep, his big body lay there motionless, his rib cage rose and fell like a calm sea, Ásdís and the children went about their business silently. Davíð slept for a long time as well, but just because he was addicted to dreams, sleep is a cavern into which he crawls, where he feels safe. Shortly after he woke, he went to visit his father, didn't follow the road but waded through the drifts covering the moors, they sat and talked for a long time, first about the Depot, you sensed something unusual, the Astronomer asked his son, with a gleam in his eyes. Yes, Davíð replied without hesitation, or at least I think so . . . I wanted to think so, but don't know how to describe it, maybe like my nerves being constantly piqued, whenever I went into the warehouse I always expected . . . well, something . . . but then, as soon as I was back among others, I felt like an idiot. Maybe I was just so eager to believe that something inexplicable could happen that I imagined it, you know; things become real the moment we come up with them in our minds. So real that Kjartan sensed them as well, and . . . no, dammit, Dad, read me something, I don't want to mull this over anymore now. Then the Astronomer rose heavily from his chair, went to the shelf, and got a book, bound in brown leather, slowly began reading the half-dead language that once ruled the world, filled the room in this nook of the world, Davíð sat there, shoulders hunched, listening, he understood little but envisioned a crenelated defensive wall, an abandoned city over which black birds hovered. From time to time, the Astronomer looked up from the book and reworded the text, whose subject turned out to be not so far from the images that the Latin had kindled in Davíð's mind. When the Astronomer stopped reading, he stood up, went and got a bottle of red wine, uncorked it, poured two glasses, they drank and Davíð asked: So do you think that the end is near?

Wouldn't that be nice? replied his father with a smile, a mischievous one, actually, and raised his glass toward the light; at least the signs seem to point to that, we have examples everywhere, all around us, on the pages of the newspapers, the covers of glossy magazines, you turn on the television and they jump off the screen; they're so obvious that we don't even notice them. But so what; Western culture had its time, many centuries, now others will take over. Great, said Davíð, looking down into his glass, down into the dark-red liquid, the dark-red color can change thoughts into dreams, no, of course it's not great, he said, I just can't shake the feeling that coincidence governs everything, that everything springs from it, including a sense of purpose; birds keep flying through the sky, and why then should we worry what culture is on top? His father shakes his head, this vision of yours is like a black hole, he says, cupping his chin in his hand, as if to support his head better, all the weight that can fit inside the human head, he drains his glass, refills it, and then says, looking distractedly at his son: I'm gathering up fragments of a dying culture. Dying? More like it's already dead, or has begun rotting alive—making me a kind of garbageman. That's not what I saw! A garbageman, decay and stars; a pretty nice combination, don't you think? Are you listening to me, the Astronomer suddenly asks when Davíð doesn't answer, doesn't even look at him, just stares into space, holding his empty glass in his hands. Once there was nothing else in the world but her breaths. What does the world's noise matter, the rise or fall of cultural worlds, coincidence or emptiness, if you don't have lips to kiss, breasts to caress, breaths that fill your ears? I wish I had a piano, Dad, he says suddenly, cutting off the heavy, gloomy thoughts of the Astronomer, who is angry, at first, at this unexpected, even superficial comment of his son, but Davíð's melancholy expression wards off all his irritation, and now, perhaps, he starts thinking of the Hungarian woman, I have a harmonica, he says, and then father and son sit under the open skylight, the evening has strewn stars across the sky, there is a bottle of whiskey between them, and the notes of the harmonica float out through the window, find themselves a star, search for a woman.

[We continue to add new stories, find it difficult to stop, but perhaps that's also because those who tell of life tend to spin long threads—everything we do is in one way or another a fight against death. But Matthías stepped out of the bus, and a few days later, the Depot reopened under his supervision, tidier, more organized than ever before, light bulbs burning in the warehouse, the forklift dashing up and down the main corridor, a computer on Matthías's desk, Macintosh Performa, customer service exceptionally speedy and everything running smoothly, nothing unexpected, no ghosts, nothing irrational. Of course we've pondered the incidents in the warehouse, have repeatedly asked Davíð and Kjartan about them, even Benedikt, we haven't dared mention them to Sigríður, of course, but haven't come anywhere close to getting an explanation. Was it all just imagination, then, pure and simple, Davíð's and Kjartan's stretched nerves, or was it really ghosts? There are many things that we don't understand, besides the fact that we tend to ask questions that tear off our clothes and leave us naked and vulnerable to the world.

Matthías turned out to be good at transforming what we consider obvious and ordinary into senselessness and absurdity. Ghosts, he says, why shouldn't we admit to them, there are so many things more preposterous than ghosts, and here's a glaring example: millions, tens of millions of people believe

173

white middle-aged American men to be boons to the nations of the world—conservative, narrow-minded, and belligerent men, blind to the finer strands of existence, dangerous to the fragile future of the Earth. But we sing their praises, instead of opposing them.

He makes a lot of sense.

And you also know that many people here, and by this we mean here in Iceland, here on this bit of earth beneath the endless, gaping sky, want nothing more than to get to sit on those people's shoulders, feel the warmth of their necks. Can you explain this to us a bit better, we're disoriented, the earth has been kicked from beneath our feet, only the void holds us up, and that's not a comfortable thought. You also know that if we continue to live as we've been doing these past decades, and now we're talking about the whole of humanity—sometimes we make such big jumps—if we don't change our way of life, our everyday life, it will be the end of us. We'll deprive ourselves of life. We are the judge, the executioner, and the condemned person tied to the stake. Yet we continue to live as if nothing were more self-evident. Senseless. We think about this sometimes, about senseless actions, senseless incidents, senseless situations, senseless life.

So, to put it bluntly, we still haven't got a concrete explanation for those days at the Depot, perhaps none is to be had, perhaps we'll find it in Lúlla's dreams, though few of us would be willing to admit that out loud, or perhaps there's an answer to be found in the story of the parish administrator. But Simmi and Gunnar have refurbished the entire electrical system in the building, the old wires were completely worn, it was sheer good fortune that they didn't cause a fire a long time ago, and ever since Matthías took over the Depot, no merchandise has been placed on the floor over the ruins. What's more, he and Kjartan partly tore up the floor there and planted a cross, a bit mad to do so, it looks really nice in the light of day, but a bit less so after dark, as if there's a pit beneath it, opening into infinite darkness. No one seems to have the courage to stay at the Depot after dusk—so far we are from defeating the darkness—whether it's inside us, beneath us, or outside us.]

Bliss

1

How is it possible for a truck driver to be so happy that nothing can ever shake him?

After Simmi and Gunnar repaired the Depot's wiring, Matthías and Kjartan broke up the floor inside the warehouse, planted the cross, and Matthías said a few words, it was as if he were convinced that his words carried beyond the grave and death, we're really not sure if he was being serious or was driven by a macabre humor, but then he told the two sworn brothers, Kjartan and Davíð, that they were all bound to devote their fullest attention to their customers, to ensure that they felt at ease, that they would return even just to chat; people, he explained, should have a sense of tranquility when they think of us; in this way, we can do our bit to help better the world. We gladly endorse these words; some people actually invent any excuse to stop by the Depot, and Benedikt shows up twice a week, plays chess with the trio and sometimes Matthías invites him to lunch. On the very first day after the Depot reopened, however, Matthías asked the truck driver Jakob to go and fetch some things of his that he had left in Reykjavík, items that he had collected in his six years of wandering: a statuette from France, a stuffed tarantula from the Amazon, and so on. Matthías had perhaps thought of renting a small flat to start with, to see if he could stand living here in the village, but Elísabet told him, you can stay with me as long as I love you. Elísabet goes regularly to the Depot and often has a lovely time there, she's a bosom friend and knows about Harpa; she's the only one who knows. Davíð doesn't pay much attention to how she's dressed, but Kjartan does, the yellow sweater, he thinks, the black dress, he thinks, and the hair that falls over her shoulders. Sometimes, however, she puts it up, in which case Kjartan would conceivably give one, two, or three fingers to undo the bun. Matthías doesn't need to sacrifice any fingers, she goes into his office with her hair in a bun, let it down, she says, and he does so. Her hair, long and dark, beautiful and devilish, falls over her shoulders, and falls in a way that can kill a man. Then, perhaps, Elísabet looks around and at the floor, where Matthías has taped down a huge map of South America, it covers the entire floor of the twelve-square-meter office, and she says: Matthías, I want to do it in Peru. And the world is so beautiful that it bursts your heart, when she says this in a tone of love combined with passion. She says this, perhaps, when she's wearing the black dress, the one that's tight above the waist but flares out below, she never wears knickers when she's got it on, and he knows this. Arequipa, she then whispers, because the town of Arequipa is next to Matthías's left ear as he lies there on his back, it's in the mountains in southern Peru, at 2,500 meters above sea level, and when he starts to turn his head slowly to the side, Elísabet takes it in her hands, leans over him in such a way that her hair covers both their faces, and mutters, my darling, darling Slav.

Sometimes Elísabet is on her way to the Astronomer's when she stops at the Depot, that winter he got himself a powerful new computer, probably the most powerful one here in the village; it might in fact take a machine like that to get a grasp on the sky, Latin, the end of the world, and a Hungarian woman. Jakob honked his horn as he passed the corrugated-iron-clad house with the computer in his truck, as if to announce: I've brought you the computer. Now, you mustn't confuse Jakob the truck driver with the other Jakob in the village, the plumber who, many years ago, suffered an accident at work and has lived since then on disability payments, though some say that the only thing wrong with him is his laziness, an uncontrollable desire to sleep in, work on crossword puzzles until late at night, wrestle with difficult puzzles, wander from one house to the next in search of a cup of coffee, gossip, and the news. The plumber is a very large man, heavyset, with a broad, strong-looking face, a deep voice, and powerful hands, it's fun to listen to such a voice, it inspires trust, is persuasive, he's also been encouraged to run for office or become a TV host, when we greet him with a handshake, his strong hands turn to sand that runs freely between our fingers. But Jakob the truck driver is completely different from his namesake, he's happy, his life is meaningful and free of shadows. Obviously, you must be wondering how it's possible nowadays, when an acrid stench arises from our culture, when we can scarcely board a plane or train without the fear of being blown up, when cameras survey our streets, when increasingly fewer people see reason to vote and democracy itself has begun to crumble—how is it possible for a truck driver to be so happy that nothing can ever shake him?

2

Few things in this world can equal driving a truck.

Jakob has been the village's number one truck driver since 1980, and even if it's exciting, and maybe much more than that, driving a big truck to and from Reykjavík, it was even better when it took just over four hours to reach the capital; today, family cars can do the same in around two hours, a truck in nearly three, such has the world shrunk, though distances between people haven't diminished. But you should have seen us when the new road over Brekkan Bluff was opened three years ago, straight and wide, instead of the old, narrow one that wound up and down, even looped back on itself, seemingly unbothered about getting to its destination and in the winters disappeared beneath the snow— how we celebrated! A dance was held at the Community Center, we got sloshed, the women had red lips, and the grass was fragrant. Jakob was the only one who didn't celebrate, a string in his heart even broke when he drove the new road for the first time, getting over the bluff in fifteen instead of fifty minutes, and the old road winding for nothing high above the new one, halfway to the sky. But Jakob isn't the type who lets sorrow darken his days, he just drives a little slower, because, we repeat: few things in the world can equal driving a truck, which is why it would be utter stupidity to hurry. Jakob is enthralled by his trips, by the movements of his truck, he drives out of the village, enjoying the softness of the steering wheel, the shape of the gearbox, the pure power of the engine, and best of all is when it rains, because nowhere else in the world can one find that combination of industriousness and tenderness than in the rhythmic strokes of the windshield wipers; Jakob sits there behind the windshield, happily gripping the wheel. Previously, he made three trips a week, winding roads, steep slopes, a good four hours brimming with bliss, but to make up for the route having been shortened so miserably, the asphalt having smothered the dust, and the undersea tunnel across Hvalfjörður, for the last four or five years Jakob has had to drive to Reykjavík and back every day; we're always needing more and more things to live. More packets of biscuits and more treadmills, thinner socks, newer televisions, we're no longer content to read the newspapers when they're two or even three days old, the world changes each day and yesterday's newspaper is completely useless; you may as well just go to the library and read about the nineteenth century. Incredible how much slower everything here went in the past, when we watch a sixty-year-old Humphrey Bogart film we get the feeling that in those days one minute was considerably longer, that more time passed between events, and that therefore it was easier to make one's way through life; even bullets flew more slowly. Today, everything goes by faster. Movies and TV programs have such sudden cuts, such quick changes of perspective, that we've nearly stopped blinking for fear of missing anything, and what then are we supposed to do with yesterday's newspaper? But our impatience increases Jakob's happiness, he drives to the capital five times a week, sets off from the village so early in the morning that the sun is still sleeping when it's winter, and the darkness is so dense that we sometimes doubt that it's capable of lifting itself up once again from the deep, over the icy mountains, to waken the beautiful and painful within us. Jakob drives south to the city, empties his truck of what needs to be emptied, then fills it with everything that we can't live without. It's almost noon by the time he has loaded the truck, Jakob drives carefully, he threads his way through the streets of the capital, tries to avoid the main thoroughfares out of inborn shyness, parks outside the bus terminal, grabs a bite for lunch, his favorite is lamb chops, he chats with two other truck drivers, some have the enormous luck to have to drive twelve hours to get home, which is such a good thing that Jakob tries very hard not to think about it. They curse the politicians, have a great many disparaging words for the Minister of Transport, are unsparing in their put-downs for a particular football coach, they talk about women but more often about cars, about spare parts, which garages are best, but never mention the caresses of the windshield wipers, some things in this world are best left unsaid, or else they get spoiled. Then Jakob heads back west. From time to time he has to wait for certain articles and will leave later, when the city is immersed in early evening twilight. In such instances, it's dark by the time he reaches Borgarfjörður, the mountains merge with the darkness, which his powerful headlights cleave, they lead the way and the truck follows. We must always follow the light.

Jakob receives a salary for his driving; with it, he pays his electrical bill, the installments on the truck, the house, the new range, buys milk and bread, yet it's absurd to talk about work in his case, for him, driving is much more a way of life, a purpose, a joy; but besides all the things we've already listed—the softness of the steering wheel, the shape of the gearbox, the caresses of the windshield wipers—we must also add the tape player and the cassettes that Jakob plays when it's not raining, when the windshield wipers sleep and the sky is dry. It's his wife, Eygló, who records the songs, lining up the greatest hits of Gylfi Ægisson, Haukur Morthens, Ási from Bær, Ellý Vilhjálmsdóttir, Elvis Presley, the Beatles, and if anyone took it upon himself to explain to Jakob the word "bliss," he would nod and think of the windshield wipers, the sounds made by the heater, the tape player.

No one would ever dream of trying to sponge a ride from Jakob, neither to nor from the capital, and not just because he's the type of person who would never be able to refuse. Eygló is the only person who gets to ride with him, but she's also his wife, and it only happens once a year, always around December 15; it's their Advent trip. For the past ten years, Eygló has had a part-time job; she sits at home entering data and figures for a company in Reykjavík, the computer screen illuminates her chubby face, her rough skin, she prepares a packed lunch for her husband, washes his clothes, cooks dinner, dries the dishes that he washes, cleans the floors, the bathroom, together they change the sheets and take care of the garden, they complement each other in the same way that the left hand does the right. It's a great relief that such people still exist; the light hasn't completely gone out yet over the human race. Eygló bites Jakob's right shoulder during orgasm, she closes her eyes, the world expands, she's torn from all contact with the earth and bites his shoulder hard, partly out of pleasure, but no less out of her deep-seated fear of losing him. Then they lie still, dead still, while the world puts itself back together, each fragment in its place, it takes patience, and then she props herself on her elbow, reaches for a jar of medicinal ointment standing on the bedside table, rubs it carefully onto his shoulder as he tries to kiss her face. Jakob thinks, and says it, too, you're so beautiful, which always makes her blush, no matter how many years have passed, and he's also the only one who has ever said this, she's short, thick, even fat, with a stumpy neck, almost colorless hair, looking most often like damp hay, such women have never been the cause of any war, tiny breasts and beefy thighs, but she has light-brown eyes that could easily remind one of the moors in bright sunlight. She runs like a little girl into the kitchen, returns with a packet of chocolate biscuits and milk, Jakob completely forgets the pain in his shoulder and says something that we prefer not to repeat, it's beautiful the way that he says it, interwoven with his breath, his voice, his brimming eyes, whereas if we put the words on paper, they would only diminish him.

The Advent trip is the high point of the year for the couple, their faces light up as it draws near, the moods of many of us become instinctively happier, even we start filling with eager anticipation. The light that plays about their trip is so strong that God must notice it; when they set off, He lies down on the bunk behind the seats. Pulls the curtain and takes a break from the world's bother, from the loquaciousness of the angels; he listens to the murmur of the engine, the low buzz of the heater, the conversations of Eygló and Jakob, perhaps hums softly along to Ási from Bær and Elvis Presley, and if the desires of the flesh awaken in the couple, when, for example, Eygló says, I find it so exciting, how you handle the gear stick, and then strokes Jakob's right thigh as he turns at the first opportunity off the highway onto a rarely traveled side road, then God steps out of the cab, goes to the side of the road to pee, throw rocks, and whistle while the two use the bunk. And then, the trip continues. And the light on the mountains and the road and the clouds and the ditches and the farmhouses and the rivers and the two of them is so beautiful.

Tekla and the Man Who Couldn't Count the Fish

1

For a long time it had been clear to us that the days of the Knitting Factory were over, and that there had perhaps never been any real basis for its operation, apart from a bet between two drunk politicians and one more reason for us to vote for the Progressive Party; and besides, for the longest time, we'd never had the imagination to do otherwise. It's also true, however, that under the management of the Astronomer, against all the laws of the market economy—so little should those be taken into account—the business had never dipped into the red; but then that damned Latin had come into play, followed by stars, the heavens between them, countless letters from all over the world, and so on. That was pretty much the end of this one little knitting factory, whether it's written with capital letters or not, but you know, everything ends, the life of a man, the life of a nation, the machinery went to another village and the sun shone into the Knitting Factory's empty premises, and the rest of us instinctively looked in another direction whenever we passed by the building, few things are as sad as a building that was once buzzing with life, purpose, but that now stands completely empty, it's depressing, plain and simple, no one to pee in its toilet, no one to open the windows. The ten hands proposed moving the whist drive from the Community Center down to the Knitting Factory, Kjartan wanted to put a pool table and ping-pong table in the room on the lower floor, to help pep up the village's social life during the long winters, Davíð pointed out that we needed a decent library, it was a bit silly having both the school library and public library under the same roof, Valli said that the building would be perfect for a gym, Helga agreed with Kjartan but wanted to add computers, slot machines, magazines, no shortage of ideas, but while most people content themselves with ideas, others take things a step further, and one day Elísabet arrived with a can of paint, a hammer, a crowbar, and a ladder, it was early May, four months after Matthías stepped out of the bus, his computer was whirring away on his desk, Kjartan and Davíð paid close attention to their customers and everything was going as smoothly as could be in the Depot, despite no one wanting to be in the place after dark; but Elísabet is there with her hammer, crowbar, can of paint, and ladder, every day and every evening we hear the noise of her hammering, disturbing the television watching of those living nearest. Elísabet didn't do much of the painting, she delegated the task to Jónas, how do you want me to paint the walls, he asked so softly that he seemed more to be breathing than speaking, entirely up to you, she replied, Jónas removed his hands from his pockets, smiled at the floor, and went to work. It took the entire summer to complete the job, he showed up at six in the morning, his cheeks still soft from sleep. Þorgrímur picked him up right before nine and brought him back home around five, Jónas painted into the evening, remarkable that something as dead as a wall can be transformed into something so full of life, how often we've hung around there counting the birds that fly together in the thousands on the outer walls, it's nice to go down there, especially in winter when the sky is lacking in birds, when time can't advance through the darkness and the water hardly wants to run from the taps. And the birds on the walls are so lively that a neighboring cat, a yellowish devil that had deprived us of far more birds than necessary, continued to leap against the building's walls the first few weeks, you could clearly see the bump this left on its head, and ever since then, it has never managed to regain its former hunting prowess—you can't say that art has no influence on life. But Elísabet brandished her crowbar, reached for her saw, set aside her drill, it distressed some people to see a woman alone with such tools, they went down to the building and asked, would you like some help with what you're doing, whatever it is? Of course, said Elísabet, you can take off your clothes, I work best with naked men around me, and preferably with full erections, she said, of course, absolutely, I need an assistant just now, hold the ladder, she said, sure, thanks, make me some coffee, go to the shop and buy me a newspaper. Some women said, she's nothing but an arrogant bitch in heat, what are these men doing offering to help, most of them are married and have trouble enough finishing their own projects at home, fixing the rain gutters, changing the glazing bars, painting the roof, they'd do well to think about their own chores instead of running down there with their brains in their dicks and their eyes on her tits. Elísabet, however, accepted Jónas's help, while Simmi tended to the wiring, and sometimes the Astronomer's ex-wife came to speak to Elísabet, and one day the bricklayer Ásbjörn, called Ási, arrived with a trowel, Ási never seemed down, one of those people who have difficulty seeing anything but the bright side of life, his smile hardly ever disappears from beneath his baseball cap, which is as heavy as a diving bell due to the hardened splashes of concrete all over it. You've certainly made some big changes here, he said, depositing a sack of cement in one corner, yes, I have big plans, replied Elísabet, tell me what they are and I'll be the most popular man in the village, you already are that, but I'll tell you all the same: I'm going to open a restaurant—and that's how we found out.

Of course it was hardly possible to have a worse idea, the ten hands flew up in eager anticipation and predicted certain bankruptcy, while those of us who longed for more life and movement sighed hopelessly, there was a range cooker in every house, some of them brand-new, people owned books full of recipes, clipped them out of newspapers, copied them down from magazines, there was really no need for a restaurant here, and anyway, you could buy hot dogs, sandwiches, beef burgers, and fries at the shop, incomprehensible that the bank lent Elísabet the money for such a blunder, what was Björgvin thinking, how could Sibbi have approved this, damn us if Elísabet didn't end up falling flat, bankrupt, disappointed, depressed, she'd have to leave the village with her breasts and her gait, the ten hands were happy—one person's tears are another person's laughter.

However . . .

On Friday, September 4, 1998, Elísabet opened her restaurant. A few days before, she'd positioned the ladder against the building, climbed up with her powerful drill, and begun unscrewing the old, weathered letters: KNITTING FACTORY. It was a sad moment for the rest of us, even Ási suddenly felt the weight of his baseball cap. Elísabet had hung up an announcement at the shop, stating that on that day, at that time, she would take down the old letters and have Jónas paint the name of the restaurant on the building, which had wreathed its way out of the vodka bottle of two MPs many years earlier. Thanks to the announcement, a small group of people had gathered outside the Knitting Factory, and now someone asks, is it really necessary, Elísabet, what, she asks in return, to take down the letters, there's something so sad about it, why do you need a new name, why does everything have to change? Because the Earth is revolving, she replies, before re-aiming her drill, but just then, Gaui comes riding down the hill at high speed, holding tightly to the handlebars because the asphalt is uneven and human life fragile.

2

Gaui has a law degree from the University of Iceland, those who have the gift of gab, but little other talent, study law, he sometimes says with a grin; he's Ási's brother. He attended high school in Reykjavík, we thought he'd moved there for good, would never return except for visits, and that was what he had thought, too; but what does anyone know? Gaui opened a law office in Reykjavík, he was industrious and astute, after eight years he had a paunch and six employees, a 300-square-meter villa with a parquet floor, and an SUV, but then misfortune hit and he drank it all away in one year, which was of course briskly done. Yet his wife, named Gerður, stuck with him, though for a time she was damn close to leaving, they have two sons and moved here to the village after his rehab, this is of course a backwoods shithole, said Gaui, just driving through it puts you to sleep, but it's a good place to build your character, gain some peace and quiet, at first they stayed in Ási's basement flat, ninety square meters. How much should I pay you in rent, brother, Gaui had asked, determinedly, because nothing stings more than charity, he took a job as a workman for the power company, his wife had a part-time job at the Dairy and the promise of extra work at the slaughterhouse in the autumn, which they definitely needed, it's incredible how much one can drink away in a year, and how much debt one can accumulate at the same time.

Ási: You can pay me with one story every Saturday night, after we finish watching *Comedy Hour* on TV; it mustn't take less than fifteen minutes, and must hold my attention the whole time. Don't be an idiot, Ási, Gaui replied. If you can't satisfy my conditions, you'll have to pay me forty thousand krónur a month. I refuse to accept. Well, in that case, the story mustn't take less than twelve minutes, but, I repeat, it will have to hold my interest. This is humiliating. Okay, then we'll stick to fifteen minutes. Listen, Ási, I blew everything, tossed it all to the wind, destroyed so many beautiful things, drank like a fish, behaved like an asshole, I was a real loser, cheated on my wife, hit my kids, I admit it all, but still, you don't have to treat me like a bum, I want to start a new life and have no place for charity. You misunderstood me, said Ási, looking down at his short, thick hands, rough from work, dry and cracked from the cement. I haven't misunderstood anything; I want to pay rent, period. And you will pay rent; with a fifteen-minute story every Saturday night. I'd call that charity, said Gaui, and why the hell are you grinning? I'm not grinning, really, no, I was smiling. I'd call it a grin, said Gaui angrily. Well, call it a grin if you want, but you've misunderstood everything, see, I'm forty-two, live alone and have done so since Dad died and Mom went to the nursing home, I make good money, nothing lacking there, I even own stocks, but it's a bit empty here sometimes in the evenings, especially on weekends, not so much on other days when I'm exhausted from work, but weekend evenings are difficult, including Friday evening, they remind me of the empty rooms, the empty kitchen chairs, leases should be required to ensure a tenant has occasional company. I didn't know that, said Gaui. What didn't you know? That you were lonely. I'm not lonely, I just get bored in the evenings sometimes, and then usually go for a walk around the village and see families gathered in front of the television or at the kitchen table, I'm a bit tired of these walks of mine and it would spare me them if you accept the terms of the lease.

Gaui and Gerður rented the basement flat for nearly two years and discovered how difficult it can be to tell a fifteen-minute story that held Ási's full attention; sometimes the stories were rubbish, but they improved over time; the stories lengthened, became something that Ási looked forward to each week, sometimes Gaui, Gerður, and the kids, too, life does indeed have its radiant sides, and then one day Ási moved into the basement and the family upstairs. Gaui no longer works for the power company, he was a laughable workman, the others bore with him out of the kindness of their hearts and their consideration for Ási, but people were constantly asking him about legal matters, about things with which they preferred not to trouble the commissioner, Guðmundur, who already had enough on his hands, and in the end the couple opened a law and accountancy office here in the village, they take on projects from all over the district, sometimes even from Reykjavík, but they've never seriously considered moving back there, nor has it crossed their kids' minds, it's nice to live here, you know, if you've got nothing against small populations, sometimes life can seem bigger in smaller places. Alcohol is the only real shadow in Gaui's life, of course he hasn't touched it in nine years, but is sometimes so shaken by the memory of it that he gets into bed and lies there for a whole week, staring at the ceiling, his wife and children slink around, trying not to make noise, we slow our cars down when we drive by. That's the only shadow, but soon the boys will go to high school, their rooms will be left empty, the dust in them will rarely stir. Life, on the other hand, is ever moving, dust can't accumulate—one day, it all changes to memory, and you're dead.

3

Gaui comes dashing down the sloping road that curves past the Knitting Factory, which is about to change into a restaurant, it's fun to go fast but he holds tight to the handlebars, because life is a thread that tears easily. Elísabet is up on the ladder with her drill, three meters above the ground, a rather mild day in August, the berries well ripened, we gather pails of them on the mountainsides and in the little dales with their overgrown farm ruins and thousands of blades of grass that write their signs in the air. Gaui stops the bicycle with a confident skid, pushes it through the group of people gathered to watch, most on their lunch breaks, the mood is serious, Elísabet is taking down a piece of the past, she's wearing blue jeans, an untucked flannel shirt, her black hair falling over its collar. Gaui stops at the bottom of the ladder, regards the letters that Elísabet has already removed, they lean against the wall, tired and disoriented, have lost their purpose, now she's removing the first "I," Gaui looks up, sees beneath her shirt her bare back, but fortunately she's wearing a black top underneath, so he continues watching without pause, it's always better to look at the person you're talking to, but then again, it's nice to see a woman's bare back—hardly anything wrong with that, either. What are you going to do with these letters, Gaui asks, raising his voice to overpower the drill. At first, she says nothing, finishes removing the "I," comes down the ladder, hands him the letter, climbs back up, she has a strong-looking jaw, it's no use entering a beauty contest with a jaw like that, Gaui asks her again and Elísabet finally says, I haven't really thought about it, I'll put them in storage, I expect. Well, I'd like to buy them from you. Elísabet stops removing the "K," looks down, long enough for her hair to slip forward and hide her face, as if she'd suddenly retreated into a dark evening, she strokes the darkness back from her face and says, ten thousand a letter. Ten thousand! shouts Gaui, looking at the people around him, now that's cheeky! Twelve thousand, says Elísabet, oh ho ho! shouts Gaui, raising his hands, and half an hour later Ási drives the letters up to the couple's office, where they were fastened to the wall, whereas Elísabet had Jónas climb the ladder with a can of paint, he painted the new name on the building's wall in yellow letters: TEKLA.

And then it was opened.

Of course it was a great event, there had never been a restaurant or bistro here, only the Co-op shop with its fryer, no need to put on nice clothes to go there, so terribly rarely that we have a chance to do so, here whole months can pass between deaths and dances, but then Elísabet opened a restaurant. Hung up an announcement in the Co-op, Tekla is opening on Friday, September 4, Davíð will entertain the guests by playing his harmonica and violin, for reservations call 434-1405, followed by the menu and the wine list. We were very pleased with the menu: lamb, poultry, and pork with unusual, sometimes exotic, side dishes, but it was the wine list that made the difference, it was still two years before a branch of the state liquor store would open here and it was a complete novelty to be able to walk into a place and order wine, we were dizzy with happiness, bloody hell, now we were going to drink! The first night, the place was packed; there were even quite a few people from the countryside who had bathed and sprayed themselves with perfume and aftershave to smother the stench of sheephouses and cowsheds, Davíð sat on a tall stool, blew a bittersweet tune on the harmonica, lightly stroked the strings of his violin, we didn't know that he could play the violin, those who play this instrument seem to have bigger hearts than others. It was a magical evening. The wind slept behind the mountains, the stars were gradually returning after the overpowering light of summer, we gain the songs of the migratory birds in spring but lose the light of the stars, in the autumn it's the exact opposite. Which is better? Birdsong sometimes seems woven of pure joy, of eager anticipation but also melancholy, it nests in our breasts, but on the other hand we often feel lonely looking at the stars, their glittering a distant hope. But that evening few people thought about loneliness or the stars, despite the sky having spread its drape of stars, and the

Astronomer walked out of the village, wrapped warmly in layers, with a thermos of coffee, sat down on an icy rock, and wrote a letter in Latin, dipping his fountain pen now and then in the black space between the stars, while his son stroked the violin strings like a lover, some hurried to swallow delicious morsels to shout bravo, those who were more experienced in the ways of the world smiled sarcastically at their provincialism because you don't applaud musicians in restaurants or churches—these places really do have much in common. Davíð smiled shyly, continued to play, sometimes looking to his left, where Harpa sat at a table with her husband and a couple of friends, but Harpa never returned his look, it was as if their lips had never met, let alone anything else, good Lord, I can't think of anything else, thought Davíð, and his violin whimpered a little, gasped, and then coiled and launched into an Argentine tango. He thought of her lips, her breaths, how she'd pulled him to her, wrapped her legs round his when he entered her, there's lust in tangos, Davíð's dark hair fell over his forehead, the violin writhed, Harpa looked up, now she looked up, really did look up, and then reached for her wineglass and drained it. Davíð continued to play and the evening passed, she looked up more often and every time she did, a string was tugged, one in his heart, one on his violin, but then night fell and Davíð and his violin were in one house, Harpa and her husband in another, they made love, she thought of Davíð the whole time.

4

Tekla, the name sounds like a type of car, yet Tekla was no car but a heroine who lived two thousand years ago, beat the man who tried to rape her, but as he was an influential man in a world dominated by men, she was condemned to death and thrown to a ferocious lioness, which changed and became gentle and kind as soon as it saw Tekla and licked her feet, and then Tekla was freed, she lived in a cave for seventy-two years and afflicted souls flocked to her, she founded a convent, this is all written on the menu. Perhaps if Tekla had lived in our days, she would have gone into politics and changed the world, provided that power didn't change her first, because power has no equal, it sings lullabies to the most fanatical idealists and turns them into conformists, docile as sleepy puppies; but that was a magnificent evening for us here in the village. We went home full, drunk, and happy, it was almost better than our dances, no fuss, no fights, no one threw up, it was almost as if it had been someone besides us. We went home and took back all the bad things we'd said about Elísabet.

But what the night hides, the light of day reveals. We woke up with our heads pounding, the noise of the children's programs on TV, we gulped down headache medicine, fed our children breakfast, found crumpled receipts in our pockets, haltingly read the unpleasant sums on them, and moaned. The ten hands hadn't shown up at Tekla, the hell we'll be there, they'd declared in unison, but were at the commissioner's office early Monday morning. Few things in this world are more beautiful than friendship, perhaps it's that more than anything else that makes the world habitable, and it was friendship that tied the ten hands together, they were a force in the village and it was no fun at all to wind up at loggerheads with them. Still, friendship isn't always enough, and a few weeks after the meeting with the commissioner, one of them was at home, it wasn't even evening, but a bright day, a Thursday, even, yet she filled her tub with warm water, went and got a utility knife, they're very sharp, you know, got into the tub, immediately cut her left wrist, then the right one, watched the blood run out into the water, perhaps thought, so that's what color life is. Fortunately, it so happened that her husband, who works for the power company, came home earlier than usual, with a gastrointestinal virus. Why? asked her friends, shocked, I don't know, she replied, looking down at the bandages on her wrists, I simply don't know, the only thing I know for sure is that it was a gastrointestinal virus that saved my life. She looked up and started laughing, then stopped suddenly and started crying, unrestrainedly, but there were four hugs waiting for her. It was beautiful and touching, and we prefer not to ruin the moment by saying that there are some things in this life that a hug can never assuage. But it was still quite some time until that Thursday and the blue utility knife when the ten hands wanted to rush straight into the commissioner's office, like a commando squad, a SWAT team charged with defending civil virtue, but Ásdís said: He's busy. We don't care. I know that, but you'll still have to sit down and wait, we're not waiting a second! Now now, said Ásdís, and then they sat down, better to be careful around Ásdís, she tried to kill her husband with a single-shot pistol normally used for sheep, set fire to his car, and has quite a lot of influence on the commissioner, better to have her on your side than against you, and there the ten hands sat and waited. From time to time Munda, the accountant, stuck her long face around her office door to take a peek at them, her blond hair gathered in a bun, as usual, it did nothing for her, lengthened her face, which was long enough already, but her husband, Sigmundur, likes her to tie up her hair, he adores his wife and fears that she would be so irresistible with her hair long and loose that he would lose her straightaway to the arms of someone better. The clock on the wall was approaching ten when the couple from the country-side finally emerged from Guðmundur's office, the farmer tall and thin, his wife short and very broad, when they stood side by side they looked most like the number 10, she was wearing a rather worn, flowery dress, the eyes beneath her brown, un-kempt hair were two deep, dim ponds. The ten hands waited for a sign from Ásdís and then marched in, Guðmundur was sitting behind his desk and sighed as if he were facing merciless forces of nature. We demand, they said without introduction, that you assign an impartial party to investigate how Elísabet could open a restaurant in the Knitting Factory building; something shifty's going on here. Why do you think that, he asks carefully, trying to maintain a neutral tone. Well, doesn't the building belong to the state, why does she get to use it like this, are there no rules about the use of such spaces, can just anyone waltz in there with all his rubbish, and where did she get the money, she must be unmasked before any more damage is done, before she sinks deeper.

Behind his desk, the commissioner looks at his computer, moves the mouse reflexively, the weekend is sitting heavily inside him, he and his wife have eaten three evenings in a row at Tekla, three evenings make a total of three bottles of red wine, a con-siderable amount of cognac, beer, violin, and harmonica music, Harpa Guðjóns was there both Friday and Saturday, and bloody hell, how well her hair went with her red dress, he sighed again, reached for his glass of water, the five women watched him, they had ten hands that transformed into a stormy forest every time the name of Elísabet was uttered. Come on, he said at last, tearing his mind away from the image of Harpa, her body beneath her red dress, she moved in such a feline way, he'd never noticed it before and needed twice as much cognac than was good for him to dampen his burning interest in her; come on, she's just industrious. Industrious! Yes, industrious and resourceful as well, there's nothing illegal about being resourceful, and nobody has edited the *District Gazette* as well as her, she . . . She's industrious, yes, that's for sure, industrious about shoving her tits in men's faces and wrapping them around her finger, you only think with your dicks and she knows it, knows that you've only got sex on your minds. It's not a crime to think about sex, he ventured to say, and a slight, very slight tremor ran through him upon saying that word, "sex."

How did she get that building for her restaurant? We want an investigation.

She's my sister-in-law.

We want an impartial investigator from Reykjavík.

You're blowing this out of proportion, you know, making a mountain of a molehill.

For example, a lawyer from the state auditor's office.

Come on, girls.

Well, then we'll press charges against her ourselves, and against you, too.

Me?

For collusion.

The commissioner sighed, his hangover had stopped hammering his head, but now began to cut a sheet of iron in two with a blunt saw; he gave up, and a few weeks later Áki arrived.

5

Áki drives into the village at the end of September in a brand-new Ford Escort, stays at Guðmundur and Sólrún's house, and is given an office alongside the commissioner's, a man of medium height, slim, delicate, his skin so thin that he appears transparent, always wearing impeccable clothes and an expensive overcoat, seldom blinks, is forty, divorced. Áki believes in numbers and organization, and also applied this belief of his to his marriage: sex on Tuesday evenings, time with his children between eight and eight thirty on Wednesday evenings, thus was everything compartmentalized and set in stone, it didn't matter what others thought, because those who don't organize their lives will be consumed in the chaos. In the end, his wife couldn't take it anymore, she said that his planning had become manic, the very essence of his life, they'd been divorced for two years when Áki drives into the village, on a quiet autumn day, the grass had paled, the migratory birds were gone, had flown off into the horizon, the slaughterhouse truck drives from farm to farm, its homemade house rattling on the truck's bed, which is empty when it leaves the village, but full of bleating lambs when it returns, a few silent sheep, an angry ram or two, and even one farmer, accompanying his animals. The truck drives down the slope, past Tekla, backs up to the slaughterhouse, two men in knee-length, dark-green smocks open the door, remove the grate at the back of the truck, drive the animals into the sheephouse, which is sometimes called the waiting room, but the wait is rarely long, the animals are driven one at a time toward the ramp that leads to the stunning platform, the slaughterman, a lanky farmer, handles the stunner with dexterity and speed, and on the upper floor wait hands eager to work. Sometimes we think of the lambs in the slaughterhouse's sheephouse, warm with life, bleating, looking around with their blue eyes, and one or two days later they're frozen carcasses. They live one summer, one short summer full of light in their veins, nothing else, the bolt shatters their forehead, above their eyes, while we're here waiting for winter.

The ten hands invite Áki for coffee, three different cakes, pancakes with cream, two types of biscuit, a brauðterta, they tell about the village, the whole village, its life, deaths, we have no churchyard, they say, and not even a church, Áki is a handsome man, you can't deny it, beautifully clean-shaven and his dirty-blond hair always in order. They invite him more often to coffee, after all, he's here because of them, ask him about his investigation, try unsuccessfully to fish something out of him, by just barely opening his thin lips, his expression turns cruel, and they think: Now that Elísabet is in trouble! After Áki has been in the village for only a week and has twice had coffee with the ten hands, he still hasn't spoken to Elísabet or set foot in Tekla; he obviously wants to approach his prey with caution, gather evidence, proof, and material first, make her nervous, he's watched her from a distance as she walks through the village.

Elísabet takes an hour-long walk every morning, in every weather, even when everything else is in danger of blowing away, she's a bit fanatical, explains the commissioner with a smile, he and Áki are standing at the window of the commissioner's office, watching Elísabet walk by, heading into the morning darkness outside the village, the empty slaughterhouse truck rattles down the road, heading into the darkness as well, clinging to its headlights so as not to get lost, school buses arrive from the countryside, unload the children, drive off, leaving the village silent once more, no movement, little happens here, says Guðmundur apologetically. Áki looks at the commissioner with those eyes that he never blinks, light blue, looking like blown glass, now I'd like to work in peace, he says, the commissioner returns his gaze and his temper flares, he sees a movement outside, Kjartan and Davíð saunter to work, Davíð in the middle of the street with his hands in his pockets, wearing a black leather jacket and dark jeans, his face deathly pale beneath his black cap, which is pulled down over his eyes, Kjartan walks on the pavement, his steps heavy, his feet a bit splayed, perhaps due to his weight, all those kilos that his skeleton is forced to carry.

Slowly, the sky brightens. Two crows glide over the Co-op. Soon the slaughterhouse van will return, its bed full of bleating, of the summer that will have turned to frozen carcasses before the week has passed, it's a Tuesday. Áki leaves, Ásdís pretends to be busy at her computer to avoid saying goodbye, but then gets up to follow him with her eyes, sees him heading toward the hill, disappear down it, there the fjord is withdrawing from the night, he's gone out, she calls in, may he rot in hell, Munda calls back, but the commissioner goes into his office, flips carefully through papers with a wrinkle of worry between his eyes. Áki passes in front of Tekla, inside everything is dark, goes into the slaughterhouse, observes the slaughterman at work and the three men at the small conveyor belt that starts beneath the stunning platform, a teenage boy with a CD player in his jacket pocket, thunderous rap in his ears, he helps turn over the creatures when they tumble in their death spasms off the platform, across from him a tall, round-shouldered man of around sixty, a drop of mucus hanging from his hooked nose, he cuts the lambs' throats, the blood gushes into the drain, the summer gushes out of them, the third man hooks one of the animals' legs to an iron hook, and the conveyor belt carries them to the upper floor, where they're turned into carcasses, then into food. Áki goes into the sheephouse, looks over the ruminating animals, it's as if they're chewing gum, which reminds him of football players, two leggers come down from upstairs, say hello to him, he gives them a little nod, they lean up against the grate, taking a break, lads of about twenty, from the countryside, each with an iron hook hanging from his belt, the gap for the hooves facing out, the handles of three knives sticking out from a holster at their hips, the slaughterhouse truck is heard approaching, Áki leans over the grate, lets his delicate, soft hand dangle, a lamb sniffs it cautiously, he looks into its eyes, listens to the muffled noise of the stunner, the thud when the beast falls onto the conveyor belt, and thinks, there's so little distance between life and death, summer and winter, he tries to think more along these lines, wants to think more but nothing comes to mind, he counts the heads in the sheephouse, then walks out, the leggers watch him with grins, you grin a lot when you're twenty, nothing can dishearten you at that age and the distance between life and death is often so long that it's useless to try to measure it. He walks down to the shore, sits on a big rock at the top of the foreshore, small waves come go come go come go come go come go, the sea is hypnotic. Quite some time passes and Áki just stares, he's neither in this world nor another, he hardly exists, little more than light-blue eyes that watch the waves come go come go, eyes that resemble blown glass. Then something moves in his head, maybe a thought, or a feeling. Today is Tuesday, in his weekly planner, between nine thirty and ten o'clock on Tuesday evenings, there's a big X, this is when he masturbates, usually to glossy American pornographic magazines, but he also has two books by Anaïs Nin. It had been a bit awkward doing so in the commissioner's guest room last Tuesday evening, but also somewhat exciting, he could hear Sólrún as he did so, she seemed to be on the phone, she has a soft voice. This is going to be nice, thinks Áki, parts his thighs slightly, calls to mind a chapter in one of the Nin books, *Delta of Venus*. No, it's not going to be nice, he thinks sadly, no change in how he feels, not a hint of an erection, he looks over the surface of the sea, which extends in three directions and in one place merges with jagged islands that scrape the horizon. It would be amusing if he could count the fish, or the tears that run down his face, down his slim cheeks, without him feeling anything, except for the numbness inside, as if his eyes have a will of their own, as if the tears are fleeing from him. A rat on a sinking ship, he thinks bitterly. There he sits, on that rock. He can't count the fish. He can't count his tears. He thinks: Why am I living?

That evening, he dined at Tekla. Soft music from a CD player, perhaps a string quartet performing the music of a long-dead composer, a pasta dish, a bottle of red wine. Several times in high school, he'd got drunk, in the late seventies, when there was little else around but aquavit and 7UP, vodka and Coke, red wine only in movies and embassies, how did it feel again to be drunk, he thought, looked over the menu, scrutinized the wine list and perhaps it was the memory of those far more daring days that inspired him to order a whole bottle, not a half, not a glass, but perhaps it was because he could neither count the fish swimming in the sea, nor the tears that ran from his eyes, in any case, he'd drunk half the bottle before his food arrived. After two glasses, he began blinking, like the rest of us. After three glasses, he looked around and nodded to the other patrons, five besides him, Dr. Arnbjörn was sitting by the window. At the seventh glass, he called Elísabet to his table and said very slowly, very carefully, a bit as if he needed to line the words up with his hands, I know a few things about you, and then he threw up over the table, the food, the floor, a little of it splashed on her, on her green sweater. Áki stared in surprise at the vomit, looked up at Elísabet and said: I couldn't count the fish.

6

It would probably be no exaggeration to say that from that moment on, everything went wrong for Áki, the man who could count neither the fish nor his tears and for that reason, lost control of his life. He dined at Tekla every night, at first we thought it was part of his investigation, Elísabet was complex, inscrutable, and it would take time to figure her out, perhaps Áki believed that as well, self-deceit is one of the most powerful tendencies in human beings. He increased his alcohol consumption quickly and steadily, finished his bottle of red wine on the fifth evening, stopped throwing up on the seventh, and then added a cognac, shambled back to the commissioner's house around one o'clock, went to work at eight thirty in the morning, even more laconic than usual, shut himself in his office, could be heard most often working on his computer. Still, he didn't look like a man in a downward spiral, he was even tidier, more impeccable than ever, ate in such a serene, discreet manner that the rest of us felt like clumsy louts in the presence of a nobleman. Of course, it did not escape our notice that he drank himself nearly unconscious every evening, but we thought that it was due to boredom, finding himself here, at the heart of monotony, and missing the cinema, the theater, musical concerts, missed hearing life's hum. Of course, here we had the slaughterhouse in full swing, Kiddi's film screenings, but what are those compared to the blood in the city's veins, and the days were growing darker and the nights longer as winter approached, pulling its dark wagon behind it. The ten hands were worried about Áki, they knew that it did no good for honest men to be in constant proximity to Elísabet, particularly if they're drunk, she being more conniving than the devil himself.

But what do we know? Nothing.

Nine days after Áki failed to count the fish in the sea, he is sitting at his table at Tekla; he had called Reykjavík, said that he needed to take sick leave, it's my heart, I'll send you the medical certificate. And now it's Thursday night, precisely a week until a woman here in the village gets into her bathtub holding a blue utility knife, a thick pile of papers on Áki's desk, have you written a novel, asks Elísabet, at which Áki's thin lips part, transforming his face into that of a predatory beast, he lays his delicate hand on the pile and says: This is about you. A detailed report on your character, your activities, all of you is here and cannot escape, would you like to read it? She leans back, takes a sip of red wine from Foggia in Italy, grabs half the stack, reads for ten seconds at most, and says, it's full of numbers. Of course, we'd be in bad shape without them, they hold everything together. She shakes her head, you're on the wrong path, I'm made solely of words, what would you like to eat?

It's Thursday evening and Kiddi is screening an excellent thriller at the Community Center, which is why there are so few at Tekla; only Áki, Arnbjörn, and four others. Arnbjörn is a regular patron at Tekla, he lives alone and has always done so, he puts on a red bow tie in the evening, aftershave on his chubby face, appears distracted, sometimes, in which case he resembles a sad bear, he always sits at the corner window, the autumn darkness on one hand, whiskey on the other, more or less. It's nice to feel a bit tipsy, one of the best sensations in this world, the landscape inside you transforms slightly, things take on a different nature, people move differently. Arnbjörn had tried to engage Áki in conversation, they had various things in common, both university-educated bachelors, both here in the village, both in their forties, those of a similar age have more and more in common as the years pass, and when we reach our forties, the past even becomes one of the more obtrusive parts of our lives. Áki has never opened up to anyone, but this particular Thursday evening takes a different turn, he has brought that pile of papers and sits there watching Elísabet as she disappears into the kitchen, looking extremely disappointed in her disinterest, the evening darkens, it settles over the village, the roofs of the houses. Áki has finished his bottle of red wine, started on his cognac, he sits down next to Arnbjörn, who closes his book, a novel in English by a French author, André Gide, Áki offers him a whiskey, make it a quadruple, he says to Elísabet, without taking his eyes off Arnbjörn, they toast, they drink, Áki is in very peculiar condition, he wants to talk, the words well up from his mouth, where were you when John Lennon was shot? What do you think is written in these papers, eh? Do you think it's possible to count the fish, and what about tears? Have you ever been to Milan? When was the last time you got laid? Is it possible to live in this village? What do you think is written in these papers? Arnbjörn tries to answer everything but is usually too late, Áki doesn't wait, he rushes onward, only slackens when Arnbjörn talks about the death of Lennon, with something of a lump in his throat, the bullet that hit my youth, he says, feeling like crying, on the one hand he has a whiskey, and on the other, the autumn darkness, it spreads itself over the village, it covers the sky, it reaches far out into space, tears, he says later that evening, actually night, by then, are the language of pain. Áki stares at Arnbjörn, raises his glass of cognac to his lips, drains it in one gulp, a double Remy Martin XO, chokes, coughs, gets up, looks at Arnbjörn until the world calms down beneath his feet, then goes out into the darkness, leaves the pile of papers behind on the table, and Arnbjörn reaches for it. Áki stays up all night, sits in the living room and drinks Sólrún and Guðmundur's wine, was probably born to drink, has real talent in that field, the level in the bottle lowers steadily, yet he speaks almost clearly when Guðmundur comes down just after three, he sits down opposite his guest, yawns, waits until sleep has removed itself completely from his body, pours himself a shot of whiskey, and says: You're sitting here drinking. Strange how good we are at saying the obvious, but don't be fooled, behind the words are perhaps the most profound of questions. Áki understands that, he knows that Guðmundur is actually asking him why he's sitting there, what incidents in his life, what pain, what tedium, what desperation put him in that armchair, passed him the bottle, while the night hung outside, drawing its strength and its darkness from the depths of the universe. In any case, replies Áki, as he fixes the button of his shirtsleeve, everything is a shambles, and then he adds, reflexively, I couldn't count the fish. Guðmundur sits up with his guest and the night passes, they drink, Áki a lot more, they speak little but play chess, what's a shambles, asks Guðmundur, if I only knew, the other answers, and when Sólrún comes down around six that morning, Áki is sleeping on the sofa, Guðmundur in the armchair, the chess pieces lie here and there on the table between them, the bottle of whiskey, two glasses, the moon hangs low in the half-dark western sky, yellow yet not yellow, and appearing almost on the verge of falling, only the frost holding it up. Sólrún spreads a blanket over Áki, wakes Guðmundur, they go back to their bedroom, still have an hour before they have to wake the children, you can do a lot of things in an entire hour in bed, and she says: Let's hold hands until the moon falls.

When Áki woke up he was alone in the house, the day had entered through the living-room window, the chess pieces still lay here and there on the table, the whiskey was gone but there was a note: Have whatever you'd like, preferably something from the kitchen. I recommend yogurt and bread. I can't exactly forbid you from drinking our wine, you're an adult, but it would be stupid of you to do so. Otherwise, make yourself at home. Sólrún.

Áki read the note, squinting from his headache, tottered to the bathroom, took a shower, had breakfast, read the note again and then ten more times, make yourself at home, why are some sentences like daggers, why do daggers so easily penetrate the skin, why can't the heart stand being stabbed? He spent all of Friday evening at Tekla, ate little, drank a lot, said few words, kept entirely to himself, but asked if he could sleep at Elísabet's, to which she replied, I've already got someone sleeping with me, and it's so hot between us that you would be burned. Áki was, however, allowed to sleep on a mattress on the upper floor of the restaurant, the moon was in the window, it was alone in the sky, and he alone here on earth, and drank a colossal amount on Saturday evening, sat at a table by the window, the sky was cloudy, but the clouds parted and there was the moon, its white rays slipped through the windowpane and mingled with the cognac in Áki's glass, how must that taste, he thought, and drained it. The moon has a peculiar taste, he woke up in an unfamiliar room, in a narrow bed, a naked woman lay against him and he was naked as well.

7

Perhaps we're reborn every time we open our eyes, which would mean that something probably dies every time we close them. Áki lay there for a long time with his eyes closed, waiting to wake from this dream in which he was lying in an unfamiliar room next to a naked woman. He opened his eyes and closed them again, opened and closed them until he realized that this was no dream. Well then, so that's how it was, he lay there in an unfamiliar bedroom, in a narrow bed, a woman breathing at his side, he could smell her body, they both lay on their backs, close together due to the constricted space. I'm dead; is eternity like this, then? The room wasn't big, he could see from wall to wall without moving his head, it seemed to be an attic room, except that it was the world that was leaning in, not the roof. In it was a worn, padded armchair, a Royal System shelving unit holding pictures of people and animals, three vases decorated with flowers, a locker or box decorated with sand and shells, a tall, narrow dresser, that was all, nor would much more have fitted, either, but outside the window hung the blue sky. He felt a little better after taking in his surroundings, after seeing that everything was in its own place, although he was still quite uncomfortable. The woman was awake, he could tell it from her breathing. Áki cleared his throat, clearly startling her, he saw her indistinctly out of the corner of his eye, her arms seemed to be crossed, where am I, he asked, his voice unrecognizable, hoarse and ragged. At Kálfastaðir. A low voice, for a woman. Is that a farm? Yes. Umm, and where is the village? They'd lain there completely motionless, he staring at the ceiling, but now she raised her arm farthest from him, the right one, pointed and said, there, and as she did so, Áki smelled her strong, almost rank body odor. His stomach spun, he broke into a sweat, don't puke, he thought, dammit, don't puke! He managed to hold it in and asked, with his eyes closed, how far is it from here? Twenty-seven kilometers, counting the side road. She didn't speak entirely unclearly, but probably didn't move her lips very much, if at all. What side road? The one leading to the farm. Is it long? Seven hundred and twenty-eight meters. Áki felt a mild current pass through his body; it was so nice when people converted their environments into exact figures, but then she raised her hand, scratched her head, he instinctively shut his eyes, waited for the stench to dull, reopened his eyes, and asked, hesitantly: What happened last night, how did I get here? There was a long silence, the woman only breathed and he waited, and then she asked, what do you remember? He thought it over, tried to recall, well, I was sitting at Tekla drinking cognac; yes, I saw the moon in the clouds . . . and then I woke up here. So you don't remember anything after that, I mean, after you saw the moon? No, he said, and he pursed his lips, thought, I'll puke if she lifts her arm again, does she ever take a bath? Well then, he sighed, they'd lain there for some time, she staring at the ceiling, which he saw when he turned his head a few millimeters, saw her rough, chubby face, thick nose, protruding mouth, unless it was just that her lips were so thick, fleshy and thick. Well then, he said, just tell me how I got here and why. Then he clung tightly to the bedside, because the world suddenly seemed to tilt so alarmingly, as if it wanted to be rid of me, flashed through Áki's head. Elísabet said it would be a great idea if you went with the two of us. With the two of you? With me and my brother. Does he live here too? Yes. Anyone else? No.

Now, on the floor below them, a radio was switched on, as if this brother wanted to verify his existence—a polite person, perhaps, because the radio played at a low volume. So you were at Tekla last night? No. Oh? We were outside. What were you doing there, were you just passing by? No, we just wanted to see who was there and what was going on, it's so easy to see inside the place in the evenings. Were you in your car, looking in? Yes. For a long time? No, maybe thirty-five minutes, before Elísabet came out. Once again, Áki felt a gentle current of well-being flow through him, now because of how precisely she kept time. Elísabet came out to you? Yes, at first we thought that she was going to make us leave, start the car, Jenni, I said. Jenni, is that your brother? Yes. And then? No, we've been having some trouble with the Toyota and it didn't start immediately, only when Elísabet had already reached us, and then I forbade him to drive off, that would have been rude. And then? She opened the door on my side, but wasn't angry or anything like that, just told us to come in, she even wanted to buy us dinner! So you went in? No, not right away, I told her that we knew nothing about sitting in restaurants and she said, well, I think you know how to sit here in your car, of course, I said, then you know how to sit at a table inside my restaurant, she said, and I immediately realized that she was right. So then you went in, asked Áki, when, for several moments, she said nothing. No, or rather, I went in but Jenni refused, he's not as sociable as me. You went in, Áki repeated, trying to breathe only through his mouth when she raised her arm again and the smell gushed out. Yes, and I had leg of lamb, even though I'd already eaten dinner and wasn't hungry, but it was just so nice of Elísabet, and it tasted so good, it was as if I'd never tasted lamb before, maybe it's true, what some people say. What do some people say? That she's got magic powers, and then that guy from the Depot was there, playing his violin, it was very pleasant and cultural as well, I was almost relieved that Jenni hadn't come in with me because he can't stand the violin, he says that it's bloody snobby, but I like all sorts of music. She stopped, and took a couple of quick breaths. Was I still sitting at the window? Yes. And I was . . . how shall I put it, still in my right mind? I think so, you were just drinking, but I didn't look at you much, she added apologetically, almost fearfully, it's just that I drink red wine so rarely and Elísabet refilled my glass and I felt so good, it was so nice to sit there and look around and . . . She stopped, held her breath, he felt that she was more or less waiting for his permission or approval to go on, he said: Yes, red wine. She began breathing again and said, there were so many people there. The doctor was there with that funny bow tie of his and Elísabet's partner in strange clothing, they sat together and sometimes spoke so loudly that I couldn't hear the violin very well, but it was still fun to listen to them, they were talking about . . . Where do I come into the picture, Áki interrupted, but half regretted it immediately, she shut up and for several long moments the only sounds were those of the wind and the radio, but finally she said softly, I talk too much, Jenni often scolds me for it. I'm sorry, he said in that unfamiliar voice, hoarse and ragged, it was rude of me to interrupt. Then she smiled, he saw it out of the corner of his eye, her face brightened, he tried instinctively to turn on his side to see her better, the bed creaked and the radio stopped playing. What am I doing, he thought, and stopped in mid-turn, leaving him lying neither on his back nor his side—the bed was so narrow that it was difficult to move in it at all. But now he saw her better, she had stiffened up, was holding the duvet in both arms, with her elbows close against her sides, he saw only her head, her neck, part of her chest, he looked at her and she tried to pull the duvet higher and the smell gushed forth again, Áki let it gush over him and acted as if nothing were out of the ordinary, he had no other choice, she looked up at him, with gray, suspicious, slightly frightened eyes beneath her short, dirty-blond hair that appeared to have been brushed so little, her skin rough and her face with that thick nose and those fleshy lips—in other words, her mouth didn't really protrude—she had on a light layer of powder, on her cheeks, around her eyes, it didn't suit her. I'm sorry, he said again, for interrupting you, but I would like to know how I got here. She looked down, now he saw only her eyelids. Elísabet said that you should go with me and Jenni. And what did I say? I don't know, you only spoke English, which I'm not very good at. And then? I thought it was a good idea to bring you here, Jenni said that it was unnecessary to take you with us, but Elísabet and I didn't listen to him. And then? Jenni had to carry you into the house and up here to my room, while I cleaned the car. You cleaned the car? You puked. Oh. It's okay. Did I want to sleep in this bed? She blushed, looked at him, and then her eyes flitted around the room as if in search of something to grasp on to, the radio downstairs was playing again. We're naked, he said finally, though there was no need whatsoever to point that out, and she blushed even more, the light layer of powder on her cheeks turned pink, her eyes darted here and there to avoid looking at him, she tried to arrange the duvet better, to pull it higher, tried to press herself into the wall, the smell returned just as she moved her arm, heavy, aggressive, but a tiny bit sweet as well, unless he was starting to become accustomed to it, he caught a glimpse of the dark hair beneath her arms, he'd never seen hair in a woman's armpits before. There they lay, he looked down at her, her gray eyes didn't stop darting for even a fraction of a second, she gripped the duvet so tightly that her knuckles whitened, and in something of a panic, Áki asked: How big is this farm of yours? He hoped that he would hear numbers again, numbers can't flee from you like people, they aren't underhand, like words. And she said: Three hundred eighteen sheep, sixteen cows, one heifer, two two-year-old bulls, and fishing rights in the river. She said this calmly, easily, even looking directly at him as she did, her voice low, her gray eyes searching his face. He grabbed the figures, held them tight, shut his eyes, let his head sink, he could no longer hold it up, his forehead bumped into something that was softer than the world, her shoulder, below it, her armpit. Three hundred eighteen sheep, sixteen cattle, one heifer, two two-year-old bulls, fishing rights in the river, a forehead against a shoulder, and his senses filled with the smell that streamed from her armpits, heavy, aggressive, sweet, and he thought, Reykjavík is the capital of Iceland, and then he thought of his studio apartment in Reykjavík's Þingholt neighborhood. It's 92.3 square meters. According to international standards (ISO 31-0), periods in decimal numerals may only be written in one place, between the integer number and the decimal fraction. 92.3 square meters, a leather sofa, two matching armchairs, glass table, range, thirty-two-inch television, twenty-six channels, there's always something to watch on television, but when he turns it off he's alone, it's only his image reflected on the screen. Alone. The number 1, in Roman numerals I or i; the smallest of integers, one man, one week, one day, one plus one, one at a time, once, not twice, if you subtract one from one, nothing remains but zero, which is nothing. Why are we living, he thought, with his forehead against the woman's shoulder, but he couldn't think of anything more to think about, just lay there with his forehead against her shoulder, his nose almost in her armpit, her strong body odor, the two of them in that bed, the sky in the distance, a bit nearer, a raven could be heard, even nearer, the wind, even nearer, the radio, much nearer was her breathing, cautious, shy breathing, I didn't know that breathing could be shy, I didn't know that there could be a zero big enough to swallow existence, I didn't know that there could be such a strong body odor, I never knew of such gray eyes, he lifted his head with difficulty, lifted it higher, so high that he saw her face and those gray eyes. He said the only thing that came to his mind, you have gray eyes, and then his penis began to harden. Very slowly, almost guardedly, yet determinedly, and those gray eyes dilated, he'd forgotten how good it was to feel his penis harden up against a warm body, he lifted his hand, grabbed the duvet, began to push it aside, at first, she held it tightly, resisting, but then let go and the duvet moved downward, he saw her small breasts with pink nipples that stiffened as he enclosed them with his lips, just for a moment, and then he watched as the duvet moved downward until it was on the floor. She had wide hips, broad thighs, and she said, I've never been with a man before. How old are you? Thirty-six. I've never been with a virgin before, he said, and thought about her maidenhead, it isn't there anymore, she whispered, as if she'd read his mind, I've used things before, I lost it when I was eighteen, when I used my hairbrush for the first time. Your hairbrush? I still have it, she said softly, so softly she could hardly be heard, and then moved her hand very cautiously, as if toward a timid animal, and closed her palm around his penis, squeezed it tightly, Áki closed his eyes, my name is Fanney, she said, and sighed. I'm Áki. I know . . . the bed squeaks a lot, Áki.

Jenni fled when she began moaning, went out to the sheephouse, sat there waiting patiently, ventured back into the house half an hour later, and began preparing the batter for pancakes.

[It's nice to wake up early here in the village. Those who live near the sea have its ever-moving surface in their living-room windows and can stand out on the veranda with a cup of coffee, perhaps barefoot, listening to the slightly hoarse prattle of the eider ducks, the coarse comments of the seagulls, the front of grayish clouds remains motionless in the windless sky, the sea barely moves, only small waves that drag a few stones deeper into the water, and they resurface to breathe. Needless to think about anything, you just exist, listen, welcome the world, the silent morning, world powers turn to dust at such moments.

Matthías gets up early, it's just him, his cup of coffee, cigarette, the sleeping sea, the eider ducks and seagulls, the tranquil sky. Elísabet is sleeping, he's outside looking at the sea, he goes back inside and watches her sleep, she breathes and the shore rocks are dragged deeper into the water. He leans over her, takes her hair in his hand and lets it slip through his fingers, her dark hair, dark as night. Everything is simpler but also poorer when she's sleeping, he goes to the living room, finds a slip of paper, writes something to her, does this sometimes, she wakes up after he has gone to work and finds a little note, perhaps in the butter dish, in the cutlery drawer, in one of her shoes, or written with a marker on the bathroom mirror: I do two things—breathe and think about you. It can take a while to clean the marker writing off the mirror, which is fine, because important messages, those that contain some sort of truth, some sort of essence, beautiful in their desperation, must not be delivered in a way that allows them to be erased easily. I do two things—breathe and think of you. It's perfectly true but at the same time it's nonsense, or at least a decent exaggeration. Matthías does many things, takes care of the Depot, he and Sólrún are the soul of the social life of the village, there's always movement around him, sometimes he receives special packages from that friend of his, the anthropologist, who may come to visit us soon, you'll recognize him as soon as he shows up, says Matthías: Louis is black, and always wears a big black hat and yellow jacket. Sometimes someone asks him, and you're happy to have returned to this backwater? To which, he replies: You can get used to pretty much any damned thing; absurdity becomes normal, and vice versa.

He's probably right, we can get used to anything, dreams in Latin and ghosts. The Astronomer lives his life outside our daily lives, just he and the sky, he and the night, he and countless letters in Latin from out in the world. It's nice to have such an eccentric here in the village, it livens up our existence, but perhaps he's not really an eccentric, just the only one who thinks rationally, with common sense and responsibility, but we don't really know what to say about his son, who smashed his violin over the head of Harpa's husband, after the latter punched Davíð twice, flooring him. It was at Tekla, and Elísabet had just run over, brandishing a pan, when Davíð sacrificed his violin, and now we have to wait and see what happens. Will Harpa leave her husband for Davíð, taking both children with her, will Davíð be able to bear it, will he be able to bear it if she doesn't want to be with him and leaves, lets some coincidence sweep her away from the village, or will he just get himself a new violin? Life is full of questions, but not answers. On the other hand, it's good to wake up early here in the village, to a familiar world where almost everything is in its place, pebbles and stones are dragged underwater and then re-surface to breathe.

Matthías always takes the same route to work. Up the slope past Tekla, past the commissioner's office, the Community Center, the post office, he wears his monkish coat, down at their house she lies there breathing, her hair nearly the color of night. When Matthías covers his head with his hood, he resembles a monk, or else a monkey, due to his swinging gait. He shows up at the Depot half an hour or three-quarters of an hour before Davíð and Kjartan, switches on the light in his office, in reception, in the warehouse, the bulbs illuminate the cross and the broken floor in the north-eastern corner, he goes there and says hello, says a few words about the weather, about politics, about whatever stirs in his heart.

Shortly after he began working there, Matthías hung up a large map of the world in reception, it reminds us that we're part of a whole, he said. We enjoy looking at the map, but it is striking how small Europe seems to be, Switzerland, for example, is barely dis-cernible, despite it having lakes and very high mountains. Gaui came to the Depot with a beautiful, clear map of Europe, and asked that it be hung up next to the world map—to put this to rights, as he worded it. But Matthías ignored his request and in-stead hung up a large map of our district. But it's not just the world and our district waiting for us at the Depot; on the counter is a stack of postcards that Elísabet bought in large quantities when she and Matthías spent a summer holiday in Germany and the

Czech Republic. Matthías, Davíð, and Kjartan encourage customers to take one home with them and display it in a prominent place, for example on the refrigerator. The postcards are all the same, a color photograph of Japanese snow monkeys submerged up to their necks in a hot spring, with just their heads above water. The monkeys take refuge in the spring when the temperature drops, sit there for days, with only their heads showing, frost and storm all around them, only hunger drives them out, but the monkeys return to the warmth of the spring as soon as they've eaten their fill. Matthías never tires of explaining that we're actually like those monkeys; the only difference being that we never need to get out to go and look for food, comfort accumulates around us, almost covering our heads. One day the Astronomer showed up at the Depot and took ten postcards, saying that he wanted to send them to his colleagues abroad, it would be fun to know what he wrote to the Hungarian woman, how do you say, I desire you, in Latin? The Astronomer laughed a lot when he saw the photograph of the monkeys, it's good to laugh, sometimes indescribably good. But life runs in every direction and then ends mid-sentence; sometimes there's nothing better than waking up early in the morning just to gaze at the surface of the sea, and let time pass by.

The sea, a cup of coffee, the prattling eider ducks, beach stones drawn underwater, then resurfacing to breathe. I do two things—breathe and think of you. We still have one more story left to tell, or rather, a particular destiny to trace to its end, events that occurred the spring and summer before Elísabet took down the letters and Áki came to the village, we weren't concerned about having this in the right order, or, we couldn't be concerned. One more story and then it's over, and yet not . . .]

What Sort of Shitty World
Would This Be Without Her?

1

Þuríður is tall and strong, she answers the phone at the health clinic, welcomes patients, dispenses medicines in the pharmacy, organizes Arnbjörn's day, makes things bearable for the nurse, Guðríður, who has a tendency to fall into depression, become enmeshed in despair—and then be barely capable of facing her days. Þuríður has a sunny nature, a kind of deep joy or luminosity seems to breathe through her skin, Þuríður's warmth and inner light have more than once woken within us the hope that life is not so bloody cursed after all, that there's a glimmer of sense to this existence. Sometimes Þuríður laughs so loudly, so powerfully, that our organs quiver within us.

But behind the laughter, within all that light and warmth, is a burning desire that has never found its refuge, she's thirty-five, just over 180 centimeters, thickset without being fat, some men find it awkward to dance with her due to her height, for a few years she's been thinking about leaving, moving away, following that ardent, esoteric desire that has started keeping her awake at night and even to rankle her joy. After all, this is a village of just four hundred souls, around five hundred more in the surrounding countryside, and the possibilities for a tall, powerful woman of thirty-five for finding herself a spouse, a companion, a partner for life are not terribly strong. She spent two nights with Arnbjörn, at his place, he once with her, at hers, but it wasn't anything deep, it was just a way to fill time, existence. She danced with Benedikt, kissed him once, it was at the New Year's party, The Good Sons on stage, and afterward they met at the Co-op and exchanged a few words, and she sat behind him at Kiddi's February film screening. But one cloudy, drizzly March evening, at around eleven o'clock, Þuríður unexpectedly appeared at Benedikt's door.

It was very dark, the drizzle had switched off the lights of the neighboring farms, Benedikt and his dog were alone in the world, they'd given up on the evening's television programs, neither of them much for books, nothing that interested them on the radio, useless to crawl into bed and go to sleep, the drizzle seemed to have swallowed his desire for sleep and its restoring grace as well. They were sitting in the living room, the dog lying there, actually, watching its master rub his hands, perhaps to feel the warmth of his own life. And then, a car was heard approaching. Its headlights, of course, half lost in the dense drizzle, but it's a car, of all things, an actual car driving up to the farm, at this late hour, and a car implies a human being, a life of flesh and blood, warmth and a voice. The dog leaped to its feet, Benedikt got up slowly, went into the kitchen, peeked out, what car is this? he asked in a low voice, but the dog didn't answer, it stood at the door, wanting to go out to check on the situation, sniff the tires, mark them, and so on. It scratched lightly at the door to draw its master's attention to the fact that he needed to open it, but Benedikt just looked out the window, didn't go straightaway to open the door, those who open their doors are actually announcing that their houses, their homes, are open to the outside world. People are strange; they may feel lonely and long for company, but when someone comes along, it's as if everything turns upside down and they want more than anything else just to retreat into themselves and be left alone—at least that's how Benedikt felt. He stood at the kitchen window and watched Þuríður approach the house, holding a small, brown suitcase! Benedikt muttered something to himself. She knocked, the dog barked. Hopefully I didn't wake you, said Þuríður with a smile when he finally opened the door, though not all the way. Benedikt looked over her shoulder, let his eyes stray out into the dark drizzle, it was as if they'd never danced together, as if she'd never pressed close against him with her lips at his left ear. May I come in, Þuríður asked, looking down at the dog, as if asking this of it, probably expecting a more positive reply from that direction, dogs are generally well disposed toward visits, it looked up at her with joyful brown eyes and wagged its tail energetically, damned social being, thought Benedikt, staring at the suitcase without knowing what he ought to say or do, surprised to see her show up like this, didn't dare to rejoice at it, almost certain that she had come only out of pity, perhaps she belonged to a religious sect and her suitcase was full of propaganda pamphlets. I was just on my way to bed, he finally said, grabbing the door handle, the dog looked in turn at the two human beings looming over it with a ridiculously happy expression and its tongue dangling from one corner of its mouth, then ran out into the farmyard to sniff the tires. Benedikt, feeling defenseless, watched the dog with an annoyed look, let me in for ten minutes, and then I'll leave, if you want, she said.

Benedikt: A suitcase for a ten-minute visit—so I guess you'd need a moving van if you were going to be staying.

She has a rather large mouth and full lips. The drizzle has wet her short, dark hair, she leaves her suitcase outside, slowly removes her knee-high leather boots, size 42. There are few things better than a late-evening cup of coffee, she says to Benedikt's back, as she follows him down the corridor, the kitchen is the first door to the right but he goes into the living room, it's more formal, thinks Benedikt, easier to keep his distance. The living room isn't terribly large, or noteworthy, he goes there only to watch TV, listen to music, or just sit there and stare, talk to the dog, read *Our Century*. In it are a brown sofa, two matching armchairs, a stereo and speakers, a big, old mahogany wardrobe with a row of carved wooden animals on top, horses, sheep, dogs, a seal, and a fox, all rather worn and dullish, his mother had pottered around with carving them thirty years ago, and then she died and his father not too long afterward; that's the way it goes, sometimes. So this is your living room, says Þuríður, as they stand there side by side, looking at the room as if they were considering buying the house; Benedikt is hardly less than 190 centimeters tall. Þuríður sits down on the sofa, won't you sit down, too, she asks gently, no, he replies, before taking a seat in the armchair in front of the TV and turning his left cheek to Þuríður; he has to look sidelong to see her. Don't worry, I won't be staying long, I said ten minutes, and in general, I keep my word; it's practically my favorite pastime. She smiles, her teeth are strong and straight, her lips red, but he only sees these things out of the corner of his eye, not wanting to look straight at her, she could mistake that for interest, and besides, he rarely looks to the side because of his nose, which juts out from his face like an important announcement. Sometimes he simply hates it, that nose, if he keeps his eyes fixed in front of him, he hardly notices it, but as soon as he glances left or right, there it is, red, ugly, ridiculously big. This is why Benedikt almost always looks straight ahead and, early on, gained a reputation for being a determined, confident, and strong-willed person.

Þuríður: You don't come to the health clinic very often.

The dog returns from the rain, Benedikt had left the door open a crack, dogs don't really care for wooden parquet, they can't retract their nails, a tick tick tick is heard from the corridor, the two humans listen and look toward the door, through which the dog walks in, it's black and in the prime of its life. Dogs aren't bound to our rules of conduct, to courtesies that tend to stiffen our lives, it just comes in and sniffs Þuríður's toes through her thin tights, then raises its head to her and waits to be petted. Benedikt is extremely disappointed in the dog. They say nothing, Þuríður concentrates on the dog, Benedikt stares straight ahead, and now he can't imagine anything better than sitting alone with his dog, maybe making coffee and playing Solitaire. It's been ten minutes, he suddenly blurts out, as if addressing the television set, though doing so would be pointless, it has no interest in listening to us, it's good to remember that before we switch it on. Well, then, there's no need for me to wait any longer, she says quite cheerfully, takes the dog's head in her hands, gives it a kiss, gets up, the dog looks at her as if prepared to give its life for her. Was that so bad, she asks with a smile, looking Benedikt straight in the eye, and now he sees her teeth between her lips, those lips that have whispered in his left ear, her lips are red, whereas her eyes are clear blue beneath her dark hair. Þuríður goes out into the corridor, the dog follows her, Benedikt follows them both, curses the dog, curses the woman's eyes. She has long legs, it can be seen quite clearly when she slips on her tall leather boots, long but not as thick as he would have expected for such a tall woman. I almost never fall ill, says Benedikt, and it takes her a few moments to realize that he's replying to her previous statement. You're lucky, she says, putting on her green coat, she dresses quickly, but calmly, her hair dark and her coat green. Then, for a second time, she looks him straight in the eye, again those clear blue eyes, says, sleep well, steps out into the drizzle, and heads for her car. Your suitcase! He pokes at her brown suitcase with his big toe, he's wearing wool socks, I'll take it with me next time, says Þuríður over her shoulder, and Benedikt has never seen such a tall woman walk away from his farmhouse. She gets in the car, the car starts, and it's too late to say anything, he's left with her suitcase, he watches the car as it drives away, watches its red taillights vanish into the darkness, into the dense drizzle, and he's at his doorway, the dog in the farmyard.

2

We all need to go and see the doctor from time to time, or to the pharmacy, if not for ourselves, then with our children, for health and development reviews; they're weighed, measured, we begin classifying ourselves right from the start, situating ourselves, changing ourselves into points on charts, we're compared against averages, vaccinated against nearly everything but sorrow, disappointment, death. Benedikt has no children, which he regrets, those who have children can point toward the sky and say, this is Venus, that is Jupiter, and as he rarely falls ill, he rarely goes to the health clinic, where Þuríður is such a powerful presence. But he danced with her at the New Year's party, she whispered in his left ear and then appeared in his farmyard in such a dark drizzle that the world lost itself. She came and she left and he'd never seen such a tall woman walk away from his door. No, never! said Benedikt to his dog in the spring, when the light had begun to erase the divide between day and night, the stars faded slowly and vanished, thousands of migratory birds came flying out of the horizon, Jónas was out on the moor with his notebook, down at the seashore with his binoculars, the tussocks gradually turned green—and Benedikt called his ex-wife. Four in the morning, no wind, the world seemed to widen. He'd been outside under the bright sky, had leaned up against the stillness, watched lambs being born, got himself a beer and suddenly found himself drunk, went into the living room, listened to music, played "The Mountains Watched Over Us" by Egó at least five times and very loudly, went back out into the tranquility, should I call Lóa, he asked his dog, who had no particular opinion about it, okay, I'll call her then, said Benedikt half an hour later. He was surprised at how unclear his voice was on the phone, his thoughts completely lucid but the words practically dissipated on his tongue or became blurred, fuzzy like wool. And then it wasn't she who answered, but some man, of course she was now living with someone, Benedikt had chosen to forget this fact but this fellow, and then Lóa too, though particularly the boyfriend, pointed out several times that it was the middle of the night, he'd woken them, and then Benedikt looked at his dog and shook his head, because it was just so absurd that anyone should think of sleeping right now, with the light streaming from the sky, the tussocks turning green in the stillness. Yet he didn't say this at first, just said, lambing's going well, okay, that's nice to hear, Benedikt, said Lóa. It's incredibly beautiful here now, he then said, unable to hold it in any longer, he stood at his kitchen window because the telephone cord was long enough, the door wide open so that the night could enter unhindered, my door is wide-open, he said, I wish I could remove the roof from my house, who ever thought of putting roofs on houses, anyway, when the night is . . . so, he said, making a sweeping gesture with his right hand to emphasize his point, and finding himself so satisfied with the gesture that he repeated it. Unfortunately, Lóa wasn't there to see it, it was only her voice—so deceptive the night can be—making that fine sweep of his hand practically useless, even entirely useless, and Lóa asked, are you drunk, and then answered her own question: you *are* drunk. Just two or three beers, he said calmly, carefully avoiding looking at the beer cans that he'd stacked into two towers next to the sink, six half-liter cans, or thinking of the shot of vodka that he'd downed to make the idea of calling Lóa seem better. Benedikt, dear, said Lóa, or rather, her voice, because the person with whom you speak on the telephone is most definitely not entirely there, he or she is missing eyes, fragrance, mass according to the laws of Newton. Benedikt stared, the night wasn't quite as bright, his dog was sleeping, the sky had drawn itself slightly away from the earth, left it behind in the void, where it turned ever so slowly, alone in space and with nothing to hold on to. And there was no longer anyone on the phone, except for Benedikt, of course, still holding the handset, his mind had wandered, did she say goodbye, had they said anything else? Yes, something, he didn't remember what, she'd said sleep well and he'd probably said yes, but of course he didn't go to bed, his bed didn't care to have company just then, he walked out, sat down against the wall of his house, felt the coolness of the night on his skin, the earth was mottled, half green, half brown, he'd regarded the vodka bottle and then woke around noon there against the wall, stiff, chilled to the bone, except for his back, against which his dog had lain, he woke from a dream, someone was kissing his face, covering it with sweet little kisses and he tried not to wake fully but, instead, just barely open his eyes to see the face of the one kissing him, to learn whose lips they were, but then woke and opened his eyes, he was lying on the ground, up against the wall of his house and his dog, rain falling on his face.

3

You mustn't think that it was always like this for Benedikt, no, no, there were weeks when he was just a farmer, a man preoccupied with his work, absorbed in putting up and repairing fences, focused on his sheep, nothing else mattered but his farm, and the sky just had to blow its bluesy harmonica for someone else. He looked forward to going home in the evening, sitting down in front of the TV, watching a good show, a good movie, listening to the radio, putting on a record or CD, it's nice to be alone, just you and your dog, life is so manageable, he goes into the village, does his shopping, stops by the Depot, often hangs around there awhile, they play chess, a four-man chess tournament, the first one to win thirty matches will be the champion, the prize a bottle of whiskey, which the winner has to drink midday, in the middle of the week at the Depot, it looks as if the title match will be between Benedikt and Matthías, Kjartan rarely wins, and almost always by sheer luck, Davíð can be a sharp, dangerous attacker but is bad at the long game, the best strategy against him is to draw things out, after twenty moves he starts losing himself in dreams, his concentration fades. These are good times for them all, and it's summer. Þuríður had come in March, left behind her brown suitcase on Benedikt's doorstep, then disappeared into the hazy drizzle along with the red taillights of her car. Benedikt brought her suitcase inside the house, but for no other reason than to keep it safe, he'd told his dog, which opened its mouth to let out its tongue, there it hung, broad and far too soft to make words. Then Þuríður returned, it was April, we're not really telling this in the right order; she turned up in the blue light of a Saturday. The frost connected the sky and the earth and this time there was no way to get lost in the haze. Benedikt had expected her to return, but certainly hadn't been waiting for her, well, yes, he had done that, in fact, and glanced at the suitcase every time he put on his coat or took off his shoes, his dog also sniffed it quite often and looked inquisitively at its master, who pretended not to understand and said nothing. But then she turned up in the blue light, and many people saw it when her red Toyota drove up the road to the farm, Benedikt knew that, what the hell do I care, he said to his dog. That visit was longer than the first, but not too long, maybe half an hour, and nothing was said or done worth recalling, he'd had a cake from the Co-op in his fridge, she had a slice, they drank coffee, talked about this and that, and then she left, both of them somewhat dissatisfied, the icy blue light should have offered up something more, thought Þuríður as she drove off and Benedikt felt discontent, without knowing precisely why, he went out to the barn, which seemed rather forlorn, tidied up there, worked hard so that the day would leave something visible behind. And the next time he went to the Depot, he was met by three grinning faces; news spreads so quickly here.

The third visit was in the month of May, toward evening, cool weather, pouring rain, everything one great quagmire, impossible to have the ewes with lambs outside and particularly not those close to giving birth, Benedikt could scarcely believe it when the dog began barking outside the sheephouse door, which opened shortly afterward and in stepped Þuríður, tall, wearing a GORE-TEX jacket and sturdy trekking boots, this was no weather for leather boots. Benedikt was a bit angry at first, despite having, without being willing to admit it, neither to himself nor to his dog, waited for her third visit, imagined it taking place on a windless day, under a clear sky, it's easier to talk to people with whom you're unfamiliar among tussocks than between walls, if things go wrong you can always grab hold of a fence post. But there she was, the rain hammered on the corrugated-iron sheets cladding the building, the dog kept her company while Benedikt continued to work, he was busy, couldn't stop for a moment, occupied himself with anything he possibly could, partly to work out his irritation but also because he didn't really understand himself when it came to this woman, who was sitting against one of the rails of the feed aisle, talking to the dog, letting a sheep sniff her fingers, smiling. Of course he'd thought about her, wondered what she was up to, what the purpose of her visits was, was she simply interested in him? He found that highly unlikely; his farm wasn't particularly big, the river that ran through it saw barely three fish per day, and several times he'd scrutinized himself in the mirror, sometimes naked, saw how tall and thin he was, his collarbone too prominent, his Adam's apple, too large in his slender neck, often seemed to live a life of its own, like a small rodent or something. His lips were thin, when he smiled he looked as if he were growling, and then there was his nose, good Lord, what in the world could ever justify such a nose! When Þuríður wasn't looking, he reached up and felt it—it nearly filled his palm, and Benedikt's hands were certainly not small. His appearance could hardly have appealed to her; she had of course kissed him at the New Year's dance, but that didn't mean anything in particular, they'd both been drunk and she'd talked about his eyes, but probably only because she found them sad. It could hardly have been his personality that attracted her, Lóa had frequently complained about him giving too little of himself, whole days could pass by without him returning to the house, and then came evening and she cooked him a nice dinner and wanted to chat, but hardly a word could be got from him, he leaned up against the silence, wadded it up beneath his head and used it as a pillow. I'm a grump, thought Benedikt, and Þuríður is not the type to have a soft spot for grumps—she must have come here out of pity, and nothing else. Benedikt's temper flares, pity is disgusting, he would rather have her hate him, it's more honest. He grabs a crowbar, despite doing nothing needing such a tool, Þuríður has stood up, is on her way over to him, she has a lovely gait, it annoys him to admit, so direct, effortless, you certainly have your hands full, she says with a smile, understandably, those who have such straight, white teeth simply must smile. He raises his hand, having forgotten about the crowbar, and wields it as if he's going to beat her, puts it down in something of a panic, why have you come, out of pity? he asks brusquely, but also unnecessarily bitterly, it wasn't supposed to come out that way, but as he asked the question, a vein seemed to open within him. She has stopped smiling, looks guilty, ashamed, or no, this is a different expression, Benedikt holds tightly to his anger, he says, making an effort to erase the bitterness from his voice, I can't stand pity, I hate it, and it's probably best that you leave, and take that brown suitcase with you, it's by the door, and he reaches down for the crowbar as if to underline his words, but what does he think he's going to do with that damned crowbar, well, just hold on to it until she's gone. But she shows no signs of leaving, she's still standing there, tall, with short, boyish hair, sturdy, Benedikt can feel her presence, unfortunately, it's like a slight pressure on his skin, he looks down at the crowbar. Maybe I've come here out of pity for myself, says Þuríður, completely calmly, if only he could speak like that, with such composure, he abruptly looks from the crowbar to her face, it's cozier looking at a woman's face than a crowbar. He's dumbfounded, not by the difference between a woman's face and a crowbar, but by her words, he's about to lift his hand to grip the back of his neck, which he frequently does when confounded, but then remembers the crowbar, I really don't know what I'm doing with this crowbar, he says embarrassedly.

So went the third visit.

Despite the pouring rain and the wind, they walked slowly

from the sheephouse back to the farmhouse, said little to each other, the words either hard to find or needless, Benedikt wasn't entirely certain, but he thought he found it nice to walk beside her and was a bit frightened by the feeling, though he did manage to ask why she'd brought her small, brown suitcase with her on her first visit, I have such a bizarre sense of humor, she answered, and besides, I wanted to do something . . . irrational, something ridiculous, because sometimes I think that's the only thing a person can do, Þuríður said, before suddenly saying goodbye, without a word more about what she meant, there was just a smile in the rain, her black, boyish hair, and then she was gone. Only then did Benedikt realize that he'd forgotten to tell her that he was going to London a couple of weeks later, but he just shook his head and said to himself, to the rain or the dog: As if that concerned her.

A week passed, two, so it goes, time goes by and we grow older, or, as it says in a poem, days come, days go, and then we die. Only in our case, things aren't so dramatic and poetic; days come, days go, and then Benedikt leaves for London. Perhaps you're surprised that he, this lonely farmer, this big-nosed recluse, is going to London, for what reason, what about his sheep, what about his dog, and do rustics like him go any farther than to Reykjavík, at most to Oslo? Well, you see, a lot of things come in the post, as we're sure you're aware, Vigdís from Brúsastaðir distributes the mail in Benedikt's area, she's one of Ágústa's infantrymen, even if it's absurd to call her an infantryman, Vigdís distributes the mail in her Japanese SUV and listens to the radio, when she drives very slowly between farms she's listening to a story on the radio or on a cassette tape, champing blue licorice pastilles, three packs a day to stay off tobacco. Vigdís left a brochure from a travel agency in Benedikt's mailbox, which is of course no novelty, our days are full of beautiful travel brochures, sunny beaches, the Caribbean, big cities fall through our mailboxes, remind us of the diversity of our planet, bringing bright color to our everyday lives, they promise us new skies in exchange for our credit cards, it's hard to resist for long. At first Benedikt didn't even look at the brochure, just put it unread in the newspaper rack, but two days later time was passing so slowly, dragging along like a decrepit old man, the sky gray and little time left for him, either, Benedikt glanced at the clock on the kitchen wall, expecting it to stop and effortlessly give way to eternity, which would be like this: he at the kitchen table, no company except for his dog, and his dog sleeping. Just then he noticed the brochure in the rack, in among old, well-read copies of the *Morgunblaðið* daily. On the cover were the words *Major Cities of the World*, which, according to the brochure, were twelve in number, Reykjavík, of course, wasn't mentioned, let alone our village, as it's not a city, and neither is Reykjavík, strictly speaking. He flipped through the cities, stopped at London, impossible to say why, he had no interest in football, which would otherwise have been a completely reasonable explanation. He hunched over the brochure, examined two street-view photographs from that city, one of Oxford Street, the other of an open-air market, where a woman, or a young lady, was holding a piece of fruit, probably a plum, he muttered after fetching his magnifying glass, maybe twenty-five years old, not much older, blond hair, with a fun-looking ponytail, she's probably playful, wearing a white T-shirt and blue denim shorts, bare feet in sandals, small knees "like kisses," a thoughtful expression, graceful shoulders, she seemed to be waiting for someone, maybe me, muttered Benedikt at the kitchen table. He looked at this woman or young lady for a few days, both with and without the magnifying glass, then booked a ticket by phone, a five-day trip, from Tuesday to Sunday.

4

He sets off at three early one June morning, the rain is the only thing still awake, his dog stands in the farmyard watching the car drive away, one ear dangling down, unable to understand why it doesn't get to go along. Benedikt looks in the rearview mirror, you can't take your dog with you to London, of course, even if the dog might enjoy it, two brown dog's eyes from the Icelandic country-side in the heart of London. Benedikt has filled the dog's bowls with food and water, Heimir and Gústa, who live next door, only one farm away, will look after it. Benedikt drives through the sleeping landscape, the windshield wipers do their job without Benedikt paying them any attention, he drives through the village, we're all fast asleep, dreams hanging over our roofs. Benedikt doesn't take the shortest route, but, instead, turns at the nursing home, drives slowly past Þuríður's house, and says out loud, I'm on my way to London for five days, and then accelerates, is at 90 kph when he passes the house of the Astronomer, who is perhaps awake even if the stars can't be seen behind the raindrops and the light.

Benedikt has a little over two hours to pass in Duty Free, he wanders from shop to shop, makes a few random purchases, mainly to pretend to have something to do, then sits down to eat a sandwich, drink a beer, pulls a postcard from his bag, looks for a moment out the window at the flat, nearly barren landscape, wet from the drizzle through which the wind slices, reaches back into the bag, takes out a pen, writes: Here I sit. Period. Looks for a long time at these three words, these stupid words. It's obvious that he's sitting writing the postcard; why point that out? Here I breathe, he adds, just in jest. Period. Then he tears the postcard in two. Ridiculous, writing a postcard; for what reason, and to whom? He leans back, sips his beer, gets up, goes and buys another postcard, sometimes you do things without knowing why, sits back down, thinks for several long moments, looks over the inhospitable landscape, writes: So I'm on my way to London, thinks for a few more long moments, then puts an exclamation mark after the words, but regrets it immediately, somehow it makes the sentence so provincial, as if it were a major event to go where thousands of Icelanders go every year. He snorts, gets up, hurries to buy another postcard, writes her name and then: So I'm on my way to London. Period, no exclamation mark. Next, he needs to provide an explanation; he writes: The world is so big. Period, which, after considerable thought, he changes into a comma: and naturally, I should have a look at some of it. That's fine, he leans back, satisfied at last, takes a big sip of beer, he's worked hard for it, feels its effects slightly, which is also nice, reads the sentence again, its tone so relaxed, so cosmopolitan, he's been abroad twice before, after all, first to Dublin, then for a holiday to a "sunny land"—that is, a trip that's not really to a particular country, but rather, to a beach, a hotel—an awful trip, the sun unbearable, the unceasing chatter of his travel companions even worse, yes, twice before, both times with a group of people from his area, but this time he's by himself, which is nice, although he misses his dog; next sentence: The Tower Bridge is in London and the famous Parliament building and countless other things, plenty to see. Period. The postcard is torn in half. Forty-five minutes until his flight, his beer is finished, what more can be said and again: why is he writing a postcard? For what purpose, what right does he have to send her a postcard, is he implying that he has some claim to her? Then he suddenly remembers Ágústa, looks over what's written on the postcard, could something be read into it? Enough for Ágústa to bring up with others, as she usually does in such instances, as if in passing, by accident, in between sentences, so that it was as if she'd never said anything, you suddenly just knew it, without having any idea how. No. Impossible to interpret what he wrote as any sort of message, no—but the very fact that he, Benedikt, wrote a postcard to her, Þuríður, might be enough. He curses softly, leans over the table, rests his forehead in his hand, these anxious thoughts of his have made him perspire, and there's an uncomfortably short amount of time until his flight, he writes, without reflecting on the words, yes, without running them by himself at all: I'll be there until Sunday. Can you record *Comedy Hour* for me? Well, now he'd gone and blown it, how stupid could he be? First, for making it seem as if he couldn't continue to live in this world if he missed one episode of *Comedy Hour*, second because he was saying, strongly suggesting, that there was something between them. Which was completely absurd, he had no right to and no interest in suggesting such a thing, he was just an idiot, with a little over half an hour until his flight. He's got to finish this up somehow, dammit, of course the best solution would be to tear up the postcard, the only sensible thing to do, yet he doesn't do so because he's a moron, but of course, one should finish what one has begun, that's just how it is. So finish it, quickly, save what can be saved, write something thoughtful, composed, no exclamation marks, just one period: It's good to get away, Iceland can be so limited—or should he write limiting, no, it's fine as it is, damned fine. Benedikt looks around, satisfied, very satisfied, bloody hell, he'd outdone himself this time, now people would see that he's no rustic recluse. Twenty minutes until departure. Twenty minutes! Benedikt jumps up, gropes for his Duty Free bag, grabs the postcard, lays it on the table, scribbles her address beneath her name, neat-looking letters in her name, standing calm and composed in the right order and not going anywhere, the letters in her address, looking, however, like a group of hyperactive neurotics, none going in the same direction, but the closing was still missing, dammit all! Well, he writes, followed by a comma, now hesitating from stress, nothing comes to mind, he just adds his name, too hurriedly for it to be legible, now no one will know who sent the postcard, that's fine, it's all ruined, he hurtles through the airport, nearly knocking three Japanese tourists to the ground in front of the post office counter, throws the card onto the counter, stammers incoherently, strews coins over the countertop, dashes off again, just manages to make his flight, sweaty, his heart racing, but soon afterward: the blue sky.

London has a great many inhabitants, considerably more than our village, and its buildings are bigger, some of them have long histories. We have a district museum, a tractor from 1936, farming implements from the 1920s, a hundred-year-old tobacco pipe, and other such things, but in London you can see the history of the world, a 4,000-year-old Egyptian mummy, even more ancient artifacts from Assyria, the world was ruled from London for hundreds of years, the Romans built a road there that's now one of the busiest shopping streets in the world, there's so much variety on London's streets that it would take numerous books to describe a single day exploring them. Benedikt is sitting in a pub with a pint of beer in his hand, watching people pass by, the heavy river of life, he thinks about the city's size, its history, the mummy, he drinks his beer and feels devastated at how all of this, the mummy, the multitude, the city's history, is nothing but rubbish, completely insignificant, compared to one single woman in a small village in a country that's far from everything except eternal winter and suffocating darkness, a land that would be completely uninhabitable if that warm ocean current didn't flow around it. Benedikt thinks for a moment about that current, the Gulf Stream, and feels almost like shedding a tear of gratitude for it, because where would Þuríður be if we didn't have the Gulf Stream? What sort of shitty world would this be if she weren't in it, what good would mummies be, history, all the people, the blue sky? Would that Tony Blair, for instance, be able to continue grinning like that, wouldn't he rather just lie there in his bed? Benedikt writes a postcard, his heart trembles as he writes: Without you, the Egyptian mummies would lose all meaning. He sits up straight, reads the sentence, has to close one eye to see properly through the fog of beer, and adds: But luckily, we have the Gulf Stream, otherwise you wouldn't exist and Blair would never grin again, yours, Benedikt. Then he carefully crosses out *yours*, you need more than six beers to be able to write *yours*, *yours* is the kind of word that takes at least ten beers, yes, *yours* is a ten-beer word. Benedikt looks at the man at the next table, the tables here are very close together, that's how it is in major cities, there are so many people, and they all have to sit somewhere. The man is a short, plump Arab wearing a very fine suit, possibly made of silk, Benedikt says to him: In the end, there's no need to say much, what matters is to use the right words, just like during the sheep roundups, when idiots are constantly running in every direction, instead of running less but always in the right direction. He tries to speak English, but his Icelandic keeps pushing its way to the fore, knocking aside the English words, yet the Arab nods in agreement and answers in a mixture of English and Arabic, Benedikt pulls his chair all the way over to the other table and says, her name is Þuríður, the Arab says what and Benedikt repeats, she is Þuríður, and then tells him that she's tall, has such eyes, tells about her leather boots, the light that radiates from inside her, the Arab looks straight at Benedikt, listens, and then takes out a photograph of an Arab woman, Benedikt looks straight at the Arab and nods; so the day passes, and the evening as well. Around midnight, Benedikt hugs the Arab, they're both choked up about having to go their separate ways, they exchange addresses, the Arab gives Benedikt his tie. The next day, it's the blue sky once more.

5

Twenty four hours after he was sitting in a London pub, not terribly far from an Egyptian mummy, a monument to life four thousand years ago, he was standing in his own farmyard, his dog close beside him, letting its tongue dangle from pure happiness, there was nothing around them but air, Benedikt could run a long way without running into anything but air, incredible, in London he could barely hold out his hand without it bumping into someone, the crowds sometimes so large that it was difficult to turn around, making him wonder if there was enough oxygen on the busiest streets, I found it hard to breathe there sometimes, he told his dog, who looked up and understood everything. Benedikt smiled, and then remembered the postcards that they'd mailed, he and the Arab, at least three, on one of them he had mentioned the Gulf Stream and the mummy, but for the life of him he couldn't recall what he'd written on the others, and they would soon arrive in the village, Ágústa's red lips would move over them, he who bares his emotions in public, who writes them on a postcard, is a fool; I'm starting to sound like a pop star or a poet, said Benedikt to his dog, come on, let's go to work, and try to get this nonsense out of our heads.

But then it happened, and now our hands are trembling a little; what shall we say, it was summer.

It was June, even for Egyptian mummies, the sheep were up in the mountains, with all their lambs that graze on Iceland moss and drink from streams, but then autumn comes and they transform into frozen carcasses, end up on the grill, in the oven, and we eat them without having any idea of what will become of that which gives their eyes such clarity. Benedikt hardly dared set foot in the village, but, naturally, had to go there for necessities, parked outside the Depot, softly asked the three co-workers whether they'd heard anything about postcards, which they in fact had, dammit, said Benedikt, and became so disconsolate that Kjartan, who'd been itching to tease him, decided he'd better not, even went over to the Co-op for him, did his grocery shopping while Davíð and Benedikt played a game of chess and Matthías said that the Co-op would soon go bankrupt, hopefully as soon as possible, thought Benedikt, and then everyone will forget my postcards. And then what will happen, asks Davíð, looking up from the chessboard, we'll be taken over by some cartel, said Matthías; oh, seventy years of Co-op history at an end, says Davíð, shaking his head, but Benedikt says nothing, because seventy years is but a flash in comparison with Egyptian mummies. You should go and see her, says Kjartan when he returns carrying bags full of groceries, Benedikt shakes his head, says no, and goes home, he doesn't dare, on his life, go and visit Þuríður, he has exposed his true self, he's completely defenseless, and if he were to meet her anywhere, it should be at home on his farm, at least there he could support himself on a fence post. Þuríður came to visit him on a cloudy day.

She stands there in the farmyard, wearing black jeans and a red sweater, and her leather boots as well, remarkable how well her dark hair goes with all the rest, the clouds, the daylight, the passing of time. Benedikt is painting his house, he's holding a paintbrush, lays it down, perhaps to be able to look at her, the clouds are up there, why is he thinking of clouds just now? Every fence post on Benedikt's land is straight as an arrow, either an obsession or else ambition on his part, though sometimes it's comforting to think that some things in this life can be put straight like that, but why are we thinking of fence posts just now, the sky is bluer than the day, the blue sky goes especially well with leather boots and dark hair, Mary Magdalene must have been wearing leather boots when Jesus saw her for the first time, and He, no doubt, had to think about the fence posts of His day in order to keep His head straight, do you think there were leather boots during Jesus's day, asks Benedikt, of course, it's completely absurd to ask such a thing, she says with a smile, those teeth can certainly nibble at me, he thinks, thanks for the postcards, she finally says, having moved closer to him. At first, there was an entire farmyard between them, but now just a few rocks, the dog's front paws were on her hips, her right hand on its head. Were there four from London, he asks hesitantly, three, she says, smiling even wider, were you that drunk, she asks, with a little laugh, but for a long moment, he says nothing, he just looks into her eyes, because what is a 4,000-year-old mummy in comparison with two living eyes? Then he says, yes, I was so drunk that I forgot about Ágústa. She certainly hasn't kept quiet about the postcards. They were for you, not the village, he says. Would you write such things if you were sober? Yes, he answers without hesitation, though without remembering exactly what he'd written on them. Þuríður takes a few steps closer, so close that you might think they were in a crowded, major city, in a crowded lift, and not in the farmyard, with such an unnecessarily large amount of space around them. Yes, he repeats, and she draws even closer, her warm, slightly sweet breath could easily melt the Greenland ice sheet, causing sea levels to rise and drowning loads of people, for example in Reykjavík and Akranes and probably in Ísafjörður, which is no more than a sand spit in the middle of a fjord, I'll never blow in the direction of the Greenland ice sheet, she promises, can you come a little closer maybe, he asks hesitantly, yes, are you sure, he asks skeptically, and she replies by moving closer, so close that he can feel her thighs and breasts, it's been so long since he felt breasts, he starts thinking about the

Egyptian mummy, but not even a 4,000-year-old death can save him, she's so tight against him that she must surely feel what is happening to him, which she does, and for which he wants to say sorry, but then she presses herself to him and Benedikt gasps, the sky trembles and time passes, probably around four thousand years. Then she moves away from him, takes two steps back, leaving him feeling uncomfortable about the excessive space around him, I'll come back tomorrow, she says, can't you come now, he asks, no, we'll let one sleepless night pass, no, let's not do that, because I can't wait, yes, you can wait, and tomorrow I'll come in a moving van, she says, and then gets in her car, starts the engine, rolls down the window, and says: We'll have tall children.

And what shall we say? Sometimes tomorrow turns out to be so far away that four thousand years are nothing in comparison, and sometimes tomorrow never comes. Þuríður drives back to the village, Benedikt and the dog stand there watching until the car is gone, and then Benedikt—and his dog—start hopping around the farmyard. Then Benedikt goes inside, finds the address of the Arab, goes and gets his Icelandic–English dictionary and starts writing a letter, Dear friend, now I can touch the sky! It's nice to write letters when you're happy, but on the other hand, it can be risky to drive a car in such a state, you're so distracted, lack concentration; and midway between Benedikt's farm and the village, Þuríður loses her focus and runs off the road in an extremely bad place, a steep slope, the car rolls three times. In the gravel at the bottom stood a big boulder, shaped over the centuries by winds and rain, it was a highly ordinary rock when the mummy was a person with desires in Egypt, but now, four thousand years later, it was shaped like a huge arrowhead. The car crashed into that rock, which penetrated the window on the driver's side, and when a human head and a rock collide, it's the head that has it worst. There that boulder had stood, all this time, just to kill a person. It took Benedikt a long time to dig it up, he began with a pickax, shovel, pinch bar, his own car up on the road, but soon had to go and get his tractor with its bucket, started early in the morning and it was nearly midnight when he managed to extract the boulder, which rocked slightly in the old hay wagon when Benedikt drove home. The boulder reached up to his chest and was quite an imposing sight out there in the farmyard where he and Þuríður had stood, and all that summer and then the autumn and all winter as well, Benedikt was out in the farmyard, in every weather, pounding on the boulder with his sledgehammer, he'd got a pair of protective goggles to keep from losing his sight, though he didn't need much of it, just enough to glimpse the boulder and it was good to hammer at it, good to break the boulder, good to feel the stone shards shoot in every direction, good to be scratched on his face and arms, but it was also almost the only thing that was good, yet not particularly good. Then came spring, on earth as in heaven, the frost withdrew slowly from the ground, the birds returned, the sun grew bigger, and the boulder was no longer in the farmyard, he had smashed it to smithereens. Benedikt leaned against the wall of the house, it was he and his dog and a brown leather suitcase in the living room, the suitcase waiting for the hand that the earth was slowly transforming. The dog is named Kolur. Benedikt and Kolur. Dogs age faster than people; in seven years, it will only be Benedikt. And what then?

A Guide to the Pronunciation
of Icelandic Consonants, Vowels,
and Vowel Combinations

ð, like the voiced *th* in *mother*

þ, like the unvoiced *th* in *thin*

æ, like the *i* in *time*

á, like the *ow* in *town*

é, like the *ye* in *yes*

í, like the *ee* in *green*

ó, like the *o* in *tote*

ö, like the *u* in *but*

ú, like the *oo* in *loon*

ý, like the *ee* in *green*

ei and *ey*, like the *ay* in *fray*

au, no English equivalent; but a little like the *oay* sound in *sway*. Closer is the *œ* sound in the French *œil*

About the Author

JÓN KALMAN STEFÁNSSON has been nominated three times for the Nordic Council Literature Prize, and his novel *Summer Light, and Then Comes the Night* received the Icelandic Literature Prize. In 2011, he was awarded the prestigious PO Enquist Literary Prize. He is perhaps best known for his trilogy: *Heaven and Hell*, *The Sorrow of Angels* (longlisted for the Independent Foreign Fiction Prize), and *The Heart of Man* (winner of the Oxford-Weidenfeld Translation Prize). A subsequent novel, *Fish Have No Feet*, was longlisted for the Man Booker International Prize in 2017.

About the Translator

PHILIP ROUGHTON is a scholar of Old Norse and medieval literature and an award-winning translator of Icelandic literature, having translated works by numerous writers, including Halldór Laxness. He received the Oxford-Weidenfeld Prize for his translation of Jón Kalman Stefánsson's *The Heart of Man* and was shortlisted for the same prize for *About the Size of the Universe*.

A Note from the Cover Designer

As I read *Summer Light, and Then Comes the Night*, I drifted with each story as the chapters passed from one unforgettable character to another. My cover design process was affected by this wandering weight. I attempted not to focus on location or a specific character on the cover, but on the tangible feeling in Stefánsson's writing: "the winter darkness pressing up against the windows of the houses" during "radiant summer light, pitch-black nights."

The scene on the cover celebrates the unique mood and atmosphere of the novel as it juggles humor and pathos and captures the everyday beauty of life. The paper stock of the printed jacket was also intentional, reflecting light and dark and the brilliance of the landscape.

—Stephen Brayda

Here ends Jón Kalman Stefánsson's
Summer Light, and Then Comes the Night.

The first edition of this book was
printed and bound at LSC Communications
in Harrisonburg, Virginia, August 2021.

A NOTE ON THE TYPE

The text of this novel was set in Minion, a serif type-
face designed by Robert Slimbach and released by Adobe
Systems in 1990. Inspired by late Renaissance-era type,
Minion's name stems from the traditional naming system for type sizes, in which minion is between nonpareil
and brevier. Designed for body text, Minion is classic
yet condensed in style, achieving a harmonious balance
between the size of letters. It is a standard font in many
Adobe programs, making it one of the most popular
typefaces used in books.

HarperVia

An imprint dedicated to publishing international voices,
offering readers a chance to encounter other lives and other
points of view via the language of the imagination.